HIGH PRAISE FROM AUSTRALIA FOR CLIFF HARDY

"Corris's story is clever, his asides wry, his language rough but whimsical. Once more Corris captures intonations of speech and nuances in gestures adeptly; that gift (and cunning similes) are the hallmarks of a thriller craftsman."

The Canberra Times

"Corris's book is tight without losing its humanity—professional without being slick. Hardy, as well as being tough and wise, is also determined, resilient. . . . Amid the footslogging, the action, the beatings Hardy receives, the twists and turns of the ingenious plot and the strongly characterized cast, there is nightmarishly grim descriptive writing."

The West Australian

"Cliff Hardy is . . . as Australian as two-up and Fosters."

The Australian

HEROIN ANNIE AND OTHER CLIFF HARDY STORIES

Peter Corris

FAWCETT GOLD MEDAL • NEW YORK

A Fawcett Gold Medal Book
Published by Ballantine Books
Copyright © 1984 by Peter Corris

Library of Congress Catalog Card Number: 83-72896

ISBN 0-449-13031-2

This edition published by arrangement with George Allen and Unwin
Australia Pty, Limited.

"The Luck of Clem Carter," "Silverman" and "Mother's Boy" were first
published in the *National Times* December 1980 to January 1981. Slightly
different versions of "Blood is Thicker" (as "The Fratricide Caper") and
"Heroin Annie" were published in *Playboy* November 1980 and June
1981. "Marriages are made in Heaven" (as "The Negative Caper") and
"Escort to an easy death" were published in slightly different form in
Penthouse January and June 1982; "California Dreamland" was published
in *Playboy* April 1983.

Manufactured in the United States of America

First Ballantine Books Edition: October 1987

For
Jim Hall

Contents

Marriages are made in heaven

"You're cold, Cliff!" Cyn banged her fist on my desk. "That's your bloody trouble, you're *cold*!" She was close to tears the way she always got when we argued. They weren't tactical tears, but they were part of the reason that I nearly always lost the arguments.

"I'm not cold," I said. "I'm warm-hearted, a loving man. I'll take you out tonight."

"I don't want to go out."

"Okay, we'll stay home. I'll cook."

The telephone rang. We were in my office where I answer the telephone, open the door, and type the letters myself, because there's no-one else to do it.

"Hardy Investigations. Warm-hearted Hardy speaking."

"Your heart's as warm as Bob Askin's. Cut out the bullshit, Cliff, I've got a job for you." It was Athol Groom, who works in advertising and agenting; he sometimes drinks where I sometimes drink.

"Terrific, Athol," I said. Athol deals in people with soft jobs; Cyn calls him a pimp, and she made a face when I said his name. "What sort of job?"

"Come down here and I'll tell you." He gave me his address.

"How long do you reckon this'll take?"

"How the hell do I know? All day, all night, all week. The longer the better as far as you're concerned, isn't it?"

1

"Yeah, I guess so. But I've gone up to seventy-five a day and expenses."

"Shit. All right. Just hurry, she'll be here soon."

"She?"

"Selina Hope. Hurry."

I put down the phone and stood up; Cyn moved away from me as if we were in a slow ballet.

"A job," I said.

"It's always a job, what we need is a talk—tonight."

"I don't know, love."

"A minute ago you were going to cook some slop for me, drink two-thirds of the wine and that."

She was looking very nice that morning, my wife. Nearly as tall as me, she was straight and slim with honey-blonde hair. She must have come directly from the architect's office where she worked because she still had draughtsman's ink on her fingers. She saw me looking, and her fine-boned, handsome face went hard.

"Cold," she said. "Selfish and cold."

I patted her arm, there were no tears, which was good. I went out.

Athol's pimping shop was in Double Bay on a steep hill. I ran the back wheels of my old Falcon into the kerb and let it sit there in a way which says to the world, "this car has a faulty handbrake"; but what can you do? Athol's decor was dominated by photographs, mirrors, and magazines. The pictures were blow-ups of models with impossible cheek bones doing mysterious things amid shadows. The magazines were glossy, and the mirrors are fine if you're a five foot nine clothes horse with the right angles and planes. When you're a thin, six foot, thirtyish man with untidy dark hair and Grace Bros. clothes, they're not so good. A lacquered, Sassooned brunette pressed a buzzer when I told her who I was, and Athol hurried out.

2

Athol Groom is one of those men in the fifties who plays squash and eats nothing so as to keep his waist down; he likes a drink though, and that slight thickening won't be denied. He has a glossy moustache, and hair and teeth to match, but he's not a phoney.

"Good to see you, Cliff, how's Cyn?" I took Athol home once, and after one look at Cyn he tried to persuade her to take up photo modelling. She laughed at him.

"All right. What's going on?"

The brunette looked at her appointment book and spoke up crisply. "Mr. Blake is due any minute, Mr. Groom."

"Right, right. Come on, Cliff, you're a bodyguard; come and meet the body."

We went down a corridor past more photographs and into Groom's office. A woman was leaning back against the big desk combing her hair. It was worth combing, a great blue-black mane that rippled and flowed under the comb strokes. Its owner had the standard tall, thin, flat body; but with a face to haunt your dreams forever. Her skin was darkish, almost olive; she had jet black eyebrows, dark eyes, and a wide, wonderful mouth. Her nose was nothing much, just exactly as straight and thin as it needed to be.

"Selina," Athol said, "this is Cliff Hardy. Selina Hope, Cliff." We nodded at each other, but I was listening to Groom's voice; this was his handle-with-care, this-side-up voice. I gathered Miss Hope was a hot property.

"We've got a little problem here, Cliff. There seems to be some creep hanging around Selina's flat, following her and such. Was he there this morning, love?"

"Yes, I think so." I expected an exotic accent of some kind to accompany the face but there was none, just good, clear, educated Australian.

"You think," Athol said sharply. Maybe he was thinking about my fee.

"Easy," I said. "Miss Hope's said the right thing. When someone's watching you it's a feeling you get more than anything else. Sort of corner of the eye thing. Is that right?"

"Yes, exactly." It's not often I say just the right thing for a beautiful woman—I'm usually considered somewhat blunt—but I did it this time. She smiled at me as if I'd won the pools. But there was some relief in that smile too—she'd been scared.

"Okay," Athol said. "Well, we all know about the weirdos in this game. It's probably some freak who's seen Selina in a bra advert and can't sleep. A few strong, silent looks from Cliff and he'll give it away. It's a pity the London job fell through though, that would've been the best cure. Next best thing is to keep busy. I've lined Selina up for two jobs today, Cliff, and I want you to stick close, and see her home. Okay?"

"Sure."

"Off you go."

I followed Selina to the back exit; she was wearing a black jumpsuit, caught tight at the ankles and loose pretty well everywhere else. Her walk was a spectacular strut that made the hair bounce on her straight shoulders. We walked across to a bright blue Mercedes sports car and she tossed me a set of keys. I threw them back.

"I'm a column gears man," I said.

She laughed and unlocked the car; I couldn't find the seat belt, couldn't fasten it, and couldn't push the seat back. She helped me with one hand and put in a cassette with the other—we took off to a roaring of guitars and electric piano.

Over the music and traffic noise I asked her about the London job. She told me that she'd been booked to be snapped outside the Houses of Parliament with a peer of the realm for a Scotch whisky advertisement, but the peer had died.

"Tough luck."

"Would have been a good trip." She dipped a shoulder and flicked the Merc around a bend, changed down and surged up a hill.

"Have you worked in London before?"

"London, Paris, New York." There was pride in her voice but no conceit. I decided I liked her.

"Have you been getting any other harassment—phone calls, letters?"

"Not a thing. Just as you said, a glimpse of someone, a feeling . . ."

"You don't know what it's about?"

"Not a clue."

I didn't like the sound of it; a good tail, one who just leaves that *feeling*, is a professional, not a sex-starved creep. Professionals work for money and the people who pay them have reasons. We drove down to Woolloomooloo near the docks; there was a fair bit of traffic and activity and she glanced around nervously as she locked the car.

"Do you have the feeling now?" I asked.

"Not sure."

"What are you doing here, an ad for overalls?"

She laughed and we walked toward a dingy-looking warehouse. "You'll see."

We went up some steps and in through a mouldy door. If the place was a nightmare outside, it was a dream within. The carpet was deep, the walls were white and the lighting was costing someone a fortune. The huge floor area was partitioned off into dressing rooms and elaborate, stylised sets. There were cameras and light fittings everywhere.

"Not overalls," I said.

"Soft drink, I believe. Come on." She led me through the maze of equipment and props, and we wound up with a photographer named Sam, his assistant, and a few cases of

5

soft drink. Sam was a Levantine; squat and heavy with a floral shirt unbuttoned to show his virile chest and stomach. All of it. His off-sider was an anorexic blonde who whisked Selina away and took me out of camera range. I asked for a sample and got a bottle of Diet-Slim cola which tasted like rusty water with saccharine added. Selina came out wearing a superformal dress, and proceeded to drape herself around some Swedish furniture while sipping tall glasses of the beverage. I got bored with this and wandered off in search of a phone. I found one behind a jungly set which was being sprayed with insect repellent by Livingstone and Stanley. I dialled the number of the terrace house in Glebe where Cyn and I practise wedded bliss. She answered in a tone that told she was keeping her head of steam up.

"It looks as if I'll be home tonight."

"You'd better be. We really need to talk, Cliff. Where are you? In some pub at the Cross, I suppose? Pissing on?"

I was still holding the Diet-Slim; I looked across to a set that featured a silver-grey Rolls Royce—a woman in a fur coat was getting out of it and smiling up at a guy in a dinner suit.

"Yeah, something like that," I said.

"I'll see you tonight." She hung up and I skirted the jungle, a schoolroom and a torture chamber back to where Sam had Selina reading while sipping: the book was *The ABZ of Love*.

Sam clicked away and the blonde moved lights and Selina smiled and smiled until I wondered at her patience. The money would have to be good. Eventually they called it a day and, after kisses all round, Selina climbed back into her jumpsuit and we were on our way.

"Lunch?" I asked.

She shook her head. "Not for me, but I'll watch you."

It was lunchtime, and things were quiet outside as we moved toward the car. Suddenly there were hurried sounds behind us, and I heard a whooshing noise and felt one side of my head tear itself loose from the middle. I crumpled, heard the sound again and my shoulder caught on fire. I went down further but managed to grab a pair of legs and pull. I looked up and saw a big guy in blue overalls pulling Selina toward a car. She screamed once and he hit her, and she was quiet. Then a knee came up into my face and I slammed down hard on the footpath.

It all took about fifteen seconds: I was going to lunch with a beautiful girl and then I had a bleeding face, dented shoulder, and no girl. And I'd be missing lunch. I brushed aside the few people who tried to help me and staggered up to Forbes Street to hail a cab. My ear and nose were bleeding and my clothes were dirty, but the Sydney cabbie is a brave soul. I gave the driver Groom's address, and mopped at the blood. My entry at the agency sent people fluttering and bells ringing: Athol came out quickly and hustled me off to wet towels and a large Scotch. I told him what had happened while I cleaned up.

"Did he hit her hard?"

"I don't think so. Why?"

"That face is just pure gold. I don't like to think of it being knocked about. What should we do now?"

I pulled a bit of loose skin off the ear and started the blood flowing again. "Call the cops," I said.

He shook his head. "I'd rather not. You've got no idea what people are like in this racket. Any police trouble involving Selina and her career could be finished just like that." He snapped his fingers. "The face has to be a pure image, untainted, see?"

"Not to mention your commission."

"Right. There must be something you can do." He was reproachful; I could have said that a bashing and an abduction were very different things from a loitering perv, but I didn't.

"Give me a bit of time on it. If I can't come up with anything pretty quick you'll have to get the cops. Where does she live? Who're her friends?"

He told me that Selina shared a flat in Woollahra with another girl, and gave me the address. He didn't know much about friends. I got to the flat quickly; my leg gave me trouble on the stairs, but never let it be said that Hardy gives in to pain. I forgot about the leg when I saw the flat door hanging on one hinge inside a shattered frame. I looked straight into the living room—torn paper, ripped and crumpled fabric and carpet made it look as if a small bomb had gone off inside. I took a few steps past the door and stopped when a woman came into the room. She looked at me and screamed.

"Easy, easy," I said. "I'm a friend, you must be Jenny."

She nodded; her face was white and her hands were flying about like frightened birds. "Who're you?" she gasped.

"Cliff Hardy." I produced some documents, thinking that they might help bring some order to the chaotic scene. The woman started swearing and I poked around in the debris while she visited terrible things on unknown persons. I gathered that she'd walked in on the violated flat just before I did; the telephone had been ripped out of the wall—the only departure from a cool, thorough bit of searching. No book, and there were a lot, was undisturbed; all lined clothes had been slashed; drawers had been tipped out and the contents sifted and all edges stuck or otherwise fastened—carpets, furniture, pictures, ornaments—had been lifted and inspected.

She picked things up and dropped them helplessly. "Why?" she said.

"It's to do with Selina. Has she been in trouble lately? Been seeing any strange people?"

"Strange? No . . . but she said there was a perv

8

hanging around." Alarm leapt in her voice and eyes. "Is she all right? Where is she?" She seemed to notice my injuries for the first time and drew the right conclusions. "Something's happened!"

"Something," I said. "I'm not sure what. Selina's been grabbed by someone, not a perv. How close are you to her?"

"Oh, we're . . . friends. I worked in TV, and I met her while she was doing a commercial. We got along, and she needed a flatmate. Grabbed? What does that mean?"

"I wish I knew." I bent down and picked up a photograph from the floor. It had been detached from a frame and the backing had been cut away. The picture was a studio portrait of a self-satisfied looking guy with good teeth and ringletted brown hair.

"Who's this?"

"Colin Short, Selina's boyfriend."

"Athol Groom didn't tell me about a boyfriend."

"He doesn't know. Selina keeps him a secret."

"Why?"

She began making piles of dismembered books. "He's a photographer. A model isn't supposed to be on with any one photographer. Shit what a mess. Why would anyone do this? What do they want, money or what?"

I squatted and helped her with the books. "They were looking for something. Selina ever mention a hiding place?"

"Come on, we're grown-up people."

"Where does Short live?"

"He's got a sort of studio just around the corner. If I could find the address book . . ." She rummaged around in the mess and came up with a notebook. She read out the address and I wrote it down. "He phoned this morning, as a matter of fact."

"What did he want?"

"God, why are we doing *this*? Something should be *done*!"

"Believe it of not, this *is* doing something. What did Short say?"

"He just wanted to know if Selina got away okay. She was supposed to go to London, the lucky . . ." She broke off and looked contrite.

"Don't worry," I said. "I know what you meant. How did Short take the news that she wasn't going?"

"Seemed upset. He kept asking me was I sure."

I grunted and stacked a few more books. Jenny told me that Selina had been keeping company with Short for nearly two years, sometimes she spent the night at his place, sometimes he stayed at the flat. I got the door into a position where it would open and close and persuaded her not to call the police—Athol Groom was handling that end of it I said. She nodded, then she dropped to her knees and started rooting urgently through the mess.

"What're you looking for?"

"The dope," she said.

I contemplated walking to Short's place, it was only a step, but the leg was throbbing so I drove. As it turned out, that was lucky. I was fifty yards from the address when I pulled into the kerb to watch something very interesting. Short, whom I recognised from the photograph, despite his white overalls and a pair of heavy industrial goggles pulled up on his head, was loading something into a blue van. He made a trip back into the studio which had a shop front directly on to the street, came out with another bundle and pulled the door closed behind him. He walked past a white Toyota station wagon which had his name and business painted on the side, got into the van and drove off. I followed.

It was a good, clear day and the traffic moved easily; a secret boyfriend seemed like a promising new factor in the situation, especially one behaving suspiciously. I didn't feel confident though. Leaving the city always made me uneasy and now there was the background buzz of tension from the fight with Cyn. We headed west at an unspectacular pace and the Blue Mountains got closer and the air heated up.

In Emu Plains we turned off the highway down the Old Bathurst Road and past the prison farm. We traveled five miles toward the mountains until the van turned off down a bumpy dirt track where I couldn't safely follow. I went on a bit and tucked the Falcon away off the road under some trees. I took the Smith & Wesson .38 out from under the dashboard, checked it over, and walked back. Half a mile along the track dropped sharply; at the foot of the hill there was a tree-fringed clearing and the van was pulled up in the middle of it. Short was mounting a camera in a tree on the left. I watched from cover up above the clearing. He fiddled, went into the clearing, went back, and then he got a second camera and stuck that in a tree on the other side. Next he took a carbine from the van, checked its action and hung it over his shoulder. He took out a small box, flicked a switch and counted to ten. His voice boomed out over the grass and set birds fluttering in the trees. He leaned back against the van, pulled down his goggles, and looked at his watch.

Ten minutes later a green Holden came over the hill. It pulled up on the edge of the clearing and two men got out; they wore business shirts and ties, and looked bulky and tough. Short's voice crackled out toward them.

"Stop," he said. "Cameras on the right and left, take a look." Their eyes swung off and Short unslung his carbine.

"The cameras are filming. There's a third one somewhere else." He lifted the rifle. "I used one of these in Vietnam. You get the picture?"

11

One of the men nodded and held up a manila envelope. "Right," Short said. "Give it to your mate. You, bring it here." He pointed with the rifle to a spot on the ground in front of him.

The envelope changed hands and the shorter of the two men came forward and held it over the place Short had indicated. He said something which I couldn't hear. Short spoke into the box again: "Back on the right hand side of the road, three tenths of a mile back you'll see a kerosene tin. It's in there."

The man shook his head; Short fired a quick burst at his feet; he dropped the envelope and jumped away. Short swung the muzzle slowly in an arc in front of him. The noise of the shots was still echoing. ". . . not a trick. Go!"

They walked back to the Holden, talking intently; they got into the car and drove off. Short stayed where he was, very alert. He ignored the envelope. He waited ten minutes then he relaxed, picked up the envelope and opened it. He let the two or three bundles of notes slide out into his hand, slipped them back and stowed them away in a pocket. Then he uncocked the rifle, put it against the wheel of the van and strolled across to the right-hand camera.

While he was working I crept down through the trees and sprinted to the van, bent low. He got the first camera down and for an awful second I thought he was going to bring it back to the van, but he put it down and moved across toward the other tree. He was whistling. I reached around for the carbine, worked the action loudly and stood up with it pointed at the middle of his back.

"Short."

He stopped whistling and swung around. I moved toward him keeping the rifle pointed at his belly. There was no self-satisfaction now in his high-coloured, handsome face. He lifted the goggles; they pinned back his hair, and I could see that it was retreating high on his temples.

"Surprise," I said.

"Smart," he said. "I suppose you want the money?"

"I might," I said. "But I really want the girl."

"What girl?" He took a few steps and I moved the gun. "Easy."

He ignored me and kept coming. "What girl?" he shouted. Despite the gun I'd lost the authority and stepped back. I said "Selina," and he swerved to one side and swung a long, looping punch at my ribs. A gun you're not going to use is useless; I dropped it and tried to punch him in the belly, but he moved and I hit his shoulder. We circled and shaped up like schoolboys; he rushed me and tried to tear my head off with a swinging right. I stepped under that and got him quick and hard in the ribs. He tried to kick but then I grabbed his leg and flipped him over. While he was wondering what to try next I got out the .38 and pointed it at his knee.

"Behave yourself, or I'll cripple you."

He nodded and sagged back on the ground. "Don't hurt Selina," he said.

"We're not communicating." I moved the gun a fraction in conciliation. "Selina was abducted this morning. I've been hired by her agent to find her. Do you know what I'm talking about?"

He sat up a bit straighter, but all the combat toughness had left him; he was pale and the hand he put up to pull off the goggles was shaking.

"I don't know," he said.

"You know something, sonny. This is a nice, quiet spot. Something nasty could happen to you here, and there's enough evidence about for me to fix it any way I like. D'you see what I mean?"

He nodded.

13

"Right. Now this was a pay-off you set up here. You're a photographer, I assume you were selling pictures, right?"

Another nod.

"You did a good job." I squinted along the line of the .38. "Who was in the pictures."

"Xavier Carlton."

"Jesus Christ." Carlton was a big-time businessman and sportsman with criminal and political associations, which every journalist in Sydney knew and kept quiet about. He was also a pillar of the Church. "Who else?"

"A girl."

"Selina. You bastard. How much?"

"Thirty thousand."

"For what?"

"Prints, negs, the lot."

I had no time for Carlton, he was a corrupt and vicious hypocrite but blackmailers are a low breed too, and this one had put his supposed girlfriend right in the shit. It was hard to understand.

"How did you set it up?"

He spoke slowly and carefully, editing as he went along. "Carlton was celebrating his Golden Slipper win, we latched on to him. He got amorous and I got some pictures."

I was sure he way lying; the careful preparations I'd seen suggested that he would have planned his move in detail— maybe down to dropping Carlton a hint or putting something in his champagne.

"You realise what you've done to the girl don't you?"

He looked away from me. "I put a note in with the film telling him she knew nothing about it. That's the truth."

I snorted. "Carlton wouldn't give a fuck. He's grabbed her and he'll break bits off her."

"She was supposed to be going away. I thought . . ."

"That he'd cool off? You picked the wrong boy. Carlton's crazy, he won't take this. He'll grill Selina till she tells him about you and he'll come after you."

"I was planning to get her away somewhere safe when I got through here. I thought she'd be okay at work today."

"You must have sent Carlton a sample. You might just have well cut her throat."

"Oh God, what can I do?"

I was thinking fast. How to get to Carlton? He'd committed himself by taking the girl and his natural inclination would be to clean up. He wouldn't take his money back and go home. What did we have? I looked at my gun and then at his gun and then at those cameras.

"How good will those pictures be?"

"The best."

"Get up." I moved back, took up the carbine, and pulled out the magazine while he stood irresolutely brushing dirt off his coveralls. I tucked the .38 away.

"Do you think you can take me?" I said.

"Maybe. Someone did recently. It depends in the circumstances."

"It always does. I don't think you can, but we haven't got the time to find out. Frankly, you make me sick, but do as I say, don't argue, don't think, and we might get her back. What do you say?"

He got up smoothly; he moved well. "Yes. I'll do whatever you say."

"Get the cameras. Let's move."

We drove back to the road and switched to my car. On the drive back to Sydney, Short told me that he'd set up the blackmail because he needed capital for his business, and money to cover gambling debts. He said he loved Selina. I didn't respond; he could've told me my name and I'd still want to check.

I hung around in Short's studio, which had a water bed and a lot of tedious albums of photographs, while he worked in his darkroom. He produced blow-ups of the faces of the two couriers and a couple of full length shots. He was right, they were good photographs.

Bill Abrahams is an ex-cop who drinks. He got shot and was invalided out of the force on a pension which keeps him alive and drunk in a room in Glebe. When he's not too drunk he can remember the face of every crim he's ever seen and after twenty-five years as a cop, that's a lot of crims. I bought a dozen cans and carted them and Short up the stairs to Bill's room. I banged on the door.

"Who is it?" Bill growled; he was capable of not opening the door if he was in the mood.

"Tooheys," I said.

He opened up and I handed in a beer. "They're cold," I said.

Bill took the beer and had a finger in the ringpull of a can faster than Ali can jab.

"C'mon in, Cliff. Good to see you. Have one?" Like all serious drinkers, Bill took a very proprietorial attitude to alcohol. We went in and I introduced Short. We sat around the laminex table by the window and opened cans. Short gulped his down and Bill looked keenly at him as he set him up with another.

"You're scared of somethin'," he said.

"He's scared of Xavier Carlton," I said. "He's gone and got himself in a bit deep and we're looking for a way out. How's the memory, Bill?"

He opened his second can. "Good as ever. It's all I've got left, sometimes I wish it wasn't so bloody good."

"I want you to take a look at these." I spoke quickly and motioned to Short to pull out the pictures; the danger with Bill is that as the alcohol level rises so does the water mark of his memories, and if they overflow the bank you never get to the point. "Anything you know about these blokes, anything."

Short spread the prints on the table; Bill hauled out his specs and examined the photo of the taller man who was holding the envelope. He stared hard at the image and then shook his head. "Don't know him."

I opened another can; Bill looked at the picture of the man who'd jumped back after dropping the envelope.

"Mustard Cleary," he said.

I let out a sour, beery breath. "And what do you know?"

"All bad. Stand-over man. Did some banks."

"Killer?"

"Could be. Did your mate here back him down?"

"Yeah."

"He won't like that at all. I wouldn't go near him without a gun, Cliff, even then . . ." He waved the beer can pessimistically.

"Where can I find him, Bill?" I got out a ten dollar note and put it under one of the empty cans. Short was looking at the pictures with an expression which was hard to interpret; he didn't look afraid, maybe it was shame.

"Mustard's a Brit originally," Bill said. "There was a pub he used to call his local. Where was it?" He drained his can and pulled another automatically. "Ultimo. The Wattle-tree, know it?"

"I know it. A rough joint."

"Certainly, that's Mustard's style. 'Course this is a few years back, could be a poofter palace now for all I know."

"I don't think so." I thanked Bill and we left him to the rest of the cans and his memories. On the drive to Ultimo Short said that it was a pity we'd left the M1 in his van, and I was inclined to agree.

It was near enough to 7 P.M., Thursday night, when we got to the pub—pension and pay night and the place was swimming along merrily on a tide of beer. The sight of a couple of women at the bar reminded me that I was going to miss my appointment with Cyn. I told Short to buy us drinks and look out for Cleary while I made a phone call.

"Cyn? I'm sorry, it's unavoidable. I . . ."

"It doesn't matter, Cliff." She sounded weary rather than angry and I took heart.

"I should be able to wind it up tonight, or maybe tomorrow. There'll be a good fee." The door to the public bar swung open and a wave of noise flowed out. I kicked it closed. "Cyn . . ."

"It doesn't matter," she said again and hung up.

I dialled again and the phone rang and rang. Back in the bar, Short had set up two Scotches, doubles, which was all wrong for comradely drinking in this sort of pub. I put the Scotch down quickly and ordered a beer. I hadn't eaten all day and the whisky on top of the beer hit me and made me incautious. I asked the barman if Mustard Cleary had been in lately.

"In earlier," he said. "In a bloody bad mood, too."

I forced a laugh. "Well, you know Mustard. Wouldn't know where he is now, would you?" The barman looked me over: I'm too thin and my clothes are too cheap to be a policeman, and Short was still wearing his coveralls. He didn't quite know how to place us so he hedged his bet.

"Marty might know." He jerked his head at a stocky man who was built like a bull; he had a bristling ginger air-force moustache and was wearing clean, starched, and ironed khaki shirt and pants. He looked up when he heard his name, and I negotiated the distance between us carrying my beer and fumbling for my makings. I reached him, pulled the tobacco out, and rolled one.

"Looking for Mustard Cleary," I said. "Smoke?" I pushed the makings across and he took them.

"What for?"

Short had come up behind me. "My mate and I have a delivery to make. He said to meet him here, we're a bit late."

He rolled a thin cigarette. "Didn't mention it to me."

"Well, it hasn't gone too smoothly. I understand he's a bit mad about it. Anyway, he'll be happy to see us, but I want to get on with it."

"What is it?"

I shook my head and ordered three beers. I lit both cigarettes and put the match away in the box, the way a con does. I was wondering how to get him out in the lane when he made up his mind suddenly.

"I can't tell you where Mustard lives because I don't know you. I can tell you where you might find him though."

I drank some beer and tried to keep it casual. "That'll do, where?"

"Said he was going fishing, didn't make much sense to me the mood he was in, but that's what he said. Mustard keeps this boat down off the lighters in Blackwattle Bay. Know the place?"

"I know it. Thanks."

"Tell him I'll have a snapper, moody bastard."

He turned back to his beer and we walked out. I looked into the bar through a window: Marty was lowering the beer I'd bought him and smoking my tobacco; he looked up at the TV set and didn't seem to be thinking of going anywhere. I headed for the car fast and Short followed me.

"I don't get it," he said. "What's going on?"

I gunned the Falcon's engine and swung out into the traffic. "What does the harbour mean to you, Short?"

"Shit, I don't know. Boats, the Opera House, the Bridge."

"Me too, but to people like Carlton and Cleary it means a good place to put bodies."

19

Short groaned and I turned off Bridge Road up the back way to Glebe, the way the taxi drivers go.

"You mean she's dead?" he said quietly.

"Not necessarily."

"Then what's the idea?"

I could hear his harsh breathing and feel his agitation; the Rafferty's rules style of the real hard men were becoming clear to him, and he must have seen his own little coup was a panto by comparison. I didn't feel like easing up on him.

"Ever hear of drowning? The lungs fill up with water and life stops. Happens every day and it's hard to prove that one person drowned another."

"Christ," he said. "Hurry."

The way he said it reminded me that he'd been in Vietnam. I turned at the cosmetics factory, cut the engines and the lights, and let the car roll down to the back of the blocks of flats near the water. Short was out of the car before me.

"How do we get down to the water?" he asked.

"There's usually a right of way." I pointed to a gap between two blocks of flats. "Have a look along there, I'll look up here." He scooted off and I moved up toward the end of one block. I turned back when I heard a low whistle; he'd found the right of way—an overgrown brick path with a derelict handrail that led down to the water. We stumbled down the path and across a stretch of grass to the half acre or so of lighter platforms linked together like chain mail. An outside light from the flats cut through the gloom but the end of the lighters and their far edges were in darkness. Dark, lumpy shapes stood up here and there, piles of boxes and other debris—cover. Across the water the container terminal was working; the machinery ground and grated and there was an occasional crash as a heavy load touched down hard.

"We go out to the end," I whispered, "and if there's nothing there we work around the sides. Keep under cover and listen for a boat, could be a motor, oars, anything."

Short nodded and we stepped over the gently lapping edge of the water onto a platform. It was slow, nervy work trying to avoid the collapsed and rotting timbers and keep under cover. About half way out we heard noises off to the left. Getting closer I could see movement; shoulders and heads against the light thrown out from the container dock. There was a boat in the pool of light and Selina Hope was sitting up in it; her hands were tied and there was something across the bottom half of her face. Mustard Cleary was picking up a box a few feet back from the water and the other man was untying a rope that ran from the boat to a cleat on the lighters. Short touched my arm and showed me the iron bar he held ready to hit with or throw. His readiness for action impressed me. I stepped out and moved up close with the .38 held out police style.

"Police," I yelled. "Don't move!"

Cleary dropped his load swearing; he ducked low and rushed the gun. I fired over his head and the sound was cancelled by a metallic crash from the container wharf, but Cleary heard it, and stopped. He bent down to grab something and I came forward quickly and crashed the gun butt down on his neck. He crumpled and I nudged him again on the way down.

When I untangled my knuckles and straightened up I heard heavy breathing and scuffling off to the side and saw that Short had moved to the edge of the lighters for a bit of hand-to-hand with the other man. The rope had been untied and the boat had drifted off a little; Selina sat ram-rod straight, watching the action with terror in her eyes. Short's opponent was swinging a bit of timber and Short was giving ground; then he seemed to lose his footing and he was hit on the shoulder. Some more swings, some more backing from

Short, then another stumble; the timber swinger jumped forward to go for the head but Short swayed aside and smashed his elbow with the iron bar. The timber hit the platform and Short put the bar to his knee, balls, and elbow again, quickly and scientifically. The guy screamed and begged him to stop. I moved in with the gun, feeling a little superfluous.

"Good," I said, but Short was hauling on the rope.

We got Selina aboard and free and she babbled and held on to Short as if he were the last sane man in a world gone mad. I eased them apart after a while and suggested that we be on our way.

"What about them?" Short asked. I was covering Cleary and his mate with my gun in a vague sort of way; Cleary was conscious but was more in a lying-down than standing-over mood. I gave Short one of my hard looks and held out my hand.

"Give me the money."

He looked pained but he handed the envelope over. I put the envelope down beside the man who was rubbing his genitals thoughtfully. "Tell Xavier to forget it," I said. "Tell him to go to confession and do the stations of the cross, and forget it. It's over, finished. Got it?"

He nodded and I patted his shoulder. "Wait here a while and then you can go home. Unless you'd like another go at him?"

He shook his head. We left them there with their aches and pains and thirty grand and walked across the lighters to the distant shore.

Back at the car Short made a clean breast of things, putting himself in the best possible light. He pleaded necessity, swore he intended to protect her, and so on. Selina had been scared witless by Carlton's boys: she said she'd done nothing but scream and cry and hadn't told them

22

anything because she hadn't understood what was happening. She still didn't, properly, but she'd seen Short fight like Lancelot in the lists for her and that was enough. They were both experiencing a sort of danger and deliverance high, and I felt like a voyeur. I drove them to Selina's place and made her promise to ring Athol Groom with the good news before she did anything else.

It was after nine on a clear, mild night but I was feeling far from clear and mild myself. There were things about Colin Short that niggled at me, but I had bigger problems. I stopped at the Toxteth and bought whisky for me and gin for Cyn. Maybe we could sit out on the bricks with the insects and take a little tobacco and alcohol and talk things out. Maybe. The house was dark and the front gate stood open but not welcomingly. I went in and found Cyn's note on the kitchen table: it said she was sorry, it said she had left and would collect her things tomorrow, it said good luck.

I poured a big drink, made some cigarettes and sat down to think. Like every married man I'd fantasised about being free; well, here it was and how did I like it? I didn't like it much. I drank some whisky and I still didn't like it. I thought that the talk wouldn't have gone well anyway and that it would have come to this and it was better to have missed that last fight. I drank and got angry and wanted the fight. She had no right to deny me the fight. Upstairs the bed was made, the ashtrays were empty, the books were stacked. She'd taken some clothes and things for beautifying herself. I looked around and mentally separated her possessions from mine. It was surprisingly easy to do.

I drank some more and self-pity ran strong and I thought sourly about Selina and Short and trust and love. I poured the rest of the whisky back into the bottle, drank two cups of strong coffee and went out to the car.

Breaking into Short's studio took about two minutes, locating his life's treasures took a little longer. Some marks on the floor and a certain artfulness about the ashes in the grate told me that all was not as it seemed. A section of the brick fireplace had been taken out to accommodate the heavy, brass-bound chest. I pulled it out, waited a few minutes to be sure that errant torch beams weren't attracting attention, and tickled it open with a skeleton key.

Colin Short was a great photographer; he had a particular talent for men in the public eye and attractive young women. I recognised a politician and radio announcer and could probably have identified a few other faces if I'd tried. A couple of films had a similar cast list.

One bundle of pictures showed a young, dark woman playing games around a swimming pool with a couple of very interested middle-aged men. The hair was different in style but it was Selina Hope. I took these pictures and a few samples of the rest and put the chest back.

I'd had some more whisky when I reached home so I was feeling rather weathered when I got to Athol Groom's establishment the following midmorning. He congratulated me and we negotiated a fee. I asked him for the dates of Selina's overseas trips and got them. The poolside pictures had a date on the back which proved to be just two weeks before one of Selina's trips.

"Hang around, Cliff," Athol said. "Selina's coming in and I know she'll want to thank you. What d'you make of this bloke of hers?"

I was about to answer when Selina came rushing in with Short tagging behind. She looked tousled and a bit underslept but marvellous. She gave me a peck on the cheek.

"You look tired," she said. "You must have a rest. I don't know how to thank you."

I wanted to tell her that Short was vermin, that he'd used her to make dirty money and probably would again. I wanted to see his sheepish bit-of-a-rascal look drop away and to see her flay him. But I couldn't; she was so purely happy, so forgiving and loving that I couldn't destroy it. I knew why I wanted to destroy it and I knew it had nothing to do with justice or her future happiness.

I shrugged. "Next time you do an ad for Scotch make sure you get a bottle for me. Could you excuse me, Selina? I want a word with Colin."

I took Short out into the corridor and showed him the pictures I'd souvenired from his collection. He went pale and plucked at a couple of bits of stubble he'd missed that morning.

"You're a lying, thieving shit," I said.

"What are you going to do?"

"You've retired as a blackmailer. If I ever hear you've gone back to it I'll drop these in the mail with a covering note."

"Don't worry," he said. "I'll burn the lot."

"I'm a born worrier. She didn't see Carlton the other day, did she?"

"No, just those two."

"That's something, maybe Carlton's smart enough to let it lie."

"We're going to New York," he said "Getting married."

"I'd keep it quiet," I said. "Just a few friends if you have any."

We went back inside and Athol opened some champagne for the occasion. I had a couple of glasses and got a decent kiss off Selina but it didn't do me any good. Later I went back to Glebe. Cyn had made a good job of cleaning her stuff out; she'd even taken the bottle of gin.

Heroin Annie

"You've got to help me, Mr. Hardy," the woman said. "Our Annie's going to end up in the gutter and I don't know what to do." The voice was adenoidal and Cockney, the bright lipstick was askew on her big, plain face and she was dropping cigarette ash all over my desk, but I liked her. Ma Parker lived in the street behind mine; she washed dishes in the local pub and sat in the sun outside her house. We talked about the weather and horses and London. I think she once thought I was a schoolteacher, but now she knew I was a private investigator and she'd brought me her troubles.

"You remember Annie, Mr. Hardy? A lovely kid she was."

I remembered Annie although I hadn't seen her for five years; back then she'd have been about thirteen and she was already tall. I remembered an oval face under straight blonde hair and not much else except the way she moved— she was graceful when she was tomboying in the street with the spotty boys or dragging home Ma's messages in a string bag.

"Tell me the trouble, Ma," I said. "I'll be happy to help if I can." I gave her a cigarette from a box of the things I keep for the weak—since I gave the habit up.

She puffed smoke and her false teeth clicked. "Annie ran off on the day she turned fourteen. She must've been planning it for a long time. I didn't know a bleedin' thing about it but she left me a note saying she had some money and not to worry. Worry! I went out of my mind with worry for nearly a year.''

I thought back but I couldn't recall noticing her distress. "I'm sorry, Ma," I said. "I don't remember it."

"Well, you were busy I expect. She was only a kid and I've got Terry and Eileen to think about. I just kept on, you know."

I nodded. I knew Ma had buried two husbands; I assumed she had a pension. I'd just let her be a walk-on character in the film of my life, the way you do. With the sensitivity suddenly tuned up like this, I looked at her clothes—they were cheap and clean except where she'd dropped ash. Ma herself seemed to be keeping up appearances okay; we were two of a kind, my clothes were cheap and getting due for a dry cleaning.

"Nearly a year, you said. How was she after that?"

"I didn't know her. She was all grown up to look at her. She got some money and took off again. The next time I saw her she was in Silverwater."

"What for?" I asked, but I'd have bet money on the answer.

"Drugs. Heroin and that—she was using them and selling them. She was giving them to kids younger than her. She got three years."

"Where? Some detention centre?"

"No, Silverwater."

"She'd be too young."

She stubbed out the cigarette; she looked old and worn but she wouldn't have been fifty. "She made me promise not to tell them her age, she said she was eighteen."

"She wanted to do her time at Silverwater?"

"That's right, Mr. Hardy. I couldn't believe it but what

could I do?" A couple of tears ran down her rouged and powdered face. It was one of those moments when I was glad I didn't have any children; she was puzzled, ashamed, and guilty, and all because this criminal was her daughter.

"What's she doing now?" I hadn't meant the words to come out so harshly, so full of hostility. She sniffed and looked at me uncertainly.

"Perhaps I oughtn't to have come. I was going to pay, you know."

That did the trick. Next I knew I was brewing her tea, stuff I never drink myself, and feeding her more cigarettes, and expressing indifference to money. The story was familiar enough: Annie had done eighteen months, came out on parole and went straight back in again on a similar charge. Now she was out again.

"Something happened to her in there, Cliff," Ma said. She was almost jaunty now, smoking away and getting down her third cup of tea. It was getting on to midday and watching her drink the muddy stuff made me think of something cold and wet in a ten-ounce glass.

"Come on, Ma, I'll run you home and you can tell me about it." We drove to Glebe and I bought her a beer in the pub opposite the trotting track. She said Annie settled down for a while after her second time inside, had a job and seemed steadier. But recently Ma had begun to have her doubts—she didn't like the look of the men who called for the girl and she had the feeling that she was heading for trouble again. She finished her first beer and I ordered another; she had a wonderful bladder.

"It's the drugs I'm worried about. She swore to me that she was finished with them, but I don't know."

"What do you want me to do, Ma? She must be a big girl now."

"She's still a kid really. You know how to investigate

people—just watch her for a day or two, see what her friends are like. And tell me if you think she's back with the bleedin' drugs."

"What will you do if she is?"

Suddenly she lost interest in the beer; there was a rough, flaky patch of skin near her nose, and she scratched it. To a turned-on eighteen-year-old she must have seemed like a survivor from the days of the Tudors. When she spoke her voice was shaky and tired. "You know, there was only ever one thing about me that Annie respected. Know what it was?"

I shook my head.

"That I was born in London. She's got a real thing about London, even reads about it. Anything on the telly about London she watches. Well, I've got a sister whose old man died a while back; and she hasn't got anyone, and she'd love to see Annie. Been looking at her photos for years and reckons she's the ant's pants. She'd pay for Annie to go over and visit her. It's the one thing that Annie'd toe the line for."

"You can't bribe people to be good," I said.

"I know that, but it's all I've got. I have to know what she's up to so's I can decide what to do."

I told her the usual things—that she might not like what turned up or that I might not be able to find out anything at all. But she'd made her mind up that this was how she wanted to handle it. She insisted on giving me fifty dollars and when I protested she turned fierce.

"I'm not bleedin' broke, you know. I work for it, and I expect to pay for work done."

I subsided. We finished our drinks and she left to walk home. I drove back to my place to have some lunch, re-arrange the bills in order of priority and kill the afternoon. Annie worked at a supermarket in Redfern, Ma had told me, and the strategy was to begin the surveillance that evening

29

to determine whether little Annie was or was not treading the path of virtue. I had fruit and wine for lunch and walked it off in the park as the shadows lengthened. It was autumn, and the ground was just beginning to soften from the occasional rain and the afternoon wind had an edge—it was a nice time to walk.

At a quarter past five I was sitting in my car opposite the supermarket. It was Wednesday and traffic and business were light; the shop window was plastered with signs offering cheap mustard pickles and dish-washing liquid. Some of the signs were torn and flapping, as if idle hands and the wind had not believed their promises.

Ma had told me that I wouldn't need a photograph to recognise Annie and she was right. When she came out at twenty to six she was recognisable from her walk; she still moved well, but there was something not proud about the way she carried her head. Her hair had darkened to a honey colour and she wore it short. In a lumpy cardigan and old jeans she headed across the pavement to a battered Datsun standing at the kerb; no-one stood aside for her and she had to push her way through. I saw her face as she got into the car; it was pale and clenched, knotted with anger and resentment.

The Datsun butted out into the traffic and I followed in my ancient Falcon like another old pensioner out for a stroll. We went down into Erskineville and the Datsun stopped outside a tattered terrace house mouldering away in the shadow of a sheet metal factory. A couple of blasts on the Datsun's horn brought a tall, thin character out from the house. He wore denims and sneakers and had to bend himself twice to get into the back of the car. I noted down the number of the house and the street and then the game began again. I don't do much tailing and I don't particularly like it, it feels too much like driving in a funeral procession.

The Datsun driver had bad manners; he cut in and bluffed out and raised several citizens' blood pressure dangerously. I stuck close and we went through the Cross and into the roller coaster of Double Bay. The apartment buildings don't look much from the outside, but the titles go for six figures; Annie and her mates were climbing the social ladder. The next stop was outside a newish three-story job with a lot of white stones to slip on and the sort of trees that have the bark peeling off them. The beanpole got out this time, and went into the building for a few minutes. When he came back he had a woman with him; in high heels she must have stood close to six feet and the purple jumpsuit affair she wore showed the world that here was someone who thought well of her body. She slid into the back seat of the car like a cat going into its basket; as she snaked her spike-shoed foot in I realised that I'd been holding my breath. I let it go and followed the Datsun down the hill into the gathering gloom.

They parked a few blocks back from Oxford Street and walked up in two pairs. The car driver was a nuggety number in jeans and a short leather jacket. The clothes accentuated the width of his shoulders and he had an easy, rolling walk like a fighter before the punches get to him. He kept his distance from Annie who mooched along with her hands stuck in the back pocket of her jeans. The beanpole and the Flamingo pranced on up ahead and a good couple of feet apart. He had a long, narrow head and crisp, curling hair; the woman had a high-tone up-market conceited strut. She didn't talk and the first act of communication she made was to take twenty dollars from her shoulder bag and hand it to the shorter man. He went into the bottle shop of a pub on Oxford Street and came out with a couple of bottles. They moved on; Annie drew closer to the leather jacket, and the tall girl tossed back a mane of platinum hair and led them to a restaurant that boasted French cuisine. A menu taped to the window told me that no main dish came in at under fifteen dollars. Through the smoked glass I saw them arrange themselves around a table and take the top off the rosé; it didn't seem likely that they'd duck out the back so I walked up past Taylor Square to a pub that has draft Guinness and honest sandwiches. Forty minutes later I was back outside the restaurant and forty minutes after that they came out. There was no wine left over and the blonde had lost some of her aloofness. The guy in the leather jacket was rock steady but the others were showing some signs. They stood on the footpath and debated something for a few minutes while I watched from across the road. A police car cruised down the strip and the blonde jerked her head at it and said something uncomplimentary. Annie lit a cigarette and the flame in her cupped, shaking hands jerked and danced like a marionette. They settled the point and walked up to the Square to a disco dive with a sign outside that read: "Drinks till two and do what you want to do."

It cost five dollars to go in which meant that this blonde, if she was still paying, was running up a fair bill for the night's fun. For the five dollars you got strobe lights and dark corners, mirrors to hate yourself in and noise. The beat of the music coming over the amplifiers was regular to the point of monotony and about as loud as the guns at Passchendaele. It was early for the action at this sort of joint; a girl was dancing with another girl and three men were dancing together on the polished floor. A few people sat drinking in plump-cushioned booths and my foursome sat up at a long bar. There were mirrors behind the bar which had the prices of the drinks written on them in white paint—a scotch cost two dollars and fifty cents, a Bloody Mary cost three dollars. I sat at the far end of the bar and ordered a beer. It wasn't an ideal place for a surveillance; alone and over thirty I stood out like a carthorse at the Melbourne Cup. Also I didn't know what to make of it:

Annie was out with some friends consuming alcohol, the fact that she had a bad case of the shakes and that three of the party looked as if they didn't have fifty cents while the other was wearing five hundred dollars on her back was interesting, but nothing more.

We all had another drink or two and I was thinking about calling it a night when he came in. His platform soles lifted him up high enough for you to call him short; he had on a dark three-piece suit with a dark shirt and a white tie. His body was plump but his head was abnormally small, it looked as if it was trying to duck down out of sight. He had a thin pasty face and stringy blonde hair, wispy on top and worn long. He looked as if he'd been made up out of leftover parts. He walked straight up to my party and the blonde bought him a green drink. They had a few giggles and then got down to what looked like serious talk, argument even. Annie shook her head a couple of times and Shorty downed his drink and made as if he was going to take the high dive off his stool. Then they all calmed down and the head shaking turned to nodding. Shorty got down and walked off toward a door with a sign over it that read "Powder your nose till it glows." Annie and leather jacket followed him, and thirty seconds later I followed them.

After the door there was a short, dark corridor and then a set of narrow, carpeted stairs. I went up the first flight, made a turn and then something like the Queen Mary hit me behind the ear. My face hit the carpet hard and a front end loader scooped me up and threw me down the stairs. I flipped over, hit my head more than once and never reached the bottom. I went down into the blackness and then down some more.

When I came out of it a cat was walking across my face and talking. I told it to be quiet and tried to brush it away but it stayed there and talked louder. At least it wasn't scratching, but I thought it might, so I opened my eyes. It wasn't dark at the bottom of the stairs anymore, there was a bright light burning about a hundred miles away and it was getting closer. I closed my eyes again.

"He's alive," a woman's voice said.

Another woman giggled. "How alive?"

I decided to kill the cat so I opened my eyes again. The light was closer this time, but not as bright, and the cat was a fur coat. Its owner also wore a pink leotard and spike heels. "What happened to you?" She had the same voice as the cat.

"I fell down the stairs."

The giggler giggled again. "Break anything?" She was small and dark with a big bright smile. She'd have been just the girl to take to an execution.

I located my arms and legs and flapped them. I didn't fly but I did manage to crawl up the wall and stand there with my head throbbing. Two versions of the big figure in the fur coat stood in front of me, I tried to fuse them into one.

"I'm okay," I said.

"Oh," said the small one, and I thought I detected a note of disappointment.

"You need a drink." Fur coat, leotard, spike heels and practical, too—my dream girl. I mumbled something and staggered through the door back to the fun parlour. There were more people around, more drinkers and dancers but no sign of the frolicsome four.

I didn't have the drink; being knocked unconscious disturbs the normal behaviour patterns. I plodded out to the street and walked two blocks before I realised I was going the wrong way. The walk back to my car was like a month on the chain gang. I stumbled and ran into things and people on the streets drew the natural conclusion; each collision sent daggers of pain stabbing into my head and only a strong mixture of pride and stupidity got me to the car. I sat in it for a while looking at the cars—the new fast ones and the old ones and the people who were just the same. When everything had settled down to a steady hum of distress, I drove home. My mirror showed me a right eye that was darkening and a swelling on the side of my head. There was no blood to speak of, and I did what I could with wet cloths and pain killers and went to bed. Just as I drifted into sleep I had one of those half-dreams where you fall off a step or a gutter, except that my step was high and over an endless void; I twitched like an electric shock victim.

I didn't wake up until nearly midday and waking up was no pleasure. My head and body ached and I felt weak as if I'd had a long illness; maybe I had, maybe it was this work I was doing. I dragged myself out to the kitchen for some food, ate it and went back to bed again. I did some more sleeping and it was dark when I came out of it to hear the phone ringing. I stumbled down the stairs.

"Mr. Hardy? Mr. Hardy, I'm worried. What's going on?" Ma's voice was urgent with concern and something else, maybe anger.

"Not sure I follow you Ma," I said. "I got knocked on the head last night by one of Annie's friends. I was going to tell you about it when I felt better. What's got you upset?"

"Annie, of course. She didn't come home last night and she hasn't been at work. I don't know where she is. I thought you might know. What happened? I mean, why'd you get hit?"

"I'm not sure, but I know your Annie's in bad company."

"The bloody drugs?"

"I think so. But one day out of sight doesn't mean anything necessarily."

"It's more than that. She was supposed to see her parole

officer today. She didn't turn up and he went to the shop. Now she's in real trouble. Mr. Hardy, Cliff, can you . . ."

I put my hand to my head, the swelling was large and pulpy and very tender to the touch. "Yeah, yeah. I'll try to find her, Ma. If she's ducking parole she won't want to see me. I might have to be rough."

"You do what you bleedin' have to."

I told her I'd work on it and keep her informed. She asked if she could help, but I couldn't see how she could. Then she said to be careful; that was nice, not many of my clients told me to be careful.

I had a cautious shower and shave and got dressed gingerly. Some food and a little wine and a careful checking of my gun made me feel better.

It was a little after six when I got to the house in Erskineville. There didn't seem to be any point in subtlety. I banged on the door, and when a hairy man in a dressing gown opened it I put the .38 to his right cheek.

"I want the tall, thin guy. Where is he?"

His mouth opened but no sound came out. I jabbed him a little with the gun. "Where?"

"He's gone. Went this morning."

"Show me."

We went down the dark hallway to a room at the back of the house. It had a bed and some basic furniture and was fairly clean. There were marks on the walls where posters had been torn off and a dust mark on the floor showed where where a bag or a box had stood. I motioned the man to stand in a corner while I looked in the cheap wardrobe: it was empty and so were the top two drawers beside it. I felt around in the bottom drawer and came out with a plastic syringe, the disposable kind. I held it up.

"Diabetic, is he?"

36

"No, no," he stammered. There were three roaches in an ashtray by the bed.

I looked at the man who was fiddling with the cord of the dressing gown. "What's his name?"

"Paul."

"Paul what?"

"I don't know."

"Where did he go?"

"Don't know."

"Don't know much, do you?"

"I don't know nothing. He stayed here a few weeks, paid his rent sometimes, not lately. I'm glad to be rid of him."

There was no point in pressing it. I put the gun away and left. Things were stirring in Annie's little circle and it wasn't too hard to guess what was causing the movement.

The next stop was Primo Tomasetti's tattooing parlour which is just down the way from my office. For a consideration Primo lets me park my car in the yard behind his establishment. I pushed the door open and entered Primo's surrealistic cavern: the parlour consists of one big room which is decorated over every inch with designs, large and small, which Primo promises to transfer to the skin. His creations range from the hetero-sexual-nautical to the most vivid, eastern-philosophy-inspired fantasies. I usually gape a bit on entering Primo's because he is capable of changing the motif of a wall overnight: I once saw disgusting imaginings involving mermaids changed into inter-galactic, time-capsule obscenities over ten hours. Primo paints on the walls and sticks needles into skin. There was a cowbell hanging from the ceiling and I rang it. Primo leapt into the room from somewhere dark and gloomy behind: that's how he moves, in jumps, except when he's wielding his tool of trade.

"Primo, caro, bonno sierra!"

He winced and adjusted the bow tie, spotted, red on

white, he wears with the business shirt, the white coat and the dark slacks.

"Cliff, you are the least talented linguist I have ever had inflicted on me." He reeled off some liquid sounds with gestures, and I watched admiringly.

"Mondo cane," I said, "L'adventura, Hiroshima mon amour. Primo, old friend, I need your help."

"At last!" He clasped his hands together and looked skywards like a bishop. "I see a Walther PPK, gun metal, under the left nipple."

"I see a little plastic bag, a sealed sachet maybe, colourless, with some white powder within."

"Stick to the wine and the Scotch, Cliff; it takes longer and you can still be interested in girls and food."

"Primo, I wouldn't touch it unless I had something terminal, you know that. Just now, for a reason, I need a little leverage. Come on, amigo, I'll pay you now and you keep ten per cent if I return it."

He looked at me like a parachutist inspecting his pack, looking for wrinkles, folds, imperfections that shouldn't be there. Then he shrugged and ducked back into the darkness. I examined the murals some more while I waited; Primo does not celebrate the drug culture, his preoccupations are carnal and his mission is the cure. He gives junk away, sells it, cuts it, feeds people, pays their hospital bills. The junkies respect him and very seldom stand over him, the cops leave him alone—he has a plan, a design, which no one else has ever understood but which most people take on trust. He came back with a flat, plastic square the size of a single serve of instant coffee. There was a teaspoon of white powder inside.

"First quality shit," he said, sounding like a dealer except that he waved my money aside.

I patted his arm, put the stuff in my pocket and went back

38

to the car. My head was aching again as I pulled up in front of the flats in Double Bay. They must have been expensive to buy or rent, because the residents were proud enough of their occupancy to put their names over the letterboxes. There was a Major Cahill, a Robert Something, a Henry Something-else and a Mr. and Mrs. and a Solomon Isaacs. The sixth flat was occupied by Samantha Coleman and her name plate was a fetching shade of pink.

I went up two flights of stairs and knocked on her door. I could hear disco music playing inside, it was loud and I had to knock again, hard. The door opened to the length of its chain, about eight inches. She was barefoot and wearing a Chinese dressing-gown; her eyes were hollow and the dark roots of her hair were showing. She looked at me, taking in the well-worn clothes and face, including the black eye.

"Yes?" Her voice was husky, accented. I caught a glimpse of suitcases on the floor behind her.

"Annie Parker," I said. "Paul, you, and a little guy with lifts in his shoes and a white tie."

Her eyes opened injudiciously; a network of tiny wrinkles sprang into life around them. "So," she said.

"I want to talk to Annie, I wanted to talk to her last night." I lifted my hand to touch the damaged eye.

"Oh, it's you, Mr. Nosey. Go away before you get hurt."

I brought out Primo's sachet and held it up for her to see. I looked around the deserted landing before I spoke.

"First quality shit," I said. "Guaranteed."

"You're selling?"

"Bargain basement, while stocks last. But I only deal with little orphan Annie."

"I'll have to make a phone call."

I waved my hand airily and the door closed. It was the sort of wait the weak-willed fill in with a cigarette. I filled it with doubt and fear. I waited longer than a phone call should have taken, unless she was discussing the pricing of oil. When the door opened she'd arranged her hair, put on her make-up and slipped into jeans and a sweater. She kept the chain on while she wriggled her feet into a pair of high-heeled sneakers.

"Have you got a car?"

"Yes."

"I'll take you to Annie, but I should tell you something first." She put her hand on the chain and jiggled it a little. "We'll be seeing a man who knows every narc in Australia, every one. Still want to go?"

I nodded; she slipped the chain and came out pulling the door shut behind her. She went down the steps wriggling her shoulders and swinging her bum as if she was trying to get herself in the mood for something exciting. I followed, watching the show with a mixture of feelings—arousal, amusement, and pity.

In the car she wrinkled her nose at the smell of age and neglect. I scrabbled in the glove box and came up with a cigarette packet containing three stand-by joints. I lit one and passed it to her.

"Thanks."

"Where are we going?"

"Wait and see." She sucked the smoke deep and held it before offering me the joint.

"No. I mean what general direction; I've got to drive it haven't I?"

"We going north, man." The accent again, South African, Rhodesian?

"North coast or north inland?"

"Coast, what d'you think. Palm Beach . . . oops, well, there it is, boy." She was enjoying the grass and she gave me a smile as she waved a hand signalling me to start the car. I started it and drove north.

"You don't smoke?" she said as she stubbed the joint out.

"Sometimes, not when I'm working. Where are you from, Samantha, South Africa?"

She giggled. "Close. Salisbury, Salisbury Sam, that's me. Greatest country in the world till the blacks took over."

"Good times, eh?"

"The best, man, the best. The best of everything. Can I have some more of that grass?"

"Help yourself." She lit up and settled back to smoke. I drove and thought. We took the turn at Pymble and headed for Mona Vale. I pulled the car up at a small mixed-business shop set back a bit from the road. Samantha looked sleepily at me and I told her I wanted chewing gum. In the shop I bought a packet of corn flour, some bananas in a plastic bag, the evening paper and the gum. I put about a quarter pound of the flour in the plastic bag and wrapped it up in some sheets of newspaper. On the way to the car I stuffed the package down in the bottom of a little bin outside the shop. I got back in the car and handed Samantha a banana.

"Drek," she said, so I gave her some chewing gum instead.

We rolled on up through the northern beaches playspots until we hit the biggest playspot of them all. It was nearly ten, and everything along the strip was going full blast—it was all chicken fat and pinballs and the popping of cold, cold cans. Samantha directed me off the main road and down a few side streets which were discreetly bordered by ti-trees and money. After the last turn, the ocean stretched away in front of us like a vast velvet cloud.

The house was one of those structures that have been pinned to a hill like a butterfly to a board. The steps down to it were steep and the house touched land only along its rear wall; the rest was supported by pillars which must have been fifty feet high at the front. Before I left the car I made a show of putting the big Colt into the clip under the dashboard. Sam watched, looking bored, but I had the short barrel .38 tucked in safe under my waistband at the back.

They were all there in the bright living room watching TV and drinking Bacardi rum—Annie, beanpole Paul, the guy in the leather jacket and the near midget. Shorty was wearing a lime-green safari suit tonight, and highly polished boots with Cuban heels. Sam headed straight for the bottle and poured herself a big slug over ice. She offered it to me and I shook my head.

"Hello, all," I said. "Hello, Annie."

She glanced up from her drink and shrugged. Leather jacket stood up and walked over to me; he had acne scars and a gold front tooth and he looked tough. I tried to look tough back.

"Name?" he said.

"No."

He flashed the tooth and spoke to Shorty. "You know him, Doc?"

Doc pushed back a strand of the stringy hair and looked at me with his pale eyes. The flesh around his face and neck was like soft, white dough.

"No," he said. "He's not a narc. Don't like the look of him, but."

I shrugged and took out the heroin. "I know Sammy and Annie and Paul and I'm pleased to meet Doc; who're you?"

"Sylvester Stallone," he said. "Let's have a look at the shit." He reached for it, but I moved it out of reach.

"You look, I talk to Annie."

"How much have you got?" Doc asked. His voice was deep and resonant, belying his appearance.

"One kilo, pure."

"Dean, you'd better have a look at that shit," Doc said. "Annie, talk to the man."

I tossed the sachet to Dean and motioned to Annie to come out on to the front balcony with me. She got up and moved sluggishly through the French windows. The others gathered around Dean ignoring the television and their drinks—they were communing with their God. The balcony ran the width of the house; it was about eight feet deep and glassed in for half of its length. Where we stood was open—out in front of us there was just the dark night and the sea. Annie stood with her back to the rail, the cigarette in her hand glowed like an angry red eye. I moved up close to her, took her hand and moved it around to the small of my back so she could feel the gun.

"Feel that? It's a .38, does nasty things. I'm going to use it on some of your friends if I have to."

"Who the hell are you?"

"My name's Hardy. You wouldn't remember me, but I live near your Mum in Glebe. She's hired me to find you and help you if I can."

"What are you doing peddling shit, then?" Her breath was heavy with tobacco and alcohol; there was a rank smell from her clothes as if they'd been slept in. She was also trembling violently.

"That was a blind to get me here. You're in a bad way, Annie, you must know that."

"Sure. What do you reckon you can do about it?"

"I can take you out of here. I know some people who've worked the cure. Your mother wants to talk to you, your parole officer's not too happy. The way you're going your life's rotting away in front of you."

She sagged against me into what I thought at first was a fit, then I realised she was laughing. The spasms shook and twisted her; she was leaf thin and impossibly light; I put my arm around her and could feel the sharp bones poking through the tight skin. I got hold of a morsel of flesh on her upper arm and pinched hard.

"What's funny?"

"Everything." She cut the laugh off with a deep breath which she expelled slowly. She looked over my shoulder into the room. "We've only got a minute. Look, Hardy, I'm working for the narcs. I don't want to, but they've got me by the tits. Understand?"

I nodded.

"There's a guy coming here tonight with some smack, a lot of it. It's a set-up. When Doc pays him, he's going to bust them all. It's arranged."

"What do you get out of it?"

Her tired features worked their way up into a sort of smile. "Freedom," she said. "That's what they've promised me. They say they'll wipe my slate."

"Any money?"

"Some, enough to get out of this bloody place. It's my one chance, Hardy. If you butt in now you'll screw it for me, and they'll come down hard on me. You know what they're like."

I did. I knew what they could do to people who got caught in their dirty world, a world in which the narcotics agents themselves were not the least dirty part. I squinted at her in the soft light, trying to gauge her levels of truth and reality, but you can't assess junkies on the normal scale— their habit over-rides everything else, straightens out their curves and throws in new ones. Anything was possible, but there was a note in her voice that could be taken for sincerity and she was Ma Parker's daughter.

"I'll buy it," I said. "When's he due?"

"Soon, any minute. I'm trying to come off it, I'm badly strung out. It has to be soon, has to be. Shit, I really didn't need you in the scene."

"We'll see. Look on me as your insurance. Why did they agree to let me come along if they've got this big score lined up?"

"Greed. Look, we can't stay out here, and I need a drink bad. I'm going back."

She moved away and I let her go. Inside new drinks were being poured and cigarettes lit. The television was still on; tennis players in coloured uniforms moved around on a red court under a blue Texas sky. Dean had slit open the sachet with a razor blade and his face was showing a little awe as he looked at me.

"You say you've got a lot of this stuff?"

"I may have exaggerated a little." I looked him up and down and let my eyes drift off over Doc and Paul. "I've got as much as you can handle anyway."

Doc spoke quickly. "We'd need to see more of it, Dean. Anyone can get hold of this amount of good shit. There's something about this that worries me . . . this packet."

Paul and Sam were working on a big joint, rolling it with a number of papers and giggling. Paul was singing a song about Rio. Dean sneered at them and went over to where Annie was standing; she had a cigarette burning and her face was drawn tight and stiff.

"What do you know about this guy, Annie?" Dean said.

"I had a girlfriend in Silverwater," I improvised. "She . . ."

"I was asking her!" The scars on Dean's skin showed out white and malignant-looking as anger pumped colour into his face. Doc was staring at the square of plastic in his hand and it was an altogether nasty situation when a soft knock sounded on the back door.

"That'll be him," Annie whispered. "This is it."

"Two big scores in one night," Sam said putting a match to the cigar-sized joint. "Let's celebrate."

"Shut up," Dean hissed. "Paul, open the door; Doc, stand back so you can get a good look at him." Dean reached inside his jacket and took out a .45 Colt automatic;

he slid the hammer back to full cock and stood where he could get a clear shot at the door. He obviously knew what he was doing, and I felt even more under-equipped and unready with the .38 tucked down behind.

Paul opened the door, and the man who came through it conjured up pictures of the *veldt* and *sjamboks*: he was about six feet tall with wide, beefy shoulders; his face was reddish and broad, topped with thin, sandy hair. He had that blue-eyed, mass-produced in Holland look, which repels most people not of the same stamp.

Doc wasn't repelled; a smile spread over his pasty face; stretched tight, his lips were like a pair of peeled almonds.

"Hendrick, dear friend," he cooed. "Hendrick, is it really you?"

The newcomer didn't smile back; his pale eyes flicked around the room, rested on me for an uncomfortable time, and then settled into a neutral, business-like glare.

"I thought it'd be you, Doc," he said. "It had the smell, you know." His accent was three shades thicker than Sam's but it was formed under the same African skies. He moved forward like a man about to take control. His grey suit would have been conservative except for the over-bold red check in it. There was a gun bulge under the left lapel and a bulge of another kind in a side pocket.

"Don't be like that, Henk," Doc said soothingly. "We're all friends here. Let's get down to business."

I took a side long look at Annie; her cigarette was burning away unheeded and extra strain seemed to have stripped the flesh from the bones of her face. I didn't know what sort of act she'd expected from her contact, but it clearly didn't include pleasant greetings from Doc. A double-cross was in the air and she could sense it. Dean acted as if comprehension was no concern of his; he held the .45 at the ready and waited.

46

Hendrick ignored Doc's patter and looked again at me. "Who's he?"

"Dealer," Doc said, "small time, nothing to interest you, Henk."

I took a chance. "Not so small," I said. "Fair sized consignment, first grade stuff." The heroin was lying on a chair arm and I pointed to it. "Sample."

The pale eyes seared me like acid. "Is that so?" he said. "Interesting." He walked over to Annie, took the cigarette from between her fingers and dropped it into her glass.

"Dirty habit, Annie," he said. His big white hand came up and he took a grip on her left breast. Annie looked down.

"I'm glad it's you we're dealing with, Henk," Doc said rubbing his hands briskly. "Annie had some story about a Vietnamese. You don't look like a Viet."

Hendrick laughed. "Well, Annie wasn't completely in the picture." He squeezed her breast harder. "It's my job to get in touch with all these desperados. But Doc here is a gentleman compared to some. I do the community a service by keeping him in business."

Sam was looking at him with her mouth slightly open— another one not repelled. Paul was well away with the grass; he'd smoked most of the joint and he was lying out on a sofa as if he was ready to levitate. Dean was still at his post.

Doc spread and waved his hands like the Pope bestowing a benediction. "There's no better smack than copper smack, let's see it, Hendrick."

He moved away from Annie and unbuttoned his jacket; the black butt of the gun curved out near his shirt pocket. He nodded at Dean. "You, put the popgun over there near the telly and then go back near the door." Dean did as he was told after a nod from Doc. Hendrick pulled out a package from his pocket and tossed it to Doc. It was wrapped in plastic, and when Doc had unwound it a couple of dozen small, linked plastic pockets rippled out like a snake.

"Hip belt," Doc said. "Good one. Annie said thirty grand, that right?"

Hendrick nodded and Doc went out of the room. When he came back he was carrying a manila envelope which he handed to Hendrick. Annie watched fascinated; maybe she was still hoping that her deal would go through, but it must have been a faint hope. Hendrick wasn't acting; he counted the money carefully and put it away in an inside pocket. He had no particular expression for thirty grand just as he had no particular expression for tit-grabbing; I wondered what he did for fun.

"This is a nice place, Doc. Had it long?"

Doc shrugged; he was looking uneasy and Dean was shifting his feet like a boxer about to start punching.

"What about a drink?" Hendrick moved towards the bottles and then suddenly darted right and picked up Dean's gun. He had the safety off and the thing on full cock in one smooth movement, the way they train them to do where he came from. Our host looked worried for a minute, but his expression changed when Hendrick pointed the gun at me.

"You know, Doc," he said, "you shouldn't deal with fly-by-nighters like this. Could get you into trouble. Is his stuff good?"

"The best," Doc said.

"Is it now? Well, I just might take him and it into custody and do myself some good." He lifted the .45 a fraction. "You wouldn't object, Doc?"

Doc licked his lips; there was reluctance in his face, greed as well, but they both had fear to contend with. He let the plastic belt slide in his hands. "No, Henk," he said. "Be my guest. Nothing rough here though."

"Of course not." He moved up to me and put the muzzle of the .45 under the point of my chin.

"Where is it?" This was what he did for kicks; he

pronounced the "where" like "vair" and there was a big, blue vein standing out under the pink skin of his temple.

"No rough stuff here, Henk," I said.

He brought his knee up accurately and I went down with that feeling of pain and violation rolling through my body. As I hit the floor I felt the gun bite into my back and I had the consoling thought that I might get a chance to shoot him where he'd placed his knee. I lay there blinking as the spasms shot through me. My wallet was in the top pocket of the denim jacket I was wearing and he bent down and lifted it out. He looked through the contents letting them drop to the floor one by one. There was only money, driver's licence and stray papers. I contemplated an attack from below but the gun in his hand was nicely directed and rock steady.

"Clifford somebody; nobody." He dropped the last paper disdainfully like an ice cream wrapper.

I sat up, controlling the pain and gathered the things from the wallet. I was about to put them back when Hendrick stood on my left hand. He bore down on it with all sixteen stone, and I screamed.

"Where?"

I shook my head. He swung his other foot at my head; I rolled away from it a bit but he connected near my ear. I felt skin tear and bones click, and there was a roaring sound getting closer. The warmth on the side of my face and neck was my blood.

"Now, Henk," Doc said.

"Shut up! How'd he get here?"

"Sam brought him," Dean said. "He said he knew Annie."

Hendrick looked at Sam with interest, she returned the look.

"He showed me the sample," she purred.

"Did he say he had it with him?" Hendrick was still looking at her, but as if he'd like to hurt her.

"He didn't say."

"Did he stop anywhere?"

"No, oh yeah, he did stop. He bought chewing gum."
She giggled. "And bananas."

"What else did he do? It's important."

Sam was pretty stoned but she gave it a good try. "Well,
he gave me some gum and he had some good grass in the
car. He didn't smoke and he's got this sort of springy step."
She giggled again.

"What?" Hendrick snapped.

"Well, I was thinking how he was Mr. Clean, you know,
not smoking and that. And outside the shop he shoved his
hand into this rubbish bin, like a derro. It looked funny but I
guess he was throwing something away."

He glanced down at me with the look he probably used
when he was kicking the kaffirs about. "Amateur!" he
sneered. I groaned and let him have his fun.

"Well, I think that winds it up here," Hendrick said.
"Get on your feet you." He helped me with a kick on the
leg and I promised him something for that too. "Annie,
you're coming with us, and you too." He waved the gun at
Samantha. "You can show us the spot."

"I don't know . . ." Sam mumbled.

"Yes, you do. Let's go."

"Hey," Dean rasped, "what about my gun?"

Hendrick looked at the .45 and slowly swung it around to
point at the bridge of Dean's nose. "It's a good piece," he
said. "I like it."

I got up slowly trying to look more wonky than I felt. I
was glad he liked the gun, a man with two guns isn't
looking around for a third; stands to reason. He herded us
out of the house and up the steps to his car, a yellow
Cortina. Annie moved listlessly and Sam tried to regain
some of her oomph, but it was a losing battle, she was
stoned and scared. Hendrick gave the keys to Annie.

"You drive and the blonde can keep you company. I'll cuddle up in the back here with Clifford."

Annie drove slowly and steadily and Sam sat rigidly beside her. I slumped back in the seat away from Hendrick and groaned from time to time. The blood had stopped flowing and the pain in my head wasn't worse than an impacted wisdom tooth. I concentrated on blaming the man beside me for the pain and the ills of the world generally.

After a while Hendrick asked Sam a few questions, and encouraged her replies with a few prods of the .45. He'd uncocked it, but I remembered the speed he'd displayed before—not yet. We slowed down and after a few false alarms Sam found the right shop. It was closed; there was forest on one side of the road and the houses on the other side were set well back from the road and behind high hedges and shrubberies. There was light from a street lamp a little way off but not much of it. There were two rubbish bins outside the shop.

He got Annie to U-turn and we pulled up twenty feet or so back from the first bin. Hendrick stuck the gun in my ribs.

"How're you feeling, man?"

"Lousy."

"Good. Now I want you to get out, go up to the right bin and retrieve something. Then bring it back here to me. If you do anything silly I'll shoot you and there'll be all the evidence I need to make it okay. Understand?"

I nodded wearily and got out of the car. There was a light breeze and it hurt the torn flesh by my ear. I limped up to the first bin, paused a minute and then went to the second. I put my hand on its rim and then collapsed, rolling on to my side where I could see back to the car. Nothing happened for several long seconds, and then Hendrick got out. He still held the .45 and he was very wary. I played dead and let him put his boot toe into my ribs. He seemed satisfied and burrowed down into the bin, still keeping the gun on target. He pulled his hand up with the package and proved he was human—for a split second he forgot me and looked at his prize. Adrenaline was flooding me—I grabbed the gun hand and pulled it down while I swung one foot at the back of his knee. He grunted and came down and I ground the fingers into the cement; I felt his little finger break and his grip relax, and I slammed the hand down again. He let the gun go and whimpered a bit. I got up fast and reached back for the .38. His eyes were wide with pain and surprise as I put the muzzle between his eyebrows.

"Henk," I croaked, "you should pick your enemies better." I kicked the .45 away into the shadows and put the .38 into the rubbish bin. "Get up."

He was good; he came up fast and threw the package at me but I was ready for that, and he missed anyway. I put a straight left on his nose and felt it give. He roared and swung wildly; I let him miss twice and then I stepped up and hooked a hard right into his mouth. The flesh split and a couple of his big, beautiful white teeth collapsed and I hit him there again. His hands went up to his face and he stepped back, then he lowered his head and charged; I stepped away and he went hard into the post which held the bin. I ripped him twice under the heart and he went down and lay still.

I was breathing hard and both hands were hurting, but it was my turn to gather guns and money. I collected the lot and picked up the plastic packet of corn flour from the roadway. Annie got out of the car and walked over to Hendrick *couchant*.

"You should've killed him," she said.

"No, he should have killed me."

The whole thing only took a couple of minutes and if any

52

cars had passed during the action their drivers must have decided it wasn't their scene. A car cruised up now with a genuine citizen aboard; he wound down the window and put his big, bald head out.

"Trouble?" he said.

"I'd taken Hendrick's ID card out of his wallet: it carried the name Hendrick Hasselt and a photograph. I put my thumb over the photo and flashed the card.

"No trouble. Making an arrest. Good of you to stop." I tried to look as if I always went about with three guns and thirty grand mad money on me. He didn't like the effect but he wasn't a fool; he nodded and drove on.

Hasselt was wearing a rather nice line in paisley ties; it looked better around his wrists and he looked better on the back seat of the car, bleeding gently over his upholstery. Sam sat in the back with him and Annie drove us to Palm Beach. We had a quiet talk on the way; as she told it, she was right in the middle between Doc and Hasselt and his colleagues. It all rang true and when I asked her how she felt about a loan and a little trip abroad she gave me the first real smile I'd seen her use.

"Can you do that?"

"I think so. I'll do it for Ma mostly. You, I'm not sure about. It depends how you feel about the junk."

"Never again." she said. "Believe me."

I didn't say anything—what can you say? They opened the door to Annie and we all trooped in. I used the .45 to impress Doc and Dean, but after dumping Hasselt in a chair they didn't need much impressing. Paul was stretched out asleep on the sofa and the little packet of heroin was nowhere to be seen.

Dean looked at Hasselt and breathed out slowly. "What happened to him?"

"He got careless and he wasn't quite as good as he

53

thought he was. Now you just be quiet and you'll get your gun back." I walked over to Doc and pushed him down into a chair, then I tickled his knee cap with the gun. "Tell Sam where the shit is, or you'll never walk again." He told her and she brought it out.

Hasselt looked bad but he was taking an interest; one side of his face was darkening fast and he was working at a loose tooth with his tongue, maybe several teeth. I took out the plastic bag and showed it to him.

"Can you cook?"

He shook his head.

"Pity," I said and dumped the cornflour in his lap, the dust flew up and he sneezed, and that caused him pain and he swore. I poured myself a small splash of Bacardi and sipped it, I could see why they drowned it with Coke.

"Now," I said, "let's all go to the bathroom." I finished my drink and we all trooped into a bathroom that had white and red tiles and good-looking plumbing. I tossed the plastic belt to Doc.

"Open it up, Doc, and pour it all into the toilet bowl."

"No," he screamed. "That's a hundred thousand . . ."

I smiled at him. "As Henk said to me a little while ago, there's enough evidence here to arrange things anyway I like. If you're found dead, Doc, clutching a hundred grand worth of heroin, no one's going to ask too many questions. Start pouring!"

He did, and the action seemed to cause him physical pain. When the water in the bowl was clouded up with the white powder I took the belt from him and held it under a running tap.

"Now, flush the toilet like a nice clean boy." He did, and a hundred thousand dollars headed for the sewer.

Back in the living room I put my .38 handy and unloaded the .45. I tossed the gun at Dean and told him to put it all down to experience. I took out the manila envelope and tapped it on the coffee table. Doc and Hasselt looked at it like cats eyeing a bird.

"I was hired to look out for Annie," I said, "and it turned out she needed it. Now you and and you have got problems." I tapped the envelope again. "Do you know what this can buy me in Sydney in the way of people to take care of you two?"

They didn't say anything, but they knew what I meant.

"Right, now Annie's going away. She might be back soon or she might not, either way it's no concern of yours. Do you get me?"

Doc nodded, Hasselt didn't move, it would have hurt him to nod.

"The same goes for me. I'll put a little of this around, and you won't even piss without me knowing about it. If I hear that you have used my name or Annie's in vain, someone will get a chunk of this and you'll be missing."

I took Annie home, and twelve days later she was off; after we worked things out with her parole officer and did an express job on her passport. I made her a small loan and paid Primo for the heroin and gave him a bit extra too. That left twenty odd thousand which I split into four lots and posted to deserving organisations. A month later I got a postcard from Annie; it had a picture of a naval gentleman on top of a high pilar; so I gathered she was in London—I couldn't read the writing.

The luck of Clem Carter

Clem Carter was the welterweight boxing champion of the Maroubra Police-Citizens Boy's Club in 1955. The title didn't mean much to most people, but it meant a hell of a lot to Clem; and it meant something to me too because I was the one he beat in the final of the tournament. He was a tough kid, Clem, working at fifteen as a brickie's mate; and he had a couple of stadium fights in the next few years while I was finishing school and not finishing university. Then I went into the army and Clem went to gaol. He got three years for grievous bodily harm, and he told me later that he had so many fights inside that he had to serve the whole time.

After fighting, cars were Clem's big thing—when he was young he stole them, later he built and raced them. I met him a few times in the early seventies when he was racing stockcars; the boxing scars on his face were overlain with marks of racing injuries, and he was drinking heavily. But he was cheerful—he was newly married and heading up north to manage a new speedway. Then someone told me that he'd been sentenced to fifteen years for armed robbery and then he was in the news—for escaping.

I didn't think much about it. I was working on a mildly interesting job, trying to locate a union official who'd gone missing with a certain amount of money. It was hard to tell whether or not he was more crooked than the people who wanted him. I got home late this night, tired from covering some far-flung addresses, and dry. I hadn't had a drink all day. I edged the old Falcon into the small yard at the back of my house, got out, locked it, and felt the hard metal bite into my ear.

"Put your gun on top of the car, Cliff."

I did, and turned around slowly. He was always a fast mover, Clem; he slid around, grabbed the gun and dropped the length of pipe he'd been holding. He could hit too, and got mean when he was hurt, so I smiled at him.

"Hi, Clem, get sick of the food?"

He jerked his head at the house. "Inside." He'd beaten me easily when he didn't have a gun, and there was only a crummy electo-plated cup riding on it, so I didn't fancy my chances now. I walked to the back door and opened it, went in, turned on lights and opened the fridge.

"Drink, Clem?"

He raised the gun. "No, you either."

"Christ, have a heart, I'm bloody dry!"

"I haven't had a drink in five years, Cliff."

"You used to like a drink."

"Yeah. Make some coffee; I see you've got the fixings. Have you got a thermos?"

I said I had, and got it out. I felt more than a little relieved, it sounded as if Clem was planning to travel. I put my car keys on the bench to help the idea along. The coffee pot is big and I gave it a full charge; and then I took a good look at Clem. He looked fit; he was quite brown and his body, under the prison denims and a knee-length plastic raincoat, looked hard. He looked a hell of a lot better than the last time I saw him and that could only mean one thing—he'd kept fit for a reason. His face confirmed that; his jaw was set firm under his battered nose and he emanated purpose and plan. I fiddled around with the coffee things, wondering what to say to him; I didn't think Clem would shoot me, but gaol does strange things to people and guns do go off.

"How'd you get out, Clem?"

He gave a short, sour laugh. "You ever been in there?"

"Yeah, just on remand, week or so."

"Remand! A playground. You should try the real thing. Well, I sucked up and got a job in the kitchen. I fixed one guard and a couple of the cons."

I poured the coffee and pushed the sugar across to him. I haven't used sugar since I went on my fitness kick a year ago. Clem ignored the sugar, sipped the coffee black. "Must have cost you," I said.

"Right." He looked at me carefully and put the gun down by his cup. "It's funny that, I had to get a mate to sell one of my cars. Joannie . . . ah, never mind, I'll sort it out."

I drank some coffee, still wanting a real drink "What're you going to do now, Clem?"

He picked up the gun. "You're driving me north. When we get there I'm going to use this on a man."

"That's crazy. That's life!"

"I didn't do that job, Cliff, he put me in."

"Still . . ."

"Don't chat about it! Five years . . . what've you been doing in the last five years?"

I finished my coffee, didn't answer.

"A few birds, Cliff? Bit of travel? I remember you used to read a lot; well, I've had plenty of time to read and to think. So I know what I'm going to do and I don't want to bloody debate it with you. Okay?"

I nodded, Clem had done a bit of self-improving in prison; he'd never have said "debate" before. He was all the more dangerous for it. I started to pour more coffee but he waved the gun. "Stick it in the thermos and make up some food, we've got a long drive."

I put together some bread, salami and cheese while Clem watched me. I took out the flagon of white wine but he shook his head.

"Let's go and get some clothes, we're still about the same size."

"A bit of luck that," I said.

He grinned at me. "Not really; I told you I've thought this out."

We weren't welterweights anymore, more like heavy middles; but a pair of my jeans and a shirt and windcheater fitted Clem well enough. I could have taken a chance while he was dressing, but he was still very quick and I knew I wouldn't have been able to use the gun on him anyway. It was a weird feeling; I was alarmed by his manner and his possession of the gun but I couldn't really believe that old Clem would harm me, and in a way I was glad of his company.

We went back downstairs and listened to the news. He listened intently but not with that inflated self-importance that leads criminals to keep scrapbooks and to want to be on TV: Clem wanted to find out what the cops were doing. The report was vague; Clem was described as dangerous and the police were appealing for help. It sounded as if they didn't have any ideas.

"They'll be looking for you up north, Clem," I said.

He rubbed his hand across his face. Some bristle was showing through but his last shave must have been a very close one. "I know," he said. "But they're pretty dim up there. I could get in and out with my eyes closed."

Suddenly I felt tired; I didn't want to go cowboying off north with Clem Carter while half the New South Wales police force chased us. I wanted a drink, several drinks, and

I felt more like reading about chases in Desmond Bagley than being in one. So I tried it; while Clem was checking the food parcel I made a grab at the gun. It wasn't much of a try, but even so Clem's speed surprised me: he side-stepped, kept the gun up out of harm's way and hit me in the pit of the stomach with his left. It was something like the left he'd dropped me with at Maroubra more than twenty years back and it had the same effect. I went down hard, and stayed down.

"You shouldn't have tried that, Cliff," he said nastily. "I can beat you anytime."

I sat on the floor, feeling my guts re-arrange themselves. "I know, Clem, I just don't like guns pointing at me. What about a truce?"

He eyed me suspiciously. "What sort of truce?"

"Put the gun away and I'll do what you say short of getting myself in too much trouble. I'll stick with you. If you shoot at anyone I'll run away. If you shoot at me I'll try to do you in any way I can."

He gave the sour laugh again. "Okay. I'll let you drop off as soon as I can."

We picked up the food, turned off the lights and went out to the car. Clem set the safety and put the .38 in the waistband of the jeans. "You drive," he said. "Take it easy, there's no hurry."

I worked the car out and we drove in silence through Glebe and Ultimo and on to the Harbour Bridge. There was rain in the air, threatening in the dark, purple-streaked sky, but the roads were still dry and the traffic was light. I told Clem I had to stop for petrol. He didn't like it much and made me keep going up the Pacific Highway until we hit a self-service place. Clem huddled down as I got out of the car.

"Don't do anything silly, Cliff."

"Hell no, this is fun. Do you want anything, smokes?"

"No, I've got no vices now. Just get on with it."

I fuelled up, checked the water and oil and tried to think of something clever but nothing came. When I got back in the car I handed Clem ten dollars.

"What's this for?"

"Give it back to me."

He did. "Now I'll consider you a client, Clem. It's as illegal as hell but it makes me feel better."

"You're full of shit, Cliff," he said but he seemed to relax a bit. The gesture was pointless, a farce, but it led him to talk about his mission.

Clem had been managing the Gismore speedway and making a fair fist of it for six months. They were taking a few thousand dollars a meeting and the prospects looked good. He bought a house which was attached to an older timber mill and this gave him a big covered space for a workshop. In his spare time he worked on improvements to his cars. According to Clem it was the owner of the speedway, a guy named Riley, who came up with the idea of holding meetings for six days running, a sort of tournament for the different models of cars. For the last meeting, Riley gave Clem the night off. He went home, collected his wife and set off for the movies, but the car broke down up in the hills. Clem was still working on it when the cops came. The speedway had been knocked over with close to $30,000 in the till. Riley, who'd taken a shotgun blast in the shoulder, identified Clem as one of the heavies. He also said that the six day meeting had been Clem's idea. The cops found a dust coat, mask and sawn-off shotgun with one barrel recently discharged in Clem's car. Clem's only witness was his wife, Joannie, and she didn't impress anyone. They searched the house and found letters from Riley giving Clem hefty advances on his salary. Clem said he'd never seen the gun or the mask or the coat before, nor the letters. Riley spent some time in hospital and he closed the speedway. The town lost jobs and entertainment. No one wanted to start a Clem Carter fan club—and he got fifteen years for armed robbery and wounding.

The way he told it impressed me. Clem was never known for his imagination and the story hung together pretty well. A few things bothered me though.

"This Riley'd be stealing his own money, wouldn't he?"

"No. He had big overheads, loans, salaries, taxes; this was a gift."

"Wouldn't he have moved on by now?"

Clem was staring ahead up the road. "You'd reckon he would, wouldn't you? But he hasn't. I expect I'll find out why when I get there."

"He'll move when he hears you're out."

"I've got a mate up there, he'll keep me informed."

"I still don't see what you reckon to get out of it."

"Revenge."

"Bullshit. You're going to kill a man for revenge, bullshit!"

"All right, Cliff, I'll tell you. I'm not going to kill him, I just said that to sound hard. You're a smart man, you must be able to guess why I'm going after him."

"The money," I said.

"Right. He hasn't touched it, it's still around somewhere and I'm going to ask him nicely where it is."

"And then . . ."

"You meet some interesting people in gaol. If I can get my hands on the money I can get out of the country, no worries."

"If you can get the money it'll prove you didn't do the job."

He sneered at me. "How?"

I could see his point—after some thought—chances were if he walked into a police station with a bag full of money they'd say thanks very much, and send him back to the slammer. Still, I was liking it less and less; it sounded like unpleasantness followed by deserted beaches or airfields. I like to do my traveling in the daylight with a lot of people taking the same risks. As I was thinking, I raised the speed a bit.

"Take it easy, Cliff, I don't want to draw any attention. I want Riley to sweat, but I don't want him to know whether I went north, south, east, or west."

We got to Newcastle around midnight, and I watched the motel signs flashing by and thought about sleep. I put the question to Clem and he uncorked the thermos for an answer. That worked for a while, but after an hour on the open road I was sagging and letting the car drift a little.

"Okay, let's not be statistics," Clem said. "Pull over when I tell you and we'll rig something up."

We turned off the highway down a dirt road which had trees, widely spaced, growing alongside. We went in through the trees and pulled up about thirty feet back from the road, pretty well sheltered. Clem rummaged around in the back of the car and came up with a long piece of flex. He wound the middle part of it around my ankle and took the two ends to tie around his foot. I stretched out in the front seat and he took the back. There was a coat and a blanket in the car and he slung the blanket over to me. It was cold and uncomfortable, and I soon needed a piss. Clem's breathing was steady but whether he was asleep or not I couldn't tell. Eventually I slept in snatches; but I was cramped, stiff, and bursting at first light when Clem stirred in the back.

"Have a good night, Cliff?"

I grunted something uncomplimentary and he laughed. "You should try to stay at the Bay, Cliff, this is a picnic."

He untied us and pushed his door open. "Splash the boots, Cliff, and let's get moving."

He looked pretty fresh, considering, although his stubble was darker and there was some tension in his movements. He kept patting the gun in his waistband. We pissed, and ate some of the food while the day got started; the sky was clear and even this distance north and Sydney there was a different taste to the air, fruity. I moved toward the door but he put his hand on my arm.

"I'll drive."

I shrugged and got in. He tapped the wheel and gear shift as if getting the weight and balance of them, and then we were off out of the trees, bumping down the track and out onto the highway. Clem drove the way he fought; very smooth, and with a feeling of power kept in reserve. He kept the speed down; I'd spent some money on the Falcon recently and it was going along nicely at sixty. I was thinking that Clem's luck was holding when the trouble started. A motorcycle cop passed us and then dropped back. Clem passed him and the cop drew up alongside and took a good look at us. He waved us in and Clem put his foot down. I looked back and saw the cop's face which was white and set under the goggles. He hunched over the handlebars and came after us with a siren screaming.

"This thing'll fall apart at eighty," I said.

"Shut up." Clem gripped the wheel and seemed to be looking ahead, beyond the turns in the road. We were climbing slighty and the bike gained quickly. Clem bent forward and his eyes flicked from the road to the rear vision mirror. I checked my seat belt and tried to console myself with the thought that the Falcon probably wouldn't even do eighty and that something would burn out if he tried— something that would slow us down and bring us to a gentle stop. Clem wasn't slowing, he pushed the speed up as we gained the flat. The bike cruised up close behind us and then Clem flicked off the bitumen and sent a hail of dust and stones flying back at the cop. That gained us some distance, the siren receded and then came back louder than ever. Clem fought the wheel as the needle touched eighty-five and the suspension and steering protested. When I thought the car was going to disintegrate he eased off and looked into the mirror, then he picked up again, eased back and studied the mirror. He grinned.

"What?" My teeth were chattering and I had to say it again to get the sound out.

"He's confused," Clem said tightly, "probably young. Give me a break and I'll shake him."

The break came in the next mile; the road narrowed over a bridge and there was a high bank quite close to the road over the bridge. Clem eased off the power, touched the brake and we probably weren't doing much more than fifty when we bumped over the bridge. He swung the wheel and the car lurched out toward the middle of the road, the bike came up on the inside and then we slipped back over to the left and crowded the bike closer to the bank. I saw the rider's head go up and then he was in a skid, sliding and slowing, and Clem kept just ahead of him, hemming him in until he went sideways into the bank. Clem picked up speed on the straight road and I kept the dark figure in sight until we went over a hill.

"Moving?" Clem said.

I drew in a sour, gummy breath. "Yeah."

"Should be okay, he wasn't going fast."

A truck roared by on the other side and Clem wiped his hand over his face. "He'll see him right. We've got to get off this bloody road, though."

We went inland south of Taree and started winding and climbing through the rich farming country. I had a map of sorts and Clem had a good eye for roads; we did some backtracking but still made pretty good progress north. After a while Clem started to whistle.

"What the hell have you got to be so cheerful about? They're going to have two men in a dark Falcon registration number KLG 343 on the air by now."

Clem looked at me, he was munching on the last of the salami and the scars and lines on his face were criss-crossing, smoothing out, and bunching up.

"You're slipping, Cliff. Notice anything about the farm houses around here?"

"No."

"Fuckin' great TV masts. This is TV territory, most of these people wouldn't listen to the local radio if you paid them and they won't watch television until the evening. Nothing to worry about till then."

I grunted. "You're wasted in a life of crime, Clem. You should be in my racket."

The remark sobered him. "Yeah," he muttered, "well, it's a bit late for that, and I mightn't be so smart anyhow, we're going to need petrol and they listen to the radio in the workshops anyway. Going to have to trust to all that bloody luck I usually have."

We bought the petrol in a small town that featured a petrol pump on the side of the road, a post office store, and a pub. Clem took some money and bought food; I bought some beer and a bottle of brandy. Clem gestured angrily at me to drive when he saw the package. I knew he wouldn't want to start a scene in the town so I opened one of the cans as I got behind the wheel.

"I said no booze, Cliff," he said when we got out of the town.

"Fuck you, Clem, I'm twitching and I need a drink. I'm not going through another night like that without a few belts. Think of it as medicine." I held one of the cans out to him but he stared out the window.

We pushed on through the afternoon scarcely talking. Clem kept looking at the map and dictating the route. He was making for some point short of Gismore and his spirits seemed to lift when we got into the ranges between Kempsey and Tamworth. The light was fading when we got to Bunda Bunda. Clem told me to stop by the single public phone booth in the town.

"Let's have some silver, Cliff." I gave him what I had, and he reached over and took the keys. He went into the booth and I saw him take the .38 out and put it to hand; then he shovelled money into the box, dialled, waited and spoke. He was grinning when he came back.

"What next?" I said.

"Night's sleep and a new car, about twenty miles off."

We turned back toward the coast and started dropping. I was tired and hungry when Clem guided us down a track to a shack at the edge of a fast moving creek. A white VW 1600, not new but younger than the Falcon, was parked behind the building which was mostly fibro with a bit of timber and a minimum of glass.

There was a gas cylinder and a two burner stove in the shack and we had a meal of tinned poison and I drank two cans of warm beer. I was sleepy and even the rickety bunks at the back of the single room looked inviting. Clem had taken the distributor from the Falcon and he looked at me as I yawned.

"Ready to pack it in, Cliff?"

"Yeah, but let's not have any of that Siamese twins act, eh?"

"You could shoot through and have the cops here in no time."

"Clem, I'm buggered. I don't know where we are. It's pitch black outside. I assume the creek goes down to the coast but I'm just not in the mood to build a raft. I'm not

67

going anywhere tonight." I took off my shoes and handed them to him.

He laughed and jabbed at me with the shoes. "All right, tell you what, you have a nice big brandy and I'll have a small one to keep you company."

He'd taken charge of the bottle and now he held it out. I set the world's bottle-opening record and we sat there in front of the kerosene lamp with a good brandy in enamel mugs. He took a sip and pulled a face. In the flickering light the strain and the years showed clearly. He drank a bit more, and squinted as if he was in pain.

I took a long pull on the smooth spirit. "What's on your mind, Clem?"

"Joannie," he said.

The room was full of light when I woke up, and Clem was shaving with a blade razor and a piece of soap; steam was lifting from a shallow enamel bowl.

"Get up you lazy bugger, and make some coffee."

I had a bit of a head and I groaned when I swung my legs on to the boards.

"You look bloody awful, I should make you take a swim in the creek."

"You'd be lucky. How'd you sleep?"

"Fair."

I made the coffee and set the mug down in front of him. He wiped his face off carefully with a torn towel. He looked healthy and fresh. I rubbed my hand over my dirty, dark-bristled face; I was the one who looked like a desperado. He offered me the razor but I couldn't see my heavy beard giving way to it.

"Look, Clem, why don't you stick here a while. I'll go up to Gismore and see what I can find out. If you can pin it on this Riley character, you're home free."

Clem sipped coffee, taking it hot and squinting against

the steam, then he shook his head slowly. "Thanks, Cliff; I know you'd give it a go but it's not on. I want him and I want the money, I'll start turning over new leaves then."

"Could be too late, Clem."

"Could be."

We tidied the cabin a bit and took the spare food and drink out to the VW. Clem took a plasitic drum out of the back and told me to siphon out the Falcon's tank. He let me pour back enough to run her a few miles and he tossed the distributor on the seat.

"It's all downhill from here," he said.

He was preoccupied on the drive toward Gismore, and so was I.

"Have you given any thought to the coppers, Clem?"

"How d'you mean?"

"Well, if this Riley set you up like you say, you'd expect a copper or two to know a little about it."

"Fine body of men, Cliff."

"Sure, but you see what I mean. If a policeman or two have an interest in keeping you fixed up for this job things could get pretty hot."

"You're so right."

"Well, you've been spotted going north, assuming that poor bugger back there could talk when they got to him. They've had plenty of time to prepare. This Riley'll have a copper in bed with him."

"I know that. I told you I'd thought about this thing, I've got a way to bring him to me quiet as a mouse."

"How?"

"You'll see."

He pushed the VW along pretty hard and when we were about still two hours out from Gismore I could tell from his driving that he was in familiar country. I wasn't; the deep green foliage and the red earth looked foreign to my city eye and the glimpses of ocean were like snapshots of exotic seas, richly coloured and mysterious.

Gismore was ten kilometres away when Clem headed up a dirt road into the hills behind the town. He seemed to take pleasure from just looking at the forest and the cleared land—there were a lot of corn fields and I have to admit they looked nice. We bounced along a couple of tracks and Clem stopped just before a sharp bend.

"Go for a stroll up the road, Cliff," Clem said. "You'll see a big open shed with an iron roof, the house is off to the right, white weatherboard. See if there's anyone about. Look innocent, mate."

I got out stiffly and walked up the track. Birds and insects in the trees were making a lot of noise and I could hear a tractor working a long way off. It was a nice clear day and I felt tense, like waiting for a dentist to start in with his drill. I stuck my hands in my pockets and wandered up to the mill which had a very rusty roof and a slab wall at the back. There was a lot of rusty machinery and a couple of long, low shapes covered with heavy polythene. I took these to be Clem's cars. On a bench in the middle of the shed a set of tools lay in a jumble of oil and dirty rags and rust. There was an almost sheer rock wall behind the shed, the track in front. The rock wall ran around to the left and the house was on the right. There was scrub and light forest behind the house. I walked across toward the house; there were no fresh tyre tracks on the dusty ground and the place had a closed-down, empty look. There were cobwebs across the screen door at the front and the back door was locked. I walked back to the car.

"All clear. What's next?"

He put the gun away and relaxed. "I'll show you around."

We went into the shed and Clem swore when he saw the neglected bench. He pointed to the closest of the covered cars. "Take a look, I want to find something here." He leaned over the bench and I bent down to lift the polythene. Clem moved fast; I didn't hear him, and then his arm was around my neck and he was pressing hard somewhere and I grabbed at the dusty plastic and everything went black.

When I came to I was sitting at the base of the bench and my arms were drawn back behind one of its legs and tied with what felt like wire.

"Sorry mate," Clem said, "I didn't think you'd go along with the next bit so I had to put you out. How do you feel?"

"Like a Tooheys," I grunted.

He laughed and loped off down the track. He was fit, purposeful, and fresh looking. I felt a thousand years old, impotent and beaten. He came back with the box of food, peeled a banana, and fed it to me slowly.

"Keep you alive for weeks that will." He found a dirty mug on the bench, rinsed it at a tap and mixed a strong brandy and water. He held the cup while I sipped it down.

"Okay?"

"Yeah. I don't like the look in your eyes, Clem; do you remember when you fought in the state finals? That army bloke?"

'Yeah, I remember."

"He was too big for you, mate, too smart and he hit too hard. I think you're going up against him again."

"No, Cliff, I'm going to win this one." He turned and went out of the shed and down the track. The wire hurt my hands but not unbearably; I tried to relax in the unnatural position and the feeling of incipient cramp eased off. Clem had cleared a space all around where I was sitting; there were no tools, no nails, no rusty hacksaw blades. Ten feet away there was enough gear to break into a bank. It was

71

early afternoon and warm; I still had on the winter shirt I'd worn in Sydney and in which I'd now slept two nights—it stank. I've always liked the north coast and fantasised often about that one big case that brings in an enormous fee which could set me up with a shack overlooking the Pacific. Right then I'd gladly have been in Melbourne, or in church or anywhere else.

I dozed and came awake to the sound of the VW being driven up to the shed. Clem got out and grinned at me.

"Bearing up?" I grunted in reply and he worked at the wire so that I had one hand free. I looked at the other hand; the wire was heavy duty stuff twisted tight and hard with pliers, I couldn't make any impression on it with my fingers. Clem handed me a hamburger and made another brandy and water.

"Sorry there's no beer, Cliff, out of the habit of it."

I looked across at the car as I bit into the hamburger. In the passenger seat I could see a vague, light shape.

"Who's that?"

Clem took the cup from me and had a swig himself. He looked confident and assured.

"That's Dorothy Farmer; she's Riley's girlfriend."

"Happy to be here, is she?"

"Not exactly, she needed some persuading. My mate in town tells me that Riley'd do anything for that girl; crazy about her, he's told me that a hundred times."

"And . . ."

"I'm going to call him, tell him I've got her and suggest he come to fetch her and bring along the money. Simple as that."

"Kidnapping, Clem; big one."

"Who's going to tell? I get the money and piss off, what's Riley going to say?"

It sounded all right—if Riley's feeling for the girl was as

strong as Clem thought. Clem went to the back of the shed and rummaged around. When he came back he was carrying a .303 rifle and a box of ammunition.

"Jesus, Clem, I thought you were confident."

"I am, but Riley's a cunning bugger, I just want to be sure. Hold tight, Cliff, I'm going to phone him."

Carrying the rifle, he went toward the house. He took a quick look in the car then he stepped up onto the porch, clubbed the window in with the butt of the rifle and reached around to open the door. He was inside for about ten minutes; I saw the girl in the car stir and her hand go up to her face. Clem helped her gently out of the car and led her into the shed. She was a plump blonde with a lot of make-up over a very scared face. There was an old car seat under the bench and Clem dragged it out and pushed the girl down into it. He put some brandy in the cup and held it out to her.

"Sorry, Dot," he said.

She tossed back the brandy and held the cup out for a refill. "You scared the shit out of me with that gun, Clem. What're you on about?" Her voice was shaky and nasal; she had a frilly blouse on and very tight jeans with high-heeled shoes. She looked as if she'd just stepped out from behind the bar, except that she was as nervous as a rabbit. Clem stood over her with the .303 across his shoulders. I was dirty-faced, stubbly and stinking with one arm lashed down with wire. She had a right to be alarmed.

Clem ignored her and I decided that it was time to recruit her to my side. "You're a hostage, Dorothy; so am I in a way. Clem's holding you because he wants something from Riley; when he has it he'll let us both go. That right, Clem?"

"That's right."

She looked at me as if I had started spouting Shakespeare. She opened her mouth to speak and then she looked at Clem; he was just faintly comic with the big rifle, but not funny enough to cause Dorothy to laugh as she did. She leaned back in the chair and bellowed. Clem swung the rifle around and at that minute I wondered just how cool he was. There was a flush in his face and his eyes looked nervous as he watched the convulsing girl.

"What . . . ," she gasped, "what makes you think Charlie Riley will do anything for me?"

"You're his girl," Clem grated. "He's nuts about you, Johnny Talbot told me."

She giggled. "Johnny Talbot told you!" She laughed again and Clem stepped forward.

"Easy, Clem," I said.

He grabbed her shoulder and shook it. "What's funny? Come on, Dot, I'm not joking."

She calmed down and looked up at him, tears had spilled eye black down her face so that she looked like a tormented mime.

"Riley hasn't laid a finger on me for two years, Clem," she said softly. "You know who he's on with now?"

"Tell me."

"Joannie, your wife. Johnny must've been too scared to tell you. Two years it's been now, Clem, near enough." She started to get up from the seat and Clem shoved her back savagely.

"Let me go," the girl said, "I'm no use to you. Let me go, Clem!"

Clem slapped her hard across her tear-daubed face. "Shut up! Just shut up and let me think!"

There was a silence and we were all thinking fast and all thinking scared. The girl was telling the truth, that was clear, but I wondered if Clem saw all the consequences.

"How did Riley take the news, Clem?" I said quietly. Clem looked at me blankly. "He was . . . sort of shocked."

"You told him to get the money and come up here."

"Yeah."

"Jesus! I know what I'd do if I was him; I'd get hold of the biggest gun I could find and come up here and blow you away. Has he got any guts, this Riley?"

"He has, he was a bookie in Sydney. He'd gone soft when I last saw him, but he used to do his own collecting."

"You're in trouble, son. There's nothing to stop him killing you, it's the best end to all his troubles. You'd better get out, Clem."

"Shit, where can I go? I was counting on getting the money."

"Ring the cops then, it's your only chance."

It was exactly the wrong advice; the words seemed to jolt him out of a defeatist mood and into something else, he checked the bolt on the rifle and patted Dorothy on the head clumsily.

"Sorry, Dot, stay put and you won't get into any trouble. It makes sense you know. I couldn't work out why she didn't come through with the money." He was talking to me now and running his left hand along the stained wood under the barrel of the rifle. I'd seen men do that before, in the army and not in the army, I'd done it myself; it meant you were ready to shoot and didn't mind being shot at. A lot of those men were dead.

"I wanted the money, but I came for Riley and I'll get him. What does he drive, Dot, something flash?"

"Volvo," she said.

"That'll do, I'll take that and head up to Queensland and get lost. Want to come along, Cliff?" He was jocular but there was a desperation in it, as if he was screwing himself up to do something.

"No thanks, Clem," I said. "Listen, have you ever shot a man?"

75

"No."

"It's not that easy."

"I'll manage. Now shut up, I need to organise this." He looked around the shed obviously picking the best cover assuming that Riley would come up the track. There wasn't much doubt about what was best—the plastic-covered cars were at right angles to each other in the middle of the shed; anyone down behind them would be protected on two sides. Dorothy and I would be off to one side, out of the line of fire from the track or the direction of the house, but with all that machinery around bullets could ricochet. I felt I had to make another try.

"Give it up, Clem, you're just going down for the second time. He might have help. All the odds are against you."

He ignored me and settled himself behind the cars with the ammunition beside him. He wriggled to get himself comfortable and then turned back toward us.

"One sound out of you two, and I'll shoot you. Got it?"

Dorothy bit her lip and shot an anguished look at me. I nodded and she did the same. Clem eased himself up to look down the track when two shots sounded clear and sharp. They hadn't carried into the shed and I squinted out past the cars; the VW sank crookedly like a wounded buffalo.

"The VW," I said, "front and back. He doesn't want you to go to Queensland."

Clem said nothing, then he tensed himself, lifted the rifle a little and let go two rounds, working the bolt smoothly; he mightn't have shot men but he knew his rifle.

"Get him, Clem?"

"No."

"Can you see his car?"

"No."

"Probably left it well back. If he's any good he's disabled it."

Clem turned on me fiercely and his head lifted up above the car. "Will you shut up, Cliff, I . . ."

A bullet whined off the bonnet of the car and two more whanged into the metal body. Clem dropped down and knocked over his ammunition. Dorothy was sobbing quietly in her chair and Clem's lips were moving silently.

"Listen, Clem," I said urgently, "you're an amateur at this and I once did it for money. You've got to go out and get him. You're pinned down as it is, he can call the shots."

"You said he might have mates."

"I was trying to persuade you to run, it's all different now. I don't think he'd bring anyone in on this. He wants you out, clean."

"Well, you tell me, if you're the professional."

"Go out the side there, get across to the house and work around behind him. Try not to kill him, Clem, they'll let you rot if you do."

"What's the odds." He put a handful of bullets into the pocket of the jeans and wriggled across to the side of the shed. He took his time, moved back and deeper into the shadow thrown by the post and then he snaked across toward some bushes by the house.

"Dorothy," I hissed. "Are you okay?"

Her answer was a sniff.

"Quick, get the pliers off the bench."

She sat frozen in the chair like an accident victim.

"Dorothy, move! There'll be bullets flying everywhere unless I can stop this! Move!"

She got up and stumbled over to the bench. "Pliers," she said.

"Right, to cut this wire. Quick, give them here."

She got them and I hacked at the wire with my left hand; I lost a bit of skin in the process but having the use of both hands again was like being given a million dollars. I bent

77

low, and scuttled across to where Clem had left the Smith & Wesson when he went back for the rifle. I held it and looked at it, and wondered what the hell difference it made. The girl was standing by the bench; she wiped the hand that had held the pliers on her blouse and left a dark, oily stain on her right breast. She glanced at it and giggled, she was close to hysteria. I took her arm and herded her across the shed to a point nearest the house. There was no sign of Clem or Riley.

"Get across there and ring the police. The window's broken by the door, you can reach in. After you've phoned, stay there; you'll be safe."

She ran across to the porch and made it into the house. I breathed out and turned my attention back to the track in front of the shed. The light was just starting to fade and a slight breeze was moving the trees and bushes. I took the .38 off safety and crouched down behind a post at the front of the shed. After ten minutes or so Riley came into view, working his way along in the scrub toward my corner of the shed. He would have been invisible from behind the cars. He looked back down the track and froze, I ducked behind a packing case and then he came on. He was doing it slow and careful and he held the short, stubby carbine lightly and ready for use. He was a big man, over six feet with a full belly and a wide, pale face. His hair was dark and thin; he wore grey slacks and white shirt, the dark hair made his thick forearms look almost black. There were big sweat patches under his arms. I waited until he had got up to the post then I tossed some sand out onto the track. He turned at the sound and I came up and put the .38 in the nape of his neck.

"Put the rifle down Riley, or I'll blow your head off."

He stood stock still for a second, I jabbed him with the muzzle and he bent and put the rifle down. He was standing there, full frontal, six feet high and three feet wide when Clem stepped out of the scrub thirty yards away. He lifted the .303 and sighted.

"Clem, don't!" I yelled.

"Move away, Cliff, I'm going to kill him." He moved a bit closer stiffly, with the rifle still up. Then from behind Clem a woman's voice screamed "No!"

Clem swung back toward the sound, I stepped away from Riley to look and saw a small figure running up the track. Then Riley bent smoothly, picked up the carbine and fired a short burst. Clem's head flew apart and he pitched backwards still holding the .303. The woman ran up the track screaming and screaming and then we heard the sirens.

Riley gave me a lot of the credit. He said he couldn't have shot Clem in self defence if I hadn't created the diversion. Dorothy told the cops I'd been tied up, how I got loose and that it was me who sent her to call them. A doctor treated me for abrasions to the wrists; my gun hadn't been fired. I was clean.

Riley told his story pretty straight; he said Clem had phoned him, told him he was holding the girl and demanded money and a car. Riley came to try to talk some sense into him and Joannie for the same reason. He said Clem had fired twice at him with the .303 and that checked out. They were a little concerned about a private citizen possessing an M1 but hell, he'd been shotgunned hadn't he?

I cleaned up in town and the police drove me back to where my car was. I drove slowly back to Sydney along the coast road. I thought of well-padded Riley with all his problems solved, and I thought of Clem's wife, a neat, dark little woman who'd stood still and said nothing. And I remembered Clem telling me that he thought she was pretty.

Silverman

If I hadn't been so busy worrying about money and my carburettor—the sorts of problems that beset your average private detective in the spring—I would have taken note of them out in the street. The car I did notice—a silver Mercedes, factory fresh. But then, that's not an impossible sight in St. Peter's Lane. We get the odd bookie dropping by, a psychoanalyst or two, the occasional tax avoidance consultant. I also saw a man and a woman in the car, nothing discordant about that really, as I went into the building and up to my office to move the bills and accounts rendered around.

I was at my desk wanting a cigarette (but fighting against it), with a slight breeze from the open window disturbing the dust, when the door buzzer sounded. I got up and let them in. The woman walked over to the solidest chair and plonked herself down in it; she needed everything the springing could give her—she must have been close to six feet and wouldn't have made the light heavyweight limit. Her hair was jet black and her make-up was vivid. Of women's clothes I'm no judge; hers looked as if they'd been made for her out of good material. She got cigarettes in a gold case out of a shiny bag, lit up, and waited for the man to do whatever he was going to do.

He was a plump, red-faced little number with lots of

chins and thin hair. His dark blue suit had been artistically cut, but the unfashionable lines of his body had easily won out. He looked like a funny, little fat man, but I had a feeling that his looks were deceptive.

"I'm Horace Silverman, Mr. Hardy," he said. "This is my wife, Beatrice. I'm in real estate."

I nodded; I hadn't thought he was a postman.

"We are concerned about our son," Silverman went on. "His name is Kenneth." I opened my mouth, but he lifed a hand to silence me. "Kenneth left home a year ago to live with other students. He was attending the university."

"Was?" I said alertly.

"Yes. He suspended his studies; I believe that's the term. He also changed his address several times. Now we don't know where he is, and we want you to find him."

"Missing Persons," I said.

"No! We have reason to believe that Kenneth is in bad company. There may be . . . legal problems."

"How bad?"

"The problems? Oh, not bad. A summons for speeding, a parking violation. Others may be pending."

"It doesn't sound serious. You'd be better off using the police, scores of men, computers . . ."

The red deepened in his face and his big, moist mouth went thin and hard; any affability he'd brought in with him had dropped away.

"I said no!" He slammed his palm down on my desk. "I'm involved in some very delicate business negotiations; very delicate, with a great deal of money involved. The slightest complication of my affairs, the slightest hint of police hanging about, and they could fall through." He got the words out with difficulty through the rising tide of his anger. He seemed intolerant of opposition. Maybe Kenneth

81

knew what he was doing. The woman blew smoke and looked concerned but said nothing.

"Okay, okay," I said. "I'm glad of the work. I charge seventy-five dollars a day plus expenses. You get an itemised account. I take a retainer of two hundred dollars."

He dipped into the bulging pocket of his suit coat and fished out a chequebook. He scribbled, ripped, and handed the cheque over—five hundred dollars.

"Do you want them shot, or tortured to death slowly?" I said.

"Who?"

The woman snorted "Horace," crushed out her cigarette in the stand and levered herself up from the chair. I gathered that they were going.

"Not so fast. I need names, addresses, descriptions, photographs . . ."

He cut me off by hauling a large manila envelope out of his other pocket and dumping it on the desk. I hoped his tailor never saw him out on the street.

"I'm busy," he said shortly. "All you'll need is there. Just find him, Mr. Hardy, and report to me." He'd calmed down; he was happiest telling people what to do.

"It could be unpleasant," I said. "He might be smoking cigarettes, taking the odd drink . . ."

"A full report, no punches pulled."

"You'll get it." I opened the door and he bustled out. She cruised after him, still looking concerned. He seemed to have brought her along just to prove that the boy had a mother.

I sat down at the desk again, propped the cheque up in front of me and opened the envelope. There were three photographs, photostats of a parking ticket and a speeding summons and of a letter, dated two months back, from the Registrar of the University of Sydney. It was directed to

Kenneth at an address in Wahroonga. There was also a sheet of Horace Silverman's business paper half-covered in type.

The typed sheet gave me the low-down on Ken. Born in Sydney twenty-one years ago, six feet tall when last measured and slim of build, fair of hair with no marks or scars. The last meeting with his parents was given and dated—a dinner eight weeks back. Two addresses in the inner suburbs were listed, and it was suggested that the Registrar's letter had been sent to Ken's home address by mistake. His interests were given—tennis, bushwalking, and politics. His major subject at university was psychology, and a Dr. Katharine Garson was listed as his student counsellor.

The photos were black and white, good quality, good size. They showed a young man in his late teens or around twenty, all three shots roughly contemporaneous. Kenneth Silverman had it all—thick, wavy hair, even features, broad shoulders. I'd have taken bets that his teeth were good. One of the pictures showed him in tennis gear, and he looked right; in another he was leaning against a sports car and he looked right in that too. I couldn't see any resemblance to Horace, maybe a little to Beatrice. There were none of those signs—weak chin, close-set eyes—that are supposed to indicate, but don't, character deficiencies. Kenneth Silverman looked healthy and happy.

Sydney University was just down the road and Silverman's last known address was in Glebe, my stamping ground. I went down to the street and along to the backyard of the tattooist's shop where I keep my car. In an ideal world, I'd find the boy in Glebe before three o'clock, deposit my cheque, draw some out, and be home in time to invite someone out to dinner.

The Fisher Library of the University of Sydney is a public

place, like the whole campus. This statutory fact has been found useful by a few Vice-Chancellors who've felt the need to call the cops in. I got there a little after midday and looked up Dr. Garson in the handbook—a string of degrees, senior lecturer in psychology. The Psychology Department was in one of those new concrete buildings that academics have allowed themselves to be herded into. They have as much personality as a bar of soap and, in my experience, they have a corresponding effect on the people who work in them. Not Dr. Garson though; she'd done her concrete cell out with pictures that actually looked like people and places, and she had a flagon of sherry sitting on the window ledge.

"A sherry?" she said when she'd installed me in a chair.

"Please; then I can show you what good manners I've got, how well I can sip and murmur appreciatively."

"Don't bother," she said pouring, "piss is piss." She set the glass on the desk near me and took a belt herself. "So you're a private detective? Some of my colleagues wouldn't allow you on the campus, let alone in their rooms."

"It's a public place."

She raised one plucked eyebrow. "So it is." She finished her sherry and poured another. She had fine bones in her wrists and even finer ones in her face.

"I want some information about a student you counselled."

She laughed. "Unlikely."

"I want to help him—find him, that is."

She sipped. "Perhaps he wants to stay lost."

"He still can if he wants to." I drank some of the sherry, dry. "I find him, report to his father and that's that."

"You don't look like a thug, Mr. Hardy, but you're in a thuggish trade. Why should I help you?"

"One, you've got an independent mind, two, Silverman might be in trouble."

She didn't jump out of her skirt at the name but she didn't treat it like a glass of flat beer either.

"Kenneth Silverman," she said slowly.

"That's right, rich Kenneth who dropped out and disappeared. His Mum and Dad would like to know why. You wouldn't be able to put their minds at rest by any chance?"

"No."

"Can't or won't?"

"Can't. I was surprised when he dropped out, he was doing well."

"What did you do about it?"

She finished her sherry with an exasperated flick. "What could I do? I counsel twenty students and teach another sixty. I wrote to him asking him to contact me for a talk. He didn't."

"Had you counselled him much?"

"No, he didn't seem to need it."

"It looks now as if he did."

"Not really, he became radical at the beginning of the year. It happens to most of the bright ones, although a bit late in his case. The process sends some of them haywire but Ken seemed to be able to handle it. His first term's work was excellent, he trailed off a bit in early second term, nothing serious, then he just suspended for no reason."

"Are you curious about that?"

"Yes, very."

"Then help me."

She took her time thinking about it. The process involved pouring some more sherry and tossing back the thick mane of chestnut hair.

"All right." She held up her glass and sunlight sifted

through the pale, amber fluid. "You'd better talk to his girlfriend, Kathy Martin."

"How can I contact her?"

"She'll be at my lecture at a quarter past two. She's a blonde with a suntan, you can't miss her."

"You won't introduce us?"

"No."

"Why not?"

She smiled. "My reputation," she said.

I finished my sherry, found out where the lecture was held, thanked her, and left.

The lecture theatre sloped steeply and had front and back entrances. I killed some time with a sandwich and coffee and was back at a quarter past two watching the acolytes roll up for knowledge. I stood up the back, and tried not to be depressed by their impossible youth. One of the last students in was a blonde with her hair tied back; she had on a simple, sleeveless dress and sandals; her arms and legs and face were very brown. She sat down and got out a clipboard and looked like business as Dr. Garson started in on R.D. Laing. I snuck out for coffee I didn't want and when I got back the students were dribbling out. I approached the blonde girl as she loped out into the quadrangle.

"Kathy Martin?"

"Yes." Up close, she was the original outdoors girl with a demoralising sheen of good health.

"My name is Hardy, I've been hired by Mr. Horace Silverman to look for his son. I understand you were a friend."

"Yes." I got the impression she wasn't a big talker.

"Well, can we have a chat?"

She looked at her watch. "I have a tutorial in an hour and I haven't done all the reading."

"It won't take long." I herded her across to a bench. She sat down after looking at her watch again.

"When did you last see Kenneth?"

"Nearly two months ago."

"Where?"

"At his place."

"Where's that?"

"He had a squat in Glebe, Sweatman Street." She gave me the number and I wrote it down.

"Why was he squatting? He had plenty of money didn't he?"

"Kenny stopped taking his family's money. He went left, extreme left."

"Did you?"

"Not so extreme."

"Did you quarrel?"

She frowned. "A bit, but we didn't split up, if that's what you mean."

"You didn't?"

"No, he was around. I saw him, we did what we usually did. You wouldn't understand."

"One day he was there and the next day he wasn't?"

"It wasn't a day-to-day thing." She tapped her battered briefcase. "Look, I really have to read this stuff."

"Won't keep you a minute. What did you do about it— Kenneth's disappearance?"

"Nothing. I said you wouldn't follow. It wasn't a disappearance. The people he was in with, they do it all the time—go north, take jobs for money, you know?"

"So you weren't worried?"

"What could I do?" she snapped. "I couldn't go to the

police or anything, they were really *out* in Kenny's terms. I didn't know his family. I just hoped he'd turn up; I still do."

"What about the people at the squat?"

"They were raided. The house was taken over."

"This was after Kenneth went missing?"

She paused. "Kenneth sounds weird. Yes, I think so, soon after."

I tried to digest the information and lost her while I did it. She got up and said goodbye in a voice that meant it. I thanked her and watched her walk away with that long, bouncy step and the thought came to me that Kenny had at least one good reason to stick around.

Sweatman Street has seen worse days; the big, two-storyed, bay-windowed houses had been broken up into flats and rooms until recently, when small, affluent families had taken them over. More European cars and four-wheel-drives than beaten-up Holdens with a rust problem. The street is down near the water and getting more leafy and smart daily and the pockets of poverty in it are not old-style—port and pension—but new-style; dope and dole poverty.

The address Kathy had given me was the last house in a terrace of twenty. It featured weeds and broken glass and peeling paint. The windows at the side and back were set too high up to see in. Around the back, I was surprised to find that all the fences dividing the yards had been removed. This left an immense space which was taken up with trees, rubbish, and children's play gear in about equal proportions.

The broken windows at the back of the house were boarded up and the door was nailed shut. I gave it an experimental tug, and a shout came from behind me.

"Hey! What're you doing?"

He was big, with a lot of hair on his head and face. His

jeans, sneakers, and T-shirt were old and dirty. I stepped down from the door and tried to look innocent.

"Just looking," I said.

He was close enough for me to see the aggression pent up in him and something else—there was a nervousness in his movements and a frozen look in his eyes that I'd seen before in speed-freaks and pill-poppers. I opened my hands in a placating gesture which he misunderstood, perhaps deliberately. He crowded up close and bumped me back against the crumbling brick wall. I wasn't ready for it, and lost a bit of breath.

"Take it easy," I said. I put out a hand to hold him back and he swept it aside. His punch was a clumsy looping effort, and I couldn't resist it; I stepped inside and hit him short, just above the belt buckle. He sagged and I grabbed him under the arms to hold him up.

"Let him go." Another man came from behind the trees; he was slighter and clean-shaven and he dropped into a martial arts pose about ten feet away from me. I let the bearded man slide down the wall.

"Don't be silly," I said. "All this is silly; I just want to ask a few questions. I'm looking for someone."

"Do him, Chris," my winded opponent said, and Chris didn't need any encouragement. He jumped up and let go a flying kick at my shoulder. It was a good, high jump, but the trick with this stuff is not to watch the acrobatics. I ducked under it and kicked the leg he landed on out from under him. He went down in a heap and the stiff-armed chop he came up with might have looked good on the mat but was way too slow in the field. I swayed away from it and hit him just where I'd hit his mate; and that was a mistake because he had washboard muscles there, but I had the combination ready and the next punch landed on his nose where there aren't any muscles, just nerves to cause pain and blood vessles to break. He yelped and threw his hands up over his face.

So I had one on the ground and one with a bloody face and no information. Then I heard a slow, ironic handclap; she was standing on the steps of the next house, dark and fat in a shapeless dress and with a cigarette between her lips.

"I didn't start it," I said inanely.

"Who cares?" She seemed to find it all funny; flesh on her face shook as she laughed and she puffed at the cigarette without touching it.

I fished out my licence card and waved it in front of Chris and his mate.

"I'm a private detective. I'm looking for Kenneth Silverman; now who's going to talk to me? There's money in it."

The woman took the cigarette out of her face and tried a fat, pursed-up smile.

"Now you're talking," she said. "Come along here."

"Don't talk to him, Fay," the bearded one said.

"Shut your head, Lenny. Come on whatever your name is, I'll talk your arse off."

I went past my opponents and followed her to a back door in the middle of the row. We went into a kitchen that was neither dirty nor clean. I smelled something vaguely familiar, and sniffed at it.

"Candles," she said. "No power in here. I can make you a coffee, though." She gestured at a small stove hooked up to a gas cylinder.

"Don't bother, thanks. Do you know Silverman?"

"Straight to it, eh? What about the money?"

I got out ten dollars and put it on the cracked linoleum-topped table.

"And another if I'm satisfied," I said.

"Fair enough." She bobbed her head and the fat bounced

90

on her and ash fell down on to her lumpy chest. "Yeah, I knew Kenny, he lived down the end there." She waved back toward the scene of my triumph. "He left when they cleared us out; no, a bit before that."

"Who's 'they'?"

"The developers—Forbes Realty. They own this terrace and a few others. Cunts!"

"What happened?"

"Came around one morning, about six o'clock, two big blokes with a guy in a suit. He told them what to do—they dumped all our stuff out; everything, every fucking thing, just out in the bloody street. Then they boarded the place up." She laughed.

"What's funny?"

"I was thinking, Lenny lost a fight that morning too—it's bullshit, that karate crap."

I grunted. "You said Silverman had gone by this time?"

She squinted at the ten dollars, remembering, or pretending to. "Yeah, he wasn't in the house that morning. No sign of him. I think some of his stuff got dumped, but I'm not sure. It was a pretty wild scene."

"Why are those two so jumpy?"

She spat the cigarette stub out onto the floor, put her thonged foot on it and fished a packet of Winfield out of her pocket.

"We've only been back a couple of weeks; it's been quiet, but you never know with that mob."

I nodded, she lit up and puffed an enormous cloud of smoke at the window. I looked around at the artefacts of the squat-packing case shelves, a hose running in through the window to the sink, the small carton of milk on the table. She read my mind.

"You're wondering what a silvertail like Kenny was doing living in a dump like this?"

I pushed the money across to her. "Yes."

She picked it up and put it away with the cigarettes.

"Kenny and the others were taking on Forbes," she spoke around the cigarette. "Kenny was living here as a political act, that's what he said."

"Who else was in the group?"

"Chris and Lennie, couple more. I think I've said enough, I don't know a bloody thing about you. Do I get the other ten?"

"You're not political yourself?"

"Shit no, I squat 'cos it's easy."

"Did they have trouble with the developers before?"

"Oh yeah, plenty—slashed tyres, windows busted— usual things."

"Anything since you moved back?"

"Not yet."

"What sort of action did Kenneth and the others take?"

"Letters to the papers, attending council meetings, street meetings about the plan. They're going to build right down to the water, you know? We won't even be able to see the bit we see now."

I gave her another ten dollars and went across to the dusty, cobwebbed window. Blackwattle Bay was an ugly, oily gleam under the dull grey sky and its Glebe shore was a blasted landscape of car bodies, timber, and scratchy grass. The view was a long way short of cheerful but there was water in it, it promised better things; it was Sydney. I thanked Fay and tramped through the back yards; Lenny and Chris weren't in sight and I pulled myself up to one of the windows of the house Silverman had occupied. It was in bad shape, there were black-rimmed holes in the floor-boards, and plumbing had been ripped out and hung limp and useless on the kitchen wall.

I drove to the post office and looked up Forbes Realty.

The address in Norton Street, Leichhardt niggled at me as I wrote it down. Back in the car I found out why—Kenneth Silverman's parking ticket had been incurred in Norton Street.

It seemed like time for some telephone research; I went home, made a drink and called a few people including Cy Sackville, my lawyer, and Grant Evans, a senior cop and friend. The results were interesting. Forbes Realty was a semi-solid firm and the word in financial circles was that it was over-extended. Its two leading shareholders were Horace Silverman and Clive Patrick. Silverman's interests were extensive and Forbes was a small part of his action. From Evans I learned that Forbes Realty had been burglarised eight weeks back and that enquiries were proceeding, also that a Constable Ian Williamson had stopped MG sports model JLM 113 registered to Kenneth Silverman and booked the driver for speeding. Evans arranged for me to talk to Williamson and that made one favour I owed him.

I reckoned I'd put in a day. It was time to tease out a few loose ends and do some thinking. I needed to know more about Forbes Realty and Kenneth's tactics, also, I was stalling: I didn't like the look of things and I might have to play a very careful hand. I bought some Lebanese food on the way home and washed it down with a few drinks. Then I took a long walk around Glebe; they were selling food and drink and fun in the main road and God knows what in the back streets and lanes. I nodded to the shop and street people I knew, and avoided the dog shit and cracks in the pavement by long habit. The water was shining under a clear sky and a slight breeze brought a salty tang to the nostrils. You wouldn't have washed your socks in the water and every tree in the place was struggling against the pollution, but it was home and I liked it. Its minute foreshore didn't need blocking out with flats.

I went home and phoned a contact in motor registry. He got back to me an hour later with the information that Silverman's car hadn't been sold, traded, stolen, or smashed in the last two months. It had disappeared. I went to sleep wondering about how Kenneth reconciled the car with his radicalism; I wondered whether Horace Silverman's delicate business negotiations involved Forbes Realty, and I wondered whether Dr. Garson would accept if I asked her out to dinner.

At ten in the morning I phoned Horace Silverman and asked him about his role in Forbes Realty. He went silent and I had to prompt him.

"I can see you've been doing your job, Mr. Hardy."

"I hope so." I was thinking fast trying to guess at his meaning and keep the upper hand. "Would you care to tell me all about it?"

There was another pause and then he spoke very deliberately. "I don't know how you found out, but it's true—Kenneth and I had a falling out over Forbes Realty."

I breathed out gently. "How bad?"

"Quite serious. He was very critical of the firm, I suppose you know why."

"Yeah. You didn't tell me he'd stopped taking your money."

"That's true too. I'm sorry I wasn't frank, Mr. Hardy. It's painful to discuss."

I could imagine his cocky little face expressing the pain, and part of it would be due to having to apologise and explain. It seemed like the right time to suggest that we weren't looking at a happy ending.

"I suppose you hoped I'd find the boy quick and easy, and none of this'd matter?"

"Yes," he said, "something like that. I take it it's not going to be easy?"

"Right. Now, tell me about Forbes Realty; do those business negotiations you mention concern it?"

He snorted. "No, not at all. That's a *very* big deal, Mr. Hardy, and I don't want to discusss it on the phone."

"Forbes is small beer to you?"

"More or less, it's a useful investment."

"Are you actively involved with the company?"

"No, not really. I paid it some attention after Kenneth made his . . . allegations."

"Were you satisfied?"

"I'm afraid I didn't enquire too deeply, other things took precedence."

I'd heard that before—from parents who wept while children with scarred arms died in hospital, and from husbands who'd come home to empty houses and notes. Silverman broke in on these thoughts: "Can you tell me what progress you've made, Hardy?" The Mr. had gone, he was asserting himself again, and I wasn't in the mood for it.

"No," I said. "I'll call again when I can."

It was close to six o'clock when I got to Erskineville; petrol fumes and dust hung in the air and Williamson, a beefy, blonde man, was sitting in his singlet on the front step of a terrace house breathing the mixture and drinking beer. We shook hands and I accepted a can.

"Evans told me to co-operate," he said popping another can. "What d'you want to know?"

I got out the photostat of the speeding summons and handed it to him. "Remember this?" I drank some beer, it was very cold.

"Yeah, pretty well. That should have come up by now. What's going on?"

"He's dropped out of sight and I'm looking for him. Can you describe him?"

Williamson took a long suck on the can. "He didn't get out of the car, so I can't be sure of his height and build—I'd guess tall and slim, maybe a bit taller and thinner than you. He was dark, narrow face . . . " He held up his hands helplessly.

"Hair?"

"Not much of it, dark and well back at the sides, peak in front, sort of."

"Age?"

"Forties."

"Clothes?"

"Suit—no shirt and tie, the jacket was on the front seat."

"Where did he get the licence from, pocket or glove box?"

"Can't remember, sorry."

"He was alone?"

"Right."

"Did you see anything in the back of the car—clothes, suitcase?"

"Can't be sure, the interior light was only on for a second."

"How was that?"

"Well, when I went up he opened the door as if he was going to get out but then he shut it again, you know those sports cars, they're short on leg room. Maybe there was something in the back, a bag, a parcel, I don't know. Why?"

"Just wanted to know if he was on a trip. You stopped him in Gymea, going south?"

"Right. He was doing 115, like it says." He tapped the document and I reached over and took it back.

"Drunk?"

"No, he was driving okay and he looked and smelled okay."

96

"Where did he say he was going?"

"Didn't ask."

"What was his voice like?"

"Well, Silverman, I don't know. He wasn't Australian, some kind of foreigner."

I finished the beer and set the can down on the wrought iron rail. "Thanks for the help and the drink."

He waved it aside. "What'll you tell Evans?"

"I'll tell him you co-operated."

"Fair enough."

The morning was grey and cool; I showered and shaved and dressed. The Smith & Wesson went into a holster under my jacket and I put a couple of fake business cards in my wallet. The wallet didn't look healthy so I banked Silverman's cheque and drew out some money in a thick stack of small notes. As I was packing it away I took another look at the speeding and parking tickets. The parking ticket was dated eight weeks back and timed at 7:30 A.M., the speeding ticket was thirteen hours later on the same day.

Norton Street was fairly busy when I arrived but I managed to park exactly where the parking attendant had booked Kenneth's sports car. The spot gave me a clear view of the Forbes office, which was a converted two-story terrace house behind a high wooden fence. I could see the windows of the upper level and down a lane which ran beside the building. The parking place was legitimate now, but ceased to be so at 7 A.M. when a clearway came into operation.

I had only the vaguest idea of what I was going to do and I tried to think which of the business cards I had was the least incredible. I decided that I knew something about books and that I might be able to gauge the probity of the firm with the right approach. The small front courtyard behind the fence was covered in bark, and there were flowers in pots on either side of the solid door. I rang the bell and the door was opened by a girl who looked too young to be working; she had big eyes swamped in make-up, a lot of straight blonde hair, five inch heels—and she still looked fifteen. I looked over her shoulder and saw a cigarette burning a hole in a piece of typing paper on her desk.

"Hey, your desk's on fire."

She spun around, shrieked and snatched at the paper which knocked the butt on the floor, where it started burning the carpet; she also knocked over a vase of flowers and spread water across the desk. She started to cry, and I went in and picked up the cigarette. I eased the big blotter out of its holder and used it to soak up the water. She stood watching me while I dried the desk and dropped the cigarette and sodden blotter into a tin wastepaper bin. I also read the letter—it advised a shopkeeper in Newtown with an unpronounceable middle-European name that his lease would not be renewed. The door had opened into what would have been the hall in the original house, but the wall had been taken out and it was now a fair sized office with two desks and several filing cabinets. The girl was fumbling on the desk for another cigarette. She got it going and sat down.

"Thanks," she said. "What can I do for youse?"

I handed her the burnt letter. "You'll have to do this again."

She looked at it. "Shit," she said.

I gave her the card that said I was a second-hand book-seller and asked to see Mr. Patrick.

"You need an appointment." She puffed smoke awkwardly and tried to look eighteen.

"I just prevented your office from burning down."

She giggled. "What do you want to see him about?"

I pointed at the card. "I want to open a bookshop; I need premises."

"Oh, you don't need Clive . . . Mr. Patrick for that; Mr. Skelton will do," she swung around to the empty desk. "He's not here . . ."

I leaned forward and dropped my voice. "Well, you know, I might have to deal with Clive. You see, this is not just an ordinary bookshop, if you get what I mean." I did everything but wink, and she got the message. Just then a short, well-stuffed guy in a pale blue suit bustled into the room. He had a high complexion, and pink showed through the thin fair hair which was carefully arranged across his skull. He shouldn't have been that heavy and thin on top, he wasn't much over thirty. The girl batted her eyes at him.

"Mr. Patrick, Mr. Henderson here wants to see you about business premises . . ."

"Give him an appointment," he barked. "Have you got the letter for that wog yet?"

She made her hands look busy on the desk. "It's almost done."

"Snap it up, Debbie." He turned without looking at me once and went out of the room. The girl looked helplessly at me.

"He's nice really," she said. "Now when are you free?"

The front door swung open and a man came through. He was tall, dressed in a narrow-cut dark suit: narrow was the word for him, he had a long, thin, swarthy face with a sharp nose, his dark eyebrows grew in a V over his yellowish, slanted eyes. He had close cropped black hair which receded on both sides and grew in a pronounced widow's peak in the front. His wolfish eyes swept over me as if he was measuring me for a coffin, then he dismissed me.

"Is Clive in, Debbie?" His voice was light and, although

it sounds corny, musical. It also carried a distinct foreign accent. Debbie looked scared, and nodded mutely. He brushed passed me and went down the corridor.

"Not Mr. Skelton," I said.

She pulled on the cigarette. "No, Mr. Szabo."

"What does he do around here?"

She shrugged and pulled the desk calendar toward her.

"Don't bother," I said, "I think I'll look for a more friendly firm." She looked hurt behind her cigarette so I was careful not to slam the door. I scouted the building and established that it had only two exits—the front door and a gate that lead out to the lane at the side. I dodged the traffic across to the other side of the road, bought a sandwich and two cans of beer and settled down to watch.

A short, plump man with ginger hair arrived after ten minutes. If he was Mr. Skelton he didn't look any more appealing than the rest of the gang. A bit after that Clive Patrick came out and drove off in a white Volvo, probably to a lunch he didn't need. Then Debbie stepped out and tottered down the street, she came back with a paper bag, a can of Coke, and a fresh packet of cigarettes.

I'd finished the sandwich and the beer and was feeling drowsy when Szabo stepped out into the lane. I whipped the camera up and started shooting. The shots in the lane wouldn't be much good, the one when he reached the street would be better. He sniffed the air like a hunting dog and looked directly across the street at me; I snapped again and could see him registering the car, my face, and the camera, and then he was moving. I dropped the camera and turned the key; a bus roared away from a stop and held Szabo up. I was clear and fifty yards away when he made it round the bus; I glanced back at him, wolfish visage and widow's peak—he didn't look happy.

I'm about as interested in photography as I am in flower

arrangement but, like a true professional, I knew the man to go to. Colin Jones was an army photographer in Malaya; if you could see it, he could photograph it. He worked for *The News* now and we met occasionally over a beer for me to tell him how much I envied his security and for him to say how much he wished his work was exciting like mine. I stopped in Glebe, phoned Colin at the paper and arranged to meet him outside *The News* building.

When I arrived Colin was standing there, smoking a cigarette and looking like a poet. The printers were on strike and there were picket lines in front of the building. The pickets were harassing the drivers who were loading the papers which were being produced by scab labour. Colin got me past the union men on the door and took me up to his smelly den.

"Contacts do?" he asked as I handed over the film.

I said they would, and wandered around the room looking at the pictures pinned on the walls; about fifty per cent of them were obscene. I used Colin's fixings to make a cup of instant coffee while I waited; the milk was slightly on the turn and the coffee ended up with little white flakes in it. I fought down the craving for sugar and a cigarette, and did some thinking instead. There wasn't much to do: Kenneth Silverman had been hanging around the Forbes Realty office one night and he hadn't been able to take his car away the next morning. That night, a Mr. Szabo of that honourable enterprise had been booked for speeding while driving south in Ken's car, which may have had a bundle in the back. It was looking worse for Kenny every minute.

Colin sauntered in and handed me the prints. The light had been bad and my hands not all that steady, but the long, vulpine mug was there clear enough—identifiable.

"Brilliant work, Cliff," Colin said ironically.

I pointed at his cigarette. "Smoking kills."

Colin tapped the prints. "I'd say this joker could kill, too. When are you going to grow up, Cliff?"

"And do what?"

He shrugged. I put the prints away and we shook hands. On the drive home I thought about what Colin had said; I was near forty and felt it; I had a house about half paid for, a car not worth a tank of petrol, two guns, and some books. I had a lot of scars and some bridge work; on the other hand, no one told me what to do, I had no office politics to contend with, and most of the bills got paid, eventually.

Musing like this is dangerous, it means defences are down and self-pity is up. I was still musing when I walked along the path to my house and only stopped when I felt something hard jab into my left kidney.

"Let's go inside, Mr. Hardy," a lilting voice said. "You've taken liberties with me, I think I'll return the compliment."

I half turned but the something dug deeper, painfully and I winced and stumbled forward.

"Take the keys out, slowly, and pretend you're coming home with the shopping."

I did it just as he said; the envelope with the prints inside was in my breast pocket and felt as big a a bible. He told me to open the door and I did that too, trying to avoid any jerky movement and cursing myself for not observing some elementary security precautions. A car is the easiest thing in the world to trace and this was just the boy to be getting my registration down as I was driving away in Norton Street. While I'd been exchanging wisdom with Colin Jones he'd been doing his job.

There was no point standing around in the hall. He prodded me with his hand, not a gun. I went, I had no booby traps, no buttons to push to release incapacitating gas; from the way he walked and held the gun I could tell that a sidestep and a sweeping movement aimed simultaneously at his ankle and wrist would get my brains all over my wall. He turned on lights as we went and that put a couple of hundred watts burning in the kitchen. He backed away and I turned around to look at him. His face was like a V—he had a narrow head with a pointed chin; his dark eyebrows were drawn together and down under the hair that receded sharply on both sides.

He moved around a little getting the dimensions of the room straight and then he advanced on me keeping the muzzle of his gun pointed at my right eye. He was good and he'd done all this before. When he was close enough, he kicked me in the knee, and as I bent over he nudged me and I sprawled on the floor. I looked up at him thinking how nice it would be to get a thumb into one of those yellow eyes.

He smiled down at me. "Don't even think about it. Now I see you have a gun under your arm and something interesting-looking in the inside pocket. Let's have the gun—easy now."

I got the gun out and slid it across the floor toward him. He lifted the pistol a fraction and I took out the envelope and pushed it across too. I started to pull myself up.

"Stay there, in fact you can lie on your face."

I could hear him fiddling with the paper and then I heard a snort.

"You're a rotten photographer, Hardy, I'm twice as handsome as this."

I didn't say anything; he was either vain or had a sense of humour; either way I couldn't see what difference it could make to me.

"Where's the phone?" I pointed and he motioned me to get up and go. The knee hurt like hell but it held my weight. The living room has some bookshelves, a TV set, and some old furniture, also a telephone. He waved me into a chair and I sat there opposite him while he dialed. The hand holding the gun was steady but he glanced uneasily at the photographs a couple of times. He still wasn't happy.

"Clive? It's Soldier, I've got Hardy; he's got a collection of pictures of me taken in Norton Street."

The phone crackled and Soldier's knuckles whitened around the receiver.

"Listen, Clive," he rasped, "you're in this. If I have to knock off this guy you're going to be part of it, not like the other one."

He listened again and when he spoke his voice had lost its musical quality, it was full of contempt. "Of course I can't. We don't know where he's been or who he's talked to. There could be copies of the pictures. It's a two-man job, Clive."

Clive evidently said he'd drop by, because Soldier put the phone down and wiped his hand over his face edgily. I didn't fancy what was coming up. It sounded like a pressure session, and Soldier looked like the boy who knew how to apply it. I felt sick and scared at the thought of what I had to do, but there was no cavalry coming. He told me to get up, and when we were both on our feet I made a slow, awkward lunge at him which gave him plenty of time to lay the flat of his gun along the side of my head. The sound inside my skull was like a rocket being launched and the colour behind my shut eyes was a blinding white, but I'd dipped with the blow a bit, and as I went down I thought *I can do it*.

I lay very stll and let the blood drip into my ear. There was a lot of blood luckily, and I was so afraid that my pulse must have slowed to ten beats a minute. He bent down to look at me, swore, and went out of the room.

Getting to the bookshelf was one of the hardest things I've ever done. It seemed to take forever, but my eyes were open and I was seeing okay when I clawed out the three volumes of Russell's autobiography and got my hands on the old, illegal Colt I keep behind there. I pulled it out of the oilskin wrapping, cocked it, and wriggled back to where I'd been. He came back into the room with a wet dishcloth in one hand and his gun in the other; his chest was thin, and covered in elegant beige silk. I shot for his leg but I was in no condition for shooting; the Colt jerked in my shaky hand and the bullet went into the embroidered pocket of the shirt. His yellow eyes flashed as the last messages his brain would ever send went through; and then blood welled and spurted and he went down backwards, awkward, and dead.

I picked up his gun and put it in my pocket and then I got the dishcloth and dragged myself to the bathroom. My face was covered in blood and I suddenly thought about his blood and vomited into the basin. After a bit more of that I cleaned myself up as best I could and went back to the phone. Horace was at home, and I told him to drive to Glebe and call me from a public box in about half an hour. He tried to order me about, but I suppose something gets into your voice after you've just killed a man, and he didn't try it for long.

My head was aching badly now, but I examined it carefully and looked into my eyes and concluded that I had a mild concussion at worst. My treatment for that was time-tested—pain-killers and whisky. I took both upstairs and sat on the balcony to wait for Clive.

He arrived in the Volvo and he was all alone. I went down and let him in. He'd sweated a bit into the neck of the pastel shirt, but he was still the image of the over-fed businessman with nothing but money on his mind. I put my gun an inch or two into his flab and moved him down the passage to the living room. I had a lot of blood on me and was feeling pretty wild from the codeine and the whisky and he just did what I said without a murmur. He was scared. He almost tripped over the corpse.

"Soldier isn't quite with us," I said.

He looked down at the bloody mess on the floor and all the golf and Courvoisier colour in his face washed away.

"You've been keeping bad company, Clive," I said. "Want a drink?" He nodded and I poured him a spash of Scotch. The phone rang, and Silverman told me where he was. Patrick was still looking at Soldier and I had to jerk his hand with the glass in it up to his mouth.

"We've got a visitor," I said. "I'm going to let him in. You sit there, if you've moved an inch when I get back I'm going to break your nose."

I got a miniature tape recorder out of a cupboard in the kitchen, and went through to answer the soft knock on the door.

Silverman started to say the things you say when you meet people with guns and beaten-up faces, but I told him to be quiet. In the living room I sat down with a Scotch and started the tape. I put Soldier's gun on the coffee table for added effect.

"What's Clive doing here?" Silverman said.

"Oh, he belongs, he murdered your son."

It stunned Silverman into silence, and set Patrick talking as I'd hoped it would. There was nothing much to it. Patrick was in deep financial trouble, and hoped for the Forbes Realty deal on the Glebe land to pull him out. But he was running short of time and he got the wind up when Silverman made a few enquiries about the firm. The squatters really got up his nose; he hired Soldier Szabo and some other muscle to help him there and Soldier was still around when Kenneth was caught snooping in Leichhardt.

"So you killed him," Silverman said quietly.

"It was an accident, Horace," Patrick muttered. "Soldier hit him too hard. It was an accident."

"Maybe," I said. "And maybe you killed him when you found out who he was. What else could you do?"

106

"It wasn't like that," Patrick said quickly.

"The body might tell us something. Of course you had to get rid of the body—you should have thought about the parking ticket."

"There was no ticket when we . . ."

"No ticket? Well, tough shit, they blow away sometimes. Did Szabo tell you about the speeding ticket?"

Patrick put his face in his hands. "No."

"What did you do with my boy?" Silverman said. All the imperiousness and arrogance had melted away. He was just a little fat man, sad, with quivering jowls and a bad colour. "Where's my boy?"

I gave Patrick a light touch on the cheek with the gun. "Answer him!"

"I don't know." He looked at Szabo; the front of the stylish shirt was dark, almost black. "He didn't tell me."

"Clive," Silverman said desperately, "I must know, we'll get you off lightly. Hardy . . ."

I didn't say anything. Something like hope flared in Patrick's face for a second but it died. He was telling the truth and he had nothing to sell.

"He didn't tell me," he said again.

After that we had the cops and an ambulance, and a doctor who looked at me and put some stitches in my head. I made a statement and Silverman made a statement, and Patrick phoned his lawyer. Eventually they all went away, and I drank a lot of Scotch and went to sleep.

They knocked down the houses anyway and built the home units which look like an interlinked series of funeral parlours. I hear the residents have trouble getting their cars in and out. Clive Patrick went to gaol for a long time, and I got paid, but nobody has ever found any trace of Kenneth Silverman.

Stockyards at Jerilderie

She was leaning against the peeling plaster wall outside my office and looking only fifty per cent likely to knock on the door. I hurried down the passage toward her, glad that I'd had a shave and that my clothes were more or less clean—business in the private enquiries game was slow; I understand it's the same in imported limousines and oil shares.

"Did you want to see me? I'm Cliff Hardy." I put a hand out which she shook as she told me her name and then I used it to open the door. Like me, the office was neater than usual; I'd used some of the idle hours I'd had lately to clean things up a bit and I'd even put a bunch of flowers in a vase on top of the filing cabinet. They were starting to droop a bit but still had a few days left in them. She sat in the chair in front of the desk and crossed her legs; they were long, thin legs and the knees jutted up high. She was a long, thin woman in fact, around thirty-five with nice, brown eyes. She wore a plain linen dress and a light beige jacket; like her they were nice, not flashy, maybe even a bit severe.

She shook her head at the cigarettes I offered and came to the point. "How honest are you, Mr. Hardy?"

"Moderately," I said. "I believe in moderation in all things."

She thought that over for a minute and looked at me like a horse buyer inspecting yearlings. As I say, I was clean and a

108

bit tanned from being under-employed; I was also a bit under-weight but that was a plus, surely. "What do you charge for being moderately honest?"

It was my turn to inspect the goods. Her clothes and leather shoulder bag weren't cheap, her short brown hair had been well cut and her teeth were good. "A hundred and twenty dollars a day and expenses," I said. "I need a retainer, but that's negotiable."

She smiled, her lips were thin, but not too thin. "If Lan Hancock walked in you'd charge five hundred a day."

"If he walked in I'd walk out. I can't stand horn-rimmed glasses."

She laughed and I saw a few more good teeth. "I hope we can do business. I want to recover something that belongs to me."

"What is it?"

"A painting."

"Aha, go on, Miss Woods."

"I don't think you're taking me seriously."

"Maybe I don't take painting seriously. *Please* go on."

She drew in an exasperated breath. "All right. I recently split with a man I'd been living with for a few years. We divided possessions, you know how it is?"

I did; I'd divided everything with Cyn my ex-wife, then she'd divided my share again seventy-five twenty-five. "Yeah," I said.

"It wasn't a very friendly parting. Leo took this painting and refuses to give it up. It has a sentimental value for me, and I've heard he's planning to sell it."

"Why don't you buy it, then?"

"It's a matter of principle; it's mine." I suppose it was then that I decided that I didn't like her. There was something frozen and emotionless in her face and maybe the lips *were* too thin. But life is a struggle, and sometimes you have to pry the jaws apart and say the words that will make people put your name on cheques.

"I see. What action do you have in mind?"

She mistook my attitude for complicity and leaned forward a bit over the desk. "I want you to break into his house and take the painting."

"No," I said.

"It means nothing to Leo. He probably wouldn't even know it had gone."

"No."

She looked at me for a minute and then she shrugged and got up. Suddenly the flowers seemed to be drooping a bit more, and the dust motes in the air swarmed thick in the beams of light that came through the clouded windows. She adjusted the strap of her bag and walked out leaving the door open. I got up, closed the door, and tried to sit the flowers a little more proudly in the vase.

Three days later, as I read in *The News*, she was dead. She'd been found in her house in Paddington with her head caved in. She was thirty-four and described as an "art dealer." I read the report, and felt vaguely sorry for her, the way you do, and vaguely pleased that I hadn't taken her on as a client and then I forgot about it. The next day I got a phone call from Detective-Inspector Grant Evans, who manages to be both an old cop and old friend. He told me that my card had been found in Susannah Woods's bag and asked if I knew anything about her.

"Yeah," I said. "She came to my office and asked me to look for a painting she'd lost."

"What d'you know about painting?"

"A bit, Cyn was keen on it."

He grunted. "You take the job?"

"No, out of my depth. Any ideas on who killed her?"

"Not really, she had this boyfriend, ah . . . Leo Porter, but he's in the clear time-wise." He read out Porter's address and number, and I wrote them down. There was a pause in the conversation.

"Why are you telling me this, Grant?"

I could imagine him sucking in his belly against his belt and poking the flab; Grant tried to balance his moral rectitude against his physical decay and the effort left him unhappy. "Well, I haven't got the time or the manpower for this one, Cliff. She hung around with artists and queers; no one cares. The Commissioner hates artists and queers. I thought I might just throw this to you—apparently this Woods woman had a valuable painting, insured for God knows how much. It's not over the fireplace just now and the company would like it back. I gather they're willing to spend a little money. Interested?"

I said I was, and he gave me the name of the man at Hawker Insurance Company—Quentin James.

"Quentin?" I said. "I bet the Commissioner just loves names like Quentin." Grant hung up on me, and since I had the phone in my hand I used it to make an appointment that afternoon to see Mr. James.

The insurance company was housed in one of those buildings which make you wonder where the world is going: the floors were made of some substance which was hard, cold, and foreign, and it was too dark in the lobby to read the signboards. I got in a lift and found that Hawkers was on the third floor, but by then the lift had shot up to the tenth and I had to ride up to the sixteenth before it came down again. Inside a smoked glass door a woman was sitting perfectly still at a desk. I walked up, and she kept her hands in her lap and only moved the minimum number of muscles for speech. It was a short speech.

"Yes?"

"Hardy, to see Mr. James."

She kept her left hand where it was and lifted her right to flick a switch. She repeated what I'd said, adding another Mr. Then she put her hands together again.

"Down the corridor to your right, Mr. Hardy." Her head inclined an inch to the right.

I wandered down the passage between the pot plants and the paintings to where a door with a laminate aping cedar bore the words "Q de V. C. James—Claims Investigation." I knocked and went in. A secretary had her back to me as she delved into a filing cabinet. She waved a hand at a door off to one side, and I gathered that Mr. Q de V. C. James was available. The door came open as I moved toward it and a tall, elegant character stepped out. He had a swathe of papers in his hand which he tossed on to the desk.

"Tania," he said breezily. "Here's the report, do your best. Hello, who're you?"

"Hardy."

"Oh, yes." He did something that used to be called beaming, I don't know what they call it now, you don't see it often. "Hardy!" he bellowed. "Private eye. Come in! Come in!"

The hearty manner and the pin-stripe, three piece suit gave an impression of aimiable idiocy, but he soon dispelled that.

"Sit down, Mr. Hardy." He waved me into a comfortable chair in his comfortable office. "Inspector Evans speaks well of you. Good man, Evans; honest cop, rare breed."

"That's right," I said.

"This is a strange case, bad smell to it. Miss Susannah Woods; shady lady I'm afraid." He picked up a folder on the desk, opened it and read: "Susannah Catherine Woods, divorced, thirty-six years, childless, journalist, art critic, artists' agent, art dealer." He gave the last word an emphasis, looked up at me and said: "And crook."

I clicked my tongue. "Maybe she's doing her time in a room full of Botticellis. What was her crime here on earth?"

"You don't like Botticelli?"

"Hypocrite," I said, "Loved little bums and tits and put in haloes to say he was sorry."

"Hmm. Well, Miss Woods insured paintings and lost them, sometimes."

"And other times?"

"She sold them; sometimes she sold the ones she lost if you follow me."

"Yeah," I said. "Why'd you take her on if you knew all this?"

"We didn't know, Mr. Hardy. This," he tapped the folder, "is the result of forty-eight hours of phoning around. She spread her business and hurt a few people."

"What's your problem?"

He looked through the folder. "Some idiot wrote a policy on a Castleton . . ." He looked up at me.

I shrugged.

He let out the bellow again, and it came to me that all this heartiness was defence and—in a word, shrewdness. "Charles Castleton," he said. "Painter, mid-nineteenth century, Australia. He's said to have perfected the colonial fence." I snorted and he laughed more normally. "It's all such incredible nonsense. Castleton was a drunk who daubed this and that. His *oeuvre* is uncertain; experts disagree. As I say, he painted fences in a particular way and this is almost his trademark. Now, Miss Woods had an authenticated Castleton; there are a few fakes about, and she insured it with us for $30,000."

I whistled. "It'd fetch that much?"

113

"Hard to say. Art insurance is a specialised field and the man who wrote this policy was good on motor vehicles. Anyway, her executors can claim the thirty thousand from us, although the whole thing is very fishy."

"In what way?"

He looked at the papers. "There's a very curious point here. Normally we insist on security arrangements in such cases; hers were acceptable, but she also informed us that she had a copy of the painting on display in her house ordinarily. She only brought out the original for knowledgeable guests and suchlike."

"Bloody confusing," I said. "Where's the copy now?"

"Still in her house, but there's no sign of the original."

"Are you sure she ever had it?" I was thinking of my conversation with her on the third last day of her life but I didn't tell him anything about that.

"Oh yes, the authentication was done by a reputable man—Dr. Bruno Ernst, an expert in the field."

I asked for and got Dr. Ernst's address and a retainer from the company. The deal was that I'd be entitled to five per cent of the claim if I recovered the painting—$1500 was three to four weeks work in my league, a nice round sum that brought out my enthusiasm and optimism.

I used the cheque I'd got from Quentin to buy myself a phone call at the desk of the frozen lady. She was still there, like a fragile, prehistoric bird trapped in the ice. I dialled Leo Porter's number and a rich, masculine voice came on the line.

"Mr. Porter? My name's Hardy, I'm working for the Hawker Insurance Company on a matter connected with the estate of Miss Susannah Woods."

"Yes." Guarded was the word for it, Horatius at the gate would have seemed relaxed by comparison.

"A small matter, Mr. Porter, I understand you have a

114

painting which had been in the joint possession of yourself and Miss Woods."

"Yes." Loquaciousness was not his middle name.

"I'm told you've offered this painting for sale, Mr. Porter; is that right?"

He gave a short laugh. "Wrong, it's worthless, it's a copy, very crude. I found it amusing."

"Could I see it?"

"Anytime Mr. . . . Hardy, except now. I'm busy. Call me later. Goodbye."

He sounded assured and hostile, and now I had more to think about. That made three Castletons, two fakes and a dinkum. It was all a bit much and I decided to bank the Hawker cheque, draw out lunch and traveling money, and do a bit of research. I had the lunch in Glebe at Lionel's crepes—one savoury and one sweet—and I put down a good bottle of hock with them. Two short black coffees fought the good fight with the wine as I walked up to the university to tap the resources of the Fisher Library.

There were three books on Castleton, all of which seemed to be based on the same slim supply of facts. He was a remittance man of sorts, good family, good with horses, and with a weakness for booze and opium which got him in the end. Falling off horses helped. Two of the books had colour reproductions of some of his paintings which looked undistinguished to me—all hazy blues and greens with an occasional streak of brown. I could see what they meant about the fences though; they wavered up hills and petered out among trees under harsh suns. Good fences. This all took a few hours; I took notes on the titles of his authenticated pictures and I browsed through a couple of books which mentioned Castleton in unimportant ways. It was mid-winter and the shadows were long on the lawns when I got out of the libary. A student pushed a pamphlet

115

into my hand. It read: LOOK AROUND YOU. THREE OUT OF FIVE OF US WILL BE UNEMPLOYED IN FIVE YEARS! VOTE RADICAL SOCIALIST FOR A FUTURE!

I walked back down Glebe Point Road to my car and sat in it wishing I'd talked to Miss Woods just a little more when I had the chance. If her racket was losing paintings and selling them, she'd have to have mates—dealers, proxies, go-betweens. I needed names, and since Grant hadn't given me any, I concluded that the cops hadn't found anything interesting in her house. But then, as Grant had said, cops had better things to do. I drove home and had a drink and a sandwich before putting on the dark clothes and the rubber-soled shoes, and taking out the wallet, which contains a few useful housebreaking tools.

I like Paddington; I've been to a few good parties there and spent a couple of those nights of sexual excess that everyone should have before they die. Miss Woods's place was a tiny cottage in a row of four in a narrow street. All four houses would have gone for a song in the 1950s and were worth more than a hundred thousand each now. There was a lane wide enough for a skinny cat behind them, and I slipped down there and over the back fence. AC-DC were playing a number on the stereo in the house next door so I didn't have to worry too much about the clink of milk bottles or the rasp of metal on metal. Her security was lousy. I was inside the place in two minutes and could have taken every Van Gogh in sight with no one the wiser. I used a narrow-beam torch to snoop around the place but the results were disappointing. Her bureau contained only a few papers, all innocuous, and if there were any hidden safes in the house they were well hidden. The imputed Castleton was on a wall in the tiny bedroom which was occupied by a big, well-used bed. I was looking at the painting when I heard the noise outside. The music next door had stopped, and I heard the glass tinkle into the sink. Then everything went very quiet before there was a scraping and rasping and the back door opened. I went down the stairs quietly, but he must have heard me. It was moonless dark and I had trouble adjusting after the torch light upstairs. I had my foot on the bottom step when he turned on the lights. I got a glimpse of him, pale and dark-haired, and then he hit me. It wasn't much, a clumsy poke in the stomach, but I was off balance, I lurched forward, grabbed him but missed, and in that cramped little house a big, hard piece of furniture leaped and crashed into the side of my head. I went down, hard, and the lights went out.

I heard myself swearing, using some exceedingly nasty language, and then it hurt to swear or to do anything except lie very still. After a bit of that I got up slowly and took hold of the stair rail; everything seemed to work reasonably well and I dragged myself upstairs. The painting was gone. I stared at the empty space for a while and when I reached up to touch my head I found I had a piece of cloth in my hand; it was cotton, looked like part of a shirt, and it was smeared and crusty with dried paint.

I put the cloth in my pocket and sat on the bed to do some thinking but my head hurt too much. Downstairs Miss Woods kept a nice supply of liquor with the fixings. I made a strong Scotch and oiled my brain with it. The treatment worked to the extent of making clear to me that we now had two missing Castletons and one still at large. I used Miss Woods's phone to call Leo Porter's number but there was no reply. Why should there be? It was Tuesday night, just right for a quiet dinner somewhere, a drink or two afterwards, and all that that might lead to. It was what any sensible, unattached, professional man would be doing with his time, but then I was only a semiprofessional myself.

I went out through the front door and slammed it closed—King Kong could have been sitting on the balcony and no one in the street would have known. Leo Porter lived a half mile away in one of the curvy, leafy iron-lace-filled streets Paddington is famous for. His front gate was open and his front door was open; I walked into the house and closed the door behind me. Leo lived in style—everything was of the best, carpets, furniture, TV, the lot. There were no paintings on the walls and that was a lot of walls, upstairs and down, six big rooms in all. My head was still hurting, so I put together some of Leo's Scotch and ice and even lit myself one of his thin panatellas. It tasted like sea-grass matting and I stubbed it out; the Scotch was good, though. After the drink I snooped through the house again but didn't find anything interesting; there was nowhere for the painting to have hung but it could have stood on the ledge above the living-room fireplace. Bad spot for a painting, though.

Leo got home about an hour later and he was very displeased to see me on his sofa with another drink in my hand. His companion was a dark, slim elegant woman who fitted cigarettes into a long holder and smoked while we talked. Leo didn't introduce us. I told him how I'd got into the house and he poked around out the back and found what I'd found—this guy's trademark, the broken glass in the kitchen.

"I could have got in another way, gone out the back and done that just for show," I said.

He grunted.

"I'm surprised you're not dashing about checking on your valuables."

"My dear fellow," he said as he made himself and the

woman a drink, "I don't have any valuables. I'm one of those lease it people, rent'em and wreck'em, you know?"

"Yeah. What business are you in?"

"Tax consulting. I'm the expert, I pay no tax myself."

"Lucky you. Did Susannah Woods pay much?"

He smiled. "Only what she had to; shrewd woman, Susannah."

The clothes horse in the armchair raised an eyebrow at that but decided to sip her drink rather than speak.

Porter looked at his slim, digital watch. "Just why are you here, Mr. Hardy?"

One good question deserves another. "Is anything missing, Mr. Porter?"

"I told you, I simply don't care, nothing here is mine."

"What about the painting?"

He spun around, nearly spilling his drink and looked through the arch into the living room. "Christ," he said. "It's gone."

"Tell me about it," I said.

"It was worthless. Who'd want to steal that?" He walked through the arch and looked at the blank space. "I used to spend some time at Susannah's place and she was often here. A civilised arrangement, you understand?"

"Yeah," I said.

"Well, we each left things in one place or another, moved things back and forth. I took a liking to this painting; don't know why, it was hardly finished really."

"Where did it come from?"

"I don't know, it just turned up in the house. She was always hanging around artists, I assumed it was just something one of them knocked up. I don't know anything about art, but this had something I liked . . . call it spontaneity."

"Was it signed?"

"Oh yes, something illegible, Castlemaine, something like that. Now what's all this about? I suppose it connects with Susannah's death?"

"Yeah, what do you know about that?"

"Nothing, except what I read and was told. I was upset of course, a horrible thing to happen. But I hadn't seen her for over a month, we were finished."

"What finished you?"

He shrugged. His dark clothes were well cut and expensive; so were the shoes with lifts in them that brought him up to about five foot eight. The woman in the chair was taller, tall enough to see the bald spot near the crown of his head. He looked at his watch again, he seemed anxious to get into a position where bald spots wouldn't show and didn't matter. "Susannah wanted me to help finance an art gallery, a crazy idea." He opened his hands and spread them shoulder-high. "Besides, I don't have any money."

I nodded and got up. "Forgive the intrusion. You were lucky, the guy who busted in here took a swing at me earlier in the night." I touched my head.

"Good God! Do you think he'll be back here?"

"Thanks for the sympathy. No, I think he's got what he wants." I finished the drink and said goodnight to Porter, whose colour wasn't so good. He looked a bit unsure of himself for the first time. The tall woman in the chair held out her glass for a refill and I gave her one of my wicked smiles and left.

I cleaned up the head wound, took some aspirin and went to bed. In the morning the head was still tender, but I'd had worse, and was anxious to try to bring about a meeting with the guy who'd given it to me. I used the telephone, and at ten o'clock I was inside Dr. Bruno Ernst's study. He lived in a little sandstone cottage in Balmain down near the wharf.

The house looked small because it was full of books and paintings, without them there would have been enough room in it for people, but apart from Ernst himself the only other thing that appeared to live there was a cat. There would probably have been some silverfish. Ernst was a short, squat guy with a fringe of white hair around a bald head, and a spade-shaped white beard. He pushed a typewriter aside on his desk and started to pack a curved pipe with tobacco. Outside a cold wind was rippling the water and flapping the ropes on boats tied up at the wharf. I sat and waited until he'd puffed enough smoke into the air.

"I understand you're an expert on Charles Castleton, Dr. Ernst."

"Bruno," he said. "Not strictly true, no-one is an expert on him, in a way there is nothing to be expert on. I have some knowledge and an interest, yes."

"You authenticated a Castleton belonging to a Miss Woods a few weeks back."

"That's right." He puffed smoke and looked a little umcomfortable. "I was never happy about it."

"Why not?"

"It was unusual. There are lost Castletons, of course. He led an erratic life, gave pictures away, paid debts and liquor bills with them. In 1884 Castleton held an exhibition in Sydney, a little tin-pot affair, but it was reported in the papers of the time and some of the paintings were described. Do you know about this?"

"Not in detail."

"The newspaper report only came to light fairly recently, and it is now taken as the best guide to Castleton's later period. Most of the paintings mentioned can be accounted for, two cannot."

"And Miss Woods had one of them?"

"Hmm, she had the painting which is called 'Stockyards at Jerilderie.'"

"Fences," I said.

"Indeed, a great many fences. This confers value on the work, a puzzling notion."

"You're sure it was genuine?"

He shrugged. "I gave my opinion that it was, no-one could be sure. But the woman had another painting of the same subject which was obviously a fraud. The materials were modern, and the technique was crude. She said she had come upon the painting by accident and averted an attempt to produce a fake version. I found this commendable, you see?"

"Yes, and this helped you to decide that the painting was genuine?"

He scratched at the squared-off beard, disturbing its symmetry. "It played a part in my judgement, yes."

"I see. Tell me, Dr. Ernst, once you've inspected and okayed a painting is there any way for anyone to know that you've given it the thumbs up?"

"Bruno. I'm sorry, I do not understand."

"Do you mark the painting in any way, Bruno?"

"Yes, indeed, with a stamp which can only be seen under ultra-violet light. The stamp carries my initials inside an octagon—I marked the Castleton with it."

I thanked him, and he insisted I have a glass of sherry with him while he showed me his paintings, books and the view. Too many paintings at once numb me, most of the books were in German, but I liked the view. The sherry was okay. As I moved toward the door, he gently suggested that he was due a consultation fee. I wrote him a cheque for fifty bucks and he waved me a goodbye with it from his doorway.

I'd left my car in Darling Street, near the police station

for safety, but I took a long walk through the Balmain streets trying to order the facts I had. The Woods woman's story to Ernst sounded phoney, but could possibly be the truth. The only trouble was that there was a third painting in the works. "Stockyards at Jerilderie" would have fitted the picture I'd seen in the Paddington house and I had to assume that Leo Porter's lost painting was of the same scene. But which one carried Ernst's mark? That seemed like the vital question, but was it? I worked up a sweat on the uphill stretch from the water and reached into my pocket for something to wipe my face with. I came up with the bit of paint-stained shirt. I looked at it and remembered what Porter had said about his former ladyfriend knocking around with artists. I also remembered the face of the man who'd hit me in the stomach. I hoofed it back to the car and drove through the ill-tempered traffic to the Cross.

Three years' friendship with Primo Tomasetti seems like a lifetime; I park my car out behind his tattooing parlour for a modest fee and he bombards me with his ideas on the good life—they involve considerable strain on the liver and prostate. Besides tattooing and mural painting, both of which he has brought to a high and erotic pitch, Primo is a bloody good man with a pencil. I stuck the Falcon on the little concrete patch at the back and came up the rear steps into the dark den where Primo plies his trade.

He was tattooing a Kiss-type design on the face of a young girl and he winked at me as I came in.

"What's her mother going to think of that?" I said.

"She never hadda mudder; she was too poor, right sweetheart?"

The girl didn't move a muscle. I watched it for as long as I could bear and then I went through to the kitchen and made coffee. Primo keeps an interesting collection of magazines back there, and I browsed through them while waiting for the coffee to perk. I made two long, strong blacks and took them back into the workshop. The girl was gone and Primo was holding his hands in front of his face and staring at them.

"I hate what I do, Cliff," he said. "It's a crime."

"Rubbish, you love it. And I know you, you put in that stuff you can wash out in six months. She was free, white, and seventeen anyway."

"I suppose you're right. Thanks," He took the coffee and I arranged some cartridge paper and pencils on his work desk while we sipped.

"You want a new name-plate designed?" he said. "A black falcon, maybe?"

"I haven't got a name-plate. When I need the name freshly written on an envelope to pin to my door I'll let you know."

He blew steam off the surface of the drink. "You got no class, Cliff."

"True. How d'you reckon you'd go at one of those identikit jobs? I describe the face, you do the drawing?"

"Sensational! It's what I've always wanted to do."

"Drink your coffee and let's have a go at it."

The floor was half-covered with crumpled paper when we finished a bit over an hour later. We got it right in the end—Primo prompted me and I abused him, and between us we caught the essence of the man I'd seen in Susannah Woods's house—his thin, peaked face, cupid bow mouth, and dark, low-growing hair. I'd have known him from the drawing and I had to hope others would too. I thanked Primo and paid him a week in advance for the parking spot. He looked hurt.

After that I tramped the art galleries of the inner city for a couple of hours getting hostile headshakes, propositions, and indifferent shrugs. I couldn't tell whether or not they were lying, and by the end of the day I felt like a visitor from Mars. They were a strange lot; most of them expressed indifference to Susannah Woods and I began to wonder what they did care about but they gave me no clues.

I decided that I *did* care who'd killed the woman and why; I wanted a drink badly and a lead nearly as badly, and gave it one last try by calling Harry Tickener. Harry is a reporter on *The News* and ten years of snooping around Sydney haven't dimmed his enthusiasm for his job. He sees a hell of a lot, hears a lot more and remembers almost all of it. I asked him a bring along the paper's art critic and promised to pay for the drinks. That made it a must for Harry, who is just a bit on the short-armed side.

We met at a pub on Broadway just across from the newspaper office. I fended off a few journos who wanted to talk about boxing—of which there isn't any anymore. Harry came in half an hour late with a paperweight sort of woman who he introduced as Renée Beale. Harry had a double Scotch of course and Renée had a Campari and ginger ale. We talked about nothing much over the drinks while Harry and the woman smoked and pushed back their hair and gave good impressions of tired workers; maybe they were. Harry lit his third Camel and squinted at me through the smoke.

"Renée's got an opening to go to, Cliff," he said.

She held up her glass. "I'll have to write it up tonight. I'll have two glasses of flagon plonk at the show and work till midnight."

"Okay," I said. "I'd like to know if you recognise this man." I pulled out Primo's drawing and handed it across to her.

She put on gold-rimmed glasses and peered at the paper. "Hey, this is good!"

"You know him?"

"Sure, this is Paul Steele, him to the life."

"What does he do?"

"Well, he . . ." She stalled by putting her glasses back in their case and sipping her drink. Then she looked across to Tickener.

"It's okay, Renée," Tickener said. "Cliff's a gentleman—he won't throw him down any stairs or anything."

I had reservations about that, but tried not to let them show in my face. Renée looked at her watch, drew smoke into her lungs, blew it out and sipped Campari.

"Paul's a painter, or was," she said. "He had a bit of a following for a while, did some very nice things. But the money and the junk got to him, and he hasn't done anything good for a long time."

"Has he done *anything*?" I asked.

"Well, he does some restoring . . ."

"And copying?" I said.

"A bit."

"Right, can you tell me where to find him?"

She gave me three possible addresses in Surry Hills and Darlinghurst, finished her drink and went off to her opening. I had another drink with Tickener and told him about the case while he blew Camel smoke around, looked at the women who came and went, and scratched at his thinning fair hair.

"You reckon this Steele character killed her to get the genuine painting, Cliff?"

"That's the way it looks."

"Why did she want the original copied?"

"This Castleton's a bit dodgy I gather, hard to prove if something's his or not. My guess is she wanted the copy to impress Ernst, help to confirm that she had the real thing—it worked too."

"Okay, but why would there be *two* copies?"

126

"I don't know, I can't figure that at all."

Harry grinned, he liked to out-sleuth me. "There's another thing, this is all pretty cold-blooded stuff—knocking the woman off, pinching the paintings, this Steele didn't sound like that sort of a bloke from Renée's story."

That was worrying me too although I didn't like to admit it. I felt I almost had the thing wrapped up but that there were some loose ends that could unravel the whole rug. There was also something else worrying me which I couldn't quite grab. I looked at the addresses and I looked at Primo's drawing and Harry and Renée's dead cigarette butts and I still couldn't get it. I said goodbye to Harry and went off indecisively to work at it.

The first address was a wash-out, no-one living in the blighted old house at all; at the second place I was offered grass but no information. The third house was in a tall, crumbling terrace wedged between rusty, graffiti-daubed factories. The street light was broken and two youths were working by torchbeam to strip a newish Commodore in the alley across from the house. One of them straightened up when I got out of my car and looked across. He picked up something from the ground.

I held up my hand. "These modern cars are so unreliable; hope you get it going again. Anyone at home in 88?"

He relaxed and spoke to his mate. The torch beam came up and hit me in the face. I let it hit.

"Junkies," one of them said. "You a narc?"

"No."

"I think they're there, why don't you take a look."

"There's no lights."

He laughed and spat into the gutter. "Squatters mate, they use candles."

I went back to my car and got the .38 from under the dash. I let the mechanics see it as I closed the door.

"Not interested in Falcons, are you?" I said.

I walked over to the house; the front door was a ruin with some of the panels replaced by cardboard. I pushed one in and put a hand through to undo the catch. In the passage way the floorboards were rotten and the walls smelled of damp. There was a chink of light under the second door along and I pushed it open with the gun held high. There were mattresses around the walls, some clothes scattered about and a candle burning crookedly in the middle of the floor. Two men were lying together on one of the mattresses. One of them turned his head to look at me, the other's eyes were closed.

"Trouble?" The accent was southern U.S., with a lot of illness and heroin in it.

"No trouble. Paul Steele here?"

"Upstairs. I'm glad there's no trouble."

I closed the door and felt my way up the stairs. The front room was showing a faint light and I could hear soft, slow voices. I crept up close and listened. There was only one voice, a woman's, and it was saying "Pauli, c'mon Pauli, Pauli?" over and over again.

I pushed the door open and the woman gave a scream and jumped off the floor and straight at me. She was big and fat, and she swung a fist into my face and followed that up with a fingernail attack. Both did some damage, and it was hard to counter while holding the gun. I gasped "Easy," and tried to duck the next swing and get at her feet, but she was quick, despite her weight. Her hand hit me again and I forgot my manners; I clipped her smartly under the chin, her knees sagged and I rushed her back against the wall which pushed all the breath out of her. I held her there while she struggled for breath.

"I'm not going to hurt you," I rasped. "Now behave, or I'll shove something in your mouth to shut you up. Understand?"

128

She nodded and I let her go keeping a cautious eye on her hands and feet. But all the fight had gone out of her and she slipped down to the floor beside the mattress on which Paul Steele lay. He'd been watching us but there was no interest in his eyes.

I bent down. "Remember me, Paul?"

There was no reaction and I reached into my pocket for the piece of cloth. He was wearing the same shirt and I dropped the torn piece onto his narrow, heaving chest.

"He's OD'd," the woman said. "What is this?"

"It's a murder investigation," I said. "A woman named Susannah Woods got killed. What's your name?"

"Morgan Lindsay," she said. "Have you got a cigarette?"

"No. Where are the paintings?"

"Over there." She pointed to the far corner of the dark room. I picked up a box of matches from the floor and went across to the corner. The three canvases were stacked carelessly against the damp wall. I struck a couple of matches and peered at them but under those conditions it was impossible to tell which version of "Stockyards at Jerilderie" was which. The woman was sitting listlessly by the ragged mattress listening to Steele's breathing which was harsh but even.

"Where'd he get the money for the heroin?" I said.

"Pinched something from that bitch's house and flogged it. It must be bad stuff though, never seen him like this before. God, I wish I had a smoke."

I looked at Steele and thought that his colour was bad, he had a sort of nineteenth century opium-den pallor and then one of the things that had been jangling around loose in my mind clicked into place. I had a short talk to Morgan Lindsay and then Steele's breathing broke up into erratic gusts and we went out to look for a phone. I talked to her some more in the street while the ambulance was coming. But when we got back to the room, Steele and his torn shirt and the ragged mattress were covered with blood and vomit, and he was dead.

I handed the three paintings over and Quentin de V. C. James pushed the buttons to get a cheque made out for me—promptly. He took the canvas with Dr. Ernst's mark on it over to the window and let the expensive light flood over it. He put it down and shook his head.

"Not my idea of $30,000 worth," he said.

I grinned. "Nobody's idea, it's a fake."

"Then they're all fakes."

"That's right, Steele did them all; the first one was a dry run which he wasn't happy with. Woods left it lying around and Leo Porter got hold of it. Then there was the deliberate fake to help authenticate the first-class fake. Steele killed her when she said she was going to burn that one and collect the insurance."

"But why? He'd have got his cut surely?"

I shook my head. "He was past that. Have a look at these." I took out Primo's picture and laid it on the desk, then I opened up one of the books on Castleton. It had as a frontispiece a photograph of Castleton taken at a time when he was ill. The hair, the face, the lines of suffering were almost identical.

"Remarkable," James said.

"Yeah, the woman filled most of it in for me. Steele was pretty nutty to begin with and the dope didn't help. He did a deep study of Castleton when he took on this commission for Woods. In the end he came to believe that he *was* Castleton or was his son or grandson—the Lindsay woman said he shifted around a bit on that point."

130

"And he cracked when she said she was going to burn the painting?"

"That's right. By then he believed it was real and that he'd painted it as a real artist."

"Is that why he went after the other pictures?"

"Probably, but I think the girl might have helped a bit there. The rough jobs probably looked more like Steele's own work; if they turned up and someone saw Steele's style in them, that would lead directly to him. The Woods woman wanted to get the rough copy back so as not to confuse the issue when she made her claim. That's why she came to me."

James was nodding sagaciously when a secretary came in and handed him an envelope. He passed it over to me and did some more beaming.

"A brilliant piece of work, Mr. Hardy, my congratulations."

"Thanks."

"One would have expected you to look a little more pleased."

I said: "Would one?" and got up and left. I was thinking of the pictures of Charles Castleton with his life sucked away by the booze and opium and Paul Steele, eaten down to the bone by smack.

Blood is thicker

He had a long, horsey face that needed a pipe stuck in it to bring it to perfection. His eyes were a washed-out blue, and his sandy hair was cut in a severe short-back-and-sides. He looked like the archetypal Aussie; a six footer, a survivor of Lone Pine and the Somme. He was from Taranaki, New Zealand. The black Oxfords were polished, the grey flannels were pressed, and his tweed jacket had been expensive and fashionable twenty years ago. The woman with him was fashionable now and anytime; she was a tall, Viking blonde, in a green silk dress with modish accessories. He was Hiram Dempsey, farmer, and she was his daughter Susan, secretary.

We were sitting in my dusty office with the linoleum decor and the streaky windows. Hiram made the introductions, mentioned the New Zealand policeman who'd referred him to me, and then let Susan take over. I could see the pride in his face when she spoke.

"We want you to look for my brother, Mr. Hardy. We understand you're very good at finding people."

I tried to look modest. "It depends how badly they want to stay lost; some dig in deep, some just stay on the surface. When did you last see this brother?"

She looked at her father. "Fifteen years?"

He nodded. "Fifteen, near enough." He had that slight

Scots burr many older New Zealanders have, slurring the hard "i" sound.

"I scarcely remember him," she went on, "I was only seven or so when he left."

"Why did he leave and where did he go?"

Hiram looked over my head out at the fierce summer sky. "Robert and I didn't get along. I'm a farmer, he wasn't. I'm a Christian, he was a sinner."

"What sort of sins?"

"Theft, drunkenness, loose living."

I thought I had the picture. "When you say theft, do you mean robberies or . . ."

"Cars."

"Right." It sounded familiar, a country boy out of his mind with boredom pinching cars, getting pissed, and screwing girls. It happens; some of them become public servants.

"Robert came to Australia, Mr. Hardy, to Sydney. My mother, she died three years ago, said that he always talked about the big city and he meant Sydney."

"He might have moved on; New York's bigger, so's London."

"No." Hiram said the word harshly. "Robert sent his mother a postcard every few years. After she died I found them; they were posted in Sydney."

"Do you have them?"

He reached into his jacket pocket and took out a slim stack of postcards held by a rubber band. He passed them across. The cards were mundane—the Bridge, the Opera House, the Zoo. The messages were minimal and written in a firm, round hand: "Dear Mum, Hope you are well. All's fine with me, loving it in Sydney and doing very well. Hope to get over to see you before too long"—that sort of thing. They were dated at two and three year intervals, with a gap

133

of four years in the middle of the sequence of seven. The last card was dated one month ago. Dempsey watched me examining it.

"He didn't know his mother had died," he said.

I looked at him, there was something unyielding about him and I decided that I'd been wrong about the pipe, the prop he needed was a Bible. "Can you tell me why you want to locate your son now, Mr. Dempsey? I gather you haven't forgiven him his trespasses."

"Don't blaspheme," he snapped. "I have less than a year to live, Mr. Hardy. I'll be joining my wife before long. I have a growth. I'm hoping that my eldest son will farm my land; it's been Dempsey land for five generations." He let out a sound that in a weaker man would be called a sigh. Some of the lines around his eyes which I'd taken to be marks of country hardiness now looked like tiredness, and there was a fragility beneath his resilience. "It's unlikely, I know," he went on, "Robert was a wastrel but he might be redeemable."

"Sure. Well, we need a starting point. I gather you have another son; would he have had any contact with his brother?"

"No. William is thirty and settled. He lives in Wollongong, he's an academic." He spoke the words without much enthusiasm; Old Dempsey must have been a hard man to please, any son who didn't have cowshit on his boots wasn't a son at all.

"He'd remember him, though. Could I have his address?" Susan gave it to me as the old man seemed to withdraw into himself. Maybe he was hoping that his Creator was a farmer. I asked for a photograph of the prodigal and she produced an old snapshot and a newspaper cutting. The photograph, which was yellowed and creased, showed a youth in his late teens standing beside a motor cycle. He

134

was smiling broadly and he had a mop of dark curling hair; he was a good-looking lad.

"That was taken of Robert just before he left," Susan said quietly. "The motorcycle was stolen."

I nodded and looked at the cutting. It was a press photo of a picket line outside a shop or an office. The caption had been cut off but two words remained of a headline above the picture—"sacks Clarke." The picketers were carrying placards which were too blurred to read; the head of one of them had been circled in red ink.

"We found this in mother's things," Susan said. "We think she believed that to be Robert in the picture."

I studied the faces; it was possible, some weight had gone on and some hair had gone off. Maybe. The mother's eye plus intuition could have been right or it could have been wishful thinking.

I turned the cutting over, on the back was part of an advertisement for motor cars. There was a picture of a Ford Falcon and the showroom's address was in Chatswood. I know a bit about Falcons because I own one; this model was a few years younger then mine, say in the early 70s.

"How would your mother have got a Sydney news-paper?"

"William used to send them when he thought there was something in them that might interest her. She was a great reader, and he sent the book pages and articles on writers and films and things." Susan looked at her father, who was sagging a little from the ramrod position.

"My father is tired, Mr. Hardy. Will you help us?"

I said I would, collected a retainer and their address in Sydney for the next few weeks. They were visiting a few relatives, winding up the old man's life.

* * *

I ushered them out, and set about earning their money by calling Harry Tickener at *The News*. He confirmed that there were people in the organisation who could identify a newspaper from the type and lay-out, and that if the cutting was from one of the half dozen papers published by his employer I could find the issue in a bound copy or a microfilm.

I walked the mile and a half to *The News* building, stopped to deposit the cheque and to buy some fruit for my lunch. These days I try to walk for an hour and eat fruit for lunch instead of sitting and drinking beer; I still miss the beer. The citizenry of Sydney were out in force in their light summer rigs; it was early summer but a lot of the women were tanned and it was a pity to take them off the beaches. Susan Dempsey had a good tan, I recalled, and looked like she'd play a great set of tennis; I'm pushing forty and the regimen has kept the fat down, but I still feel furtive when I have randy thoughts about females twenty years my junior. There's a bit of Hiram Dempsey in us all.

Tickener was too busy to talk as usual. He introduced me to a sub on one of the papers, who instantly identified the cutting.

"*The Sunday Post*," he said. He was a little roly-poly man who scratched his head a lot with a pencil. "Only ran for a year or so, that narrows it down."

"Still a lot of looking."

"Yeah. Hold on. Who's this Clarke?"

I said I didn't know.

"Rings a bell," he said. "Yeah, around that time. Come on we'll look him up in the cuts."

We went down to the library and he pulled out a metal drawer crammed with quarto size manila envelopes. All had names on them followed by occupations. Some were thin as if they could contain only a single sheet, others bulged fatly.

Thomas Clarke's file was thinnish. He was a unionist involved in a strike at a food processing plant in Wollongong in 1972. Clarke had refused to work with non-unionists and had been sacked. Reading between the lines of the cuttings, the message was that Clarke had been trying to unionise the plant and had run foul of the management. The strike lasted two months, and the unionists won. A large item on Clarke's sacking had been published in *The Sunday Post*, and it included my photograph. The men were picketing a supermarket in Wollongong which stocked the company's products; a heavy man in the centre of the picture was identified as Clarke, the others shown were described as his "supporters."

The sub made photostats of a few of the cuttings for me; I thanked him and left the building. Outside it was hot and cheerful, I felt pretty cheerful myself; I like the south coast, especially when someone's paying me to go there. I walked back to the office, drove home to Glebe and packed a bag. I put in swimming trunks and a towel but I left the snorkel and speargun behind.

If you stay on the highway the drive to Wollongong is a two hour bore, if you turn off and go through the national park and the string of mining towns along the coast from Stanwell Park, it's a lot better. I took the slow route and drove past the camp sites and beaches that would soon be filling up with holidaying hedonists. Packed in between the sea and the scarp on which the land slips so that people can't hang their timber and glass fantasies off it, the coal towns don't seem to have changed much in the past twenty years. The ocean was a deep blue and crashing in firmly as if rehearsing for a long, hot summer. There were one or two caravans already in place, forerunners of the tent and caravan cities that would spring up soon and last until April.

It was after six o'clock when I reached Wollongong; I checked into a motel down near the beach and went for a swim. My body was winter pale and the water was icy cold. It was a brief visit to the beach. I went back to the motel, showered and changed and watched the evening news on TV. After a couple of beers and a barbecued steak at the pub opposite the motel I was ready to go to work.

Dr. William Dempsey lived in one of the fashionable hillside suburbs of Wollongong. I spoke on the telephone to his wife, who was also a New Zealander, and easily intrigued by the story of her husband's long lost brother. Dr. Dempsey was lecturing at the university that evening and expected home soon after eight; I was invited for nine. As soon as I hung up I regretted that I hadn't asked what subject he taught—in my experience physicists and historians are as different as Afrikaners and Bantus. I arrived on time, and a thirtyish woman with a well-dressed, good figure let me in and took me through to a room which had a big window occupying most of one wall. The house was well up, and in the day the window would be full of first-class ocean view.

She got me a Scotch and soda which was about three times too strong. She stood in the doorway looking agitated, her carefully prepared black hair was a bit astray.

"I'm sorry he's late, Mr. Hardy. He's never late as a rule. The meal's ruined."

There was a noise from the back of the house and she went off to deal with it. The room had some comfortable chairs, a TV set and a coffee table; there were magazines and books on the table and more books on the floor near one chair and a whole lot more in a big bookcase. I took a sip of the Scotch and went over to look—they were mostly novels and biographies, but here and there others books had been stuck in or laid across the top of the rows. These were studies of work-places, unions, and aspects of the labour movement. Some had Dempsey's name in them and so did some of the novels. He could be a political scientist, economist, or sociologist, it's hard to tell these days, but the novels ruled out physics.

Mrs. Dempsey, who'd introduced herself as Rosemary, came back carrying a Scotch that looked nearly as strong as mine. She was very edgy.

"That was Graham, our eldest," she said, "I'd promised him his father would come in and say goodnight, I don't know what to do."

"Have a drink and sit down." She was in that distracted state that comes from listening to your own fears. An outside voice is welcome and usually obeyed. She sat down and sipped mechanically.

"Have you rung the university?"

"Yes, just before you arrived. He left the lecture theatre on time."

"Would he stop off on the way, for cigarettes, wine?" She shook her head.

"Might have had a breakdown."

"He's more than an hour *late*!" She looked at me as if I were an idiotic child. "If he had a breakdown he'd call the NRMA and he'd call *me*!"

"Let's give him a few minutes." I forced her to talk and learned that Dempsey was a senior lecturer in sociology. He had a Ph.D. from the ANU, and they'd been in Wollongong for five years. I sipped the Scotch and tried to think of more to say but her eyes were screaming at me. I got up.

"Okay, I'll go and have a look for him. I'm sort of retained by the family anyway."

She told me that Dempsey was a tall, thin man with spectacles, who'd been wearing light drill trousers and an army-style shirt. The car was a red VW beetle. I told her I'd call as soon as I knew anything and advised her to get a friend over for support. She said she would. I drove the obvious route to the university and heard no sirens, saw no flashing red or blue lights. It was a Monday night, quiet, with four TV channels available.

Dempsey was teaching a special course in industrial sociology, his wife had told me, and most of the students were adults who'd be rushing off to their own families and activities. The lectures were held in a set of halls at the northern end of the campus. I located them on the campus map and parked in the roadway at the front. The lights in the grounds were modern and bright but the lecture halls were in darkness. The doors were heavy jobs of the self-locking kind that could be operated by the last person out. I walked around the building and found a car park about fifty yards back surrounded by a chest-high hedge. I saw the shape of a VW in the corner of the park and broke into a run.

William Dempsey was lying on the ground beside the car with his feet under the hedge. One side of his face was covered with blood and it had flowed up into his hair and down into his shirt, soaking into one of the pockets. He wasn't wearing spectacles. He was breathing evenly and the blood still oozed from a cut running along where his hair was parted. I opened the car door; there was a set of keys in the ignition and a briefcase on the passenger seat. Light from the car washed over Dempsey and he groaned. I squatted down beside him and told him to lie still.

He lifted one hand and let it flop back, then he tried a leg. "Who're you?"

I told him and said I was going to ring for an ambulance."

"No, wait." His voice was weak but urgent. "Rosemary told me you'd be coming." He screwed up his eyes and looked at me. The eye on the blood-smeared side came into life as well as the other, which was a comfort. "Don't call an ambulance, just help me."

"Nothing doing," I said. "Your skull might be cracked, you could die in an hour. Lie back and wait."

"I won't." Something in the way he said it, something petulant, almost childish and yet determined, made me listen to him. "If you go off I'll get in that car and drive it."

"You wouldn't get out of the car park."

He lifted his head, groaned and let it fall back. His voice was weaker. "Hardy, if you ring my wife she'll have a doctor waiting for us at home. If he says so, I'll go to hospital; but I don't want to if I don't have to. This is political."

The last word was spoken so softly I had to bend down to hear it.

"This bashing, it's political?"

"Yes," he whispered.

It sounded like everything I usually like to avoid. But he meant what he said enough to take a risk and incur some pain saying it. That was worth something, also I admired his taste in novels.

"I'll bring my car around, it's bigger. Take it easy." I jogged back to the road and drove around behind the lecture halls to the car park. Dempsey clenched his teeth as I lifted him into the back seat but he didn't make a sound. Moving him I noticed more blood, down one side of his chest and on his back. I got him more or less stretched out with something soft under his head. He closed his eyes and I lifted the unbloodied lid with a finger; it looked all right.

"Bag," he said.

I got his case from the VW and took the keys out of the lock. There was a crook-lock lying on the floor and I put it on and secured it, then I locked the car. I looked back at him before starting; he opened his eyes and tried to give me a wink. I thought about the strong Scotch I'd left on Rose-mary Dempsey's table, and hoped it would still be there. I drove out of the quiet campus and through the almost empty streets as smoothly as you can in a fifteen-year-old Falcon.

Dempsey's house was unnaturally bright, the way houses are when there's a crisis on. Rosemary Dempsey had a neighbour, a woman as well-turned-out as herself, with her and they were drinking coffee and smoking when I walked in. When I got into the light I saw that some of Dempsey's blood had got on my shirt. Rosemary went white when she saw me.

"Oh, Christ." She jumped up and knocked her coffee over, the dark liquid soaked the cloth and dripped on the floor. "What happened? Where is he?"

"Calm down," I said. "He's in the car and he's alive."

We got him into the house and on to a divan on the sun porch. The neighbour turned out to be a nurse and she got busy cleaning Dempsey up and checking him over. He was conscious, but in a lot of pain and not making much sense.

"He said there was a doctor you could contact," I said.

Rosemary looked at the other woman. "Zelda?"

"The cut needs stitching," Zelda said.

"I'll call Archie." She went out quickly and I followed her through to the sitting room. My Scotch was sitting where I'd left it and I took a good slug of it. Rosemary was holding the phone, waiting for an answer; she pointed to the Scotch bottle on the coffee table and gave me a full candlepower smile. She was a very attractive woman in a slightly sculptured way. I re-made the drink and went back to the sun porch. Dempsey's colour wasn't too bad, and Zelda was holding his head up to a glass of water.

"Who's Archie?" I said.

She grinned at me. "Archie Pappas," she said. "He's the

142

local communist doctor. You knew the Dempseys were commos, of course?"

The wood under my feet was polished pine, the whisky in my glass was Black Label. "No, I didn't know that."

"Sure," she said. "Raving reds."

The doctor arrived just as I was finishing the drink. He was dark and squat with a spread waist. He butted a cigarette and bustled across to the divan. After looking at the cut which was clean now and gaping open, he got a medical torch out of his bag and looked into Dempsey's eyes.

"He's bleeding from his side and at the back, doctor," I said.

"Who's he?" Pappas grunted.

Rosemary glanced at me blankly as if she didn't know the answer, then she remembered—I was the one who'd brought her husband home and stopped her tearing her hair out. "This is Mr. Hardy," she said. "He's a sociologist."

Pappas kept on doctoring. "Oh, really, what's your field, Mr. Hardy?"

"Criminology," I said.

Zelda gave an amused snort but the doctor didn't seem to notice; he prepared a syringe and I got the idea that I wasn't going to get much information out of Dempsey that night. The needle went in and the doctor cleaned up. "He'll be okay," he said. "I've stitched the cut on his head and put a dressing on the ribs. There's no fracture; concussion, but not too bad."

"No hospital," I said.

He glanced at Rosemary. "No, not necessary."

I stood aside and let Rosemary escort him out. He gave me a nod and went quickly, I heard Rosemary say something to him near the door but not loudly enough to catch it.

Zelda came over and stood closer to me than she needed to. I didn't mind, she was tall and slim and she had nice eyes. She looked as if she'd have a sense of humour.

"Funny doctor," I said. "A criminal assault and no questions asked. Are politics really so hot around here?"

"Sometimes," she said. "Bill Dempsey's in the middle of something very hot just now. I thought that was why you're here."

"No."

"Well, I'm curious; why are you here, Mr. Hardy?"

"Cliff. I'm sorry I can't tell you, a family matter."

"You tell me and I'll tell you why Bill got bashed."

"Sorry, perhaps Mrs. Dempsey . . ."

"Mrs. Dempsey what?" Rosemary came back into the room and leaned against the door. She looked drawn and tired and her hair definitely needed a comb.

"I'm prying, Rosemary. I want to know all about this mystery man. Tell him to talk to me."

"This is Zelda Robson, Mr. Hardy," Rosemary said wearily. "She's my best friend and you can talk to her. She'll tell me everything you say anyway. I'm sorry, I don't think we can do much about your enquiry tonight. Perhaps tomorrow."

"Right. I'll check with you. Just quickly, I take it you don't know anything about your husband's brother?"

"Nothing."

"Okay, thank you."

"Don't think me rude, please. I'm washed out, but thank you very much for what you've done."

"Come on, Cliff." Zelda had me by the arm and moved me across to the back door. Rosemary watched us go with an expression that was hard to interpret—it might have been approving, or maybe she'd just seen the film before.

We went across some grass, a paved courtyard and

through a gate in a brushwood fence. Zelda's house seemed to be a slightly smaller version of the Dempsey's; it boasted a lot of timber and glass and was straining a bit too hard to be natural. She held on to my arm while she gathered up a bottle of Scotch and some ice cubes in the kitchen, and ushered me through to her living room. It was carpeted, with a sofa and a couple of big chairs; these were covered with skins and furs and you could have copulated in comfort almost anywhere in the room. She made us big drinks and we sat down opposite each other, about four ion-charged feet apart.

"Well." Her voice was deep, almost mannish and the bones of her face and jaw cried out for fingers to run along them.

"Cheers." I took a long sip of the Scotch.

She laughed. "I think this is called fencing." She tucked one bare foot up under her; she was wearing tight black slacks and a white silk blouse. "Bill's trying to save a mine and a railway line and stop a road."

"That sounds like fun. Who's he up against?"

"Do you know anything about the mines in this neck of the woods, Cliff?"

I shook my head. "No."

"They're basic to the character of the place. Miners are terrific people. There's a strong democratic spirit around here, the miners keep it alive and they've stopped this part of the world becoming a great McDonaldland. You know what I mean?"

"Yeah, I noticed some of the towns coming down; they still look like people might live in them. There must be big money trying to change all that, though."

"That's what the Dempseys are fighting. There's a mine in behind here, about thirty miles in. It's small but it pays its way and the coal comes out by rail. There's pressure on to build a road and move the coal that way."

"Pressure from who?"

She held up her hand and ticked off on fingers. "The truckies want it, people who'll be paid for the land want it, and believe me, some of them only bought the land yesterday. The big mines want it so they can argue that all the coal here travels by road and they need a subsidy."

"What about the unions?"

"Some for and some against."

"Charming, and Dempsey's leading the fight?"

"Right. He's held public meetings, organised petitions, written to everyone who can read. He's writing a book on the politics and economics of it, hot stuff."

"Shouldn't he be teaching at the university?"

She gave a short, barking laugh. "He works it into his lectures, he sets essays on it. He's had students interviewing truck drivers and mine management."

"That'd make him popular. It's one of this crew that bashed him tonight?"

"Bound to be."

"Where does the Communist Party fit in?"

She leaned forward to pick up her glass; I could see down her blouse, see the line and shape of her breasts. "That's another story," she said. "Now you tell me why you're here."

I told her; but I wasn't far into it before she crossed the gap and we were kissing and she was touching me and I was touching her. We went through to the bedroom and she took her clothes off and my clothes off and there was a good deal of laughing while we got used to each other. It didn't take long; she lay under me and we moved well together, and we made a very good job of it. After, I held her small, tight breasts in my hands and she held me, she wasn't shy.

In the morning we did the usual things—drank coffee, hugged and kissed and wondered what would happen next, if anything. I finished telling her about my assignment for the patriarch Dempsey, and I learned that she was divorced, with two children, of whom the father had the custody. She didn't want to talk about that. I admired her figure and the quick, deft way she did things around the house while I waited to see the Dempseys again. On an impulse, I pulled out a copy of the newspaper clipping and pointed to the man in the crowd scene with his head circled.

"Know him, Zelda?"

She took a quick, casual look. "Sure, who doesn't?"

"I don't. Who is he?"

"Tommy Gibbons, bad news."

"What's his game?"

"Don't know what you'd call him, he's a sort of bodyguard or protector."

"Who does he protect?"

"Harry Belfrage; he's a trucker and lots of other things."

"Like what?"

"Oh, security services, he moves money I think and guards buildings, you know."

"Yeah. This Gibbons, he used to be a unionist, why'd he change sides?"

She shrugged, it was nice to watch. "I don't know; I don't follow this sport myself, I just get it from Bill and Ro. What's the connection? If Gibbons has any tie-up with the lost brother it means he's a hood."

I was staring out of the window at her well-kept but unfussy garden; she preferred trees and shrubs to flowers and there were big stones arranged in a circle that looked to be for sitting and drinking on. She snapped her fingers in front of my face.

"I see there's a great mind at work. Look, I have to go out soon, Cliff . . ."

"Okay, can I ring the Dempseys?"

"Ring? They're just over there."

"I don't have time for the chitchat, and I suspect he won't be up to seeing me."

She pointed to the phone, turned hard on her heel and went out. I made the call and got Rosemary, who confirmed what I'd thought. Bill was still drowsy and she wasn't letting anyone near him. I said I'd call later, and hung up. I sat thinking for a minute and then located Belfrage's business address in the directory. When I went through the house I found that Zelda had left. I wrote a note on a paper napkin telling her where I was staying and saying I'd ring her later, and left it under the Scotch bottle.

I drove back to the motel for a shave and a shower. They saw me come, knew I hadn't slept there, saw me go, and not one of them batted an eye. As I drove off I remembered the first time I'd stayed, guilt-ridden, at a motel; the car had stalled and the luggage was faked and the manager had looked like he was about to call the cops. Now you couldn't faze them if you checked in with Les Girls.

The Belfrage Trucking and Security Company was a huge area enclosed by a high cyclone wire fence. About twenty big trucks, Macks, Internationals, and others, were parked on a strip of tarmac that looked big enough to handle a Concord. There were workshops and other buildings inside the compound and up near the front gate a long, low structure with a curved roof like a Quonset hut.

It was past ten o'clock on what was going to be a warm day. I sat in my car with a drop of sweat trickling down my neck and admitted to myself that I only had a vague idea of what to do next. To bust in on Gibbons and Belfrage demanding to see birth certificates seemed a sure way to land in the hopsital, if not the harbour. I sat and watched, wishing I could smoke so as to convince myself that I was thinking. But I didn't smoke anymore. Suddenly, I had something to watch: the door to the main building flew open and a dark, stocky man moved almost at a trot across to a Holden ute parked nearby. I was the best part of a hundred yards away, but I could hear his voice raised in anger and tell from his movement that he was not happy. Another man appeared in the doorway—a big, middle-aged character with a pink shirt and a face to match—and he wasn't happy either. He was yelling and the first man was yelling, and then a bloke in overalls came sprinting on to the scene. He did a bit of yelling too, and some arm-waving as he unlocked and swung oepn the big gate which held a metal plate with Belfrage Trucking and Security printed on it. The dark man gunned the ute and roared out of the gate; he bounced inside the vehicle as he drove over a gutter and passed within twenty feet of me heading toward town. I got a good look at him; he was the man in the photograph, aged a few years, and with his features distorted by ungovernable anger.

I got out of my car and moved quickly toward the gate. The two men were talking across a distance of thirty feet and the gate stayed open. The overalled man started to swing it to as he saw me. I held up my hand.

"Business with Mr. Belfrage," I said. "That him?"

He nodded and let me through. I walked toward Belfrage who stood in the doorway watching me. He looked unhealthy; his grey hair was cropped short around his bullet head and seemingly thousands of veins had broken in his nose and face. He looked as if he was pumped-up and over-heated, ready to burst. I wiped my hand on my trousers and stuck it out in front of me.

"Mr. Belfrage, my name's Hardy; I might want to lease a truck—quarrying job."

He ignored my hand and turned back inside as he spoke.

"Talk to Eddie."

It followed that Eddie was the man in the overalls. I went over to him as he locked the gate. He was short, almost jockey-sized, with a sharp intelligent face under a red baseball cap. His overalls had BTS in big blue letters on the pocket. Unlike his boss, he shook my hand. I told him my business and he asked me a few questions about where the quarry was and what sort of material it yielded. I was vague and tried to get him on to trucks, about which I knew more than quarries.

I nodded back at the gate as we walked toward the trucks. "What was all that about?"

He grinned. "Tommy blew his stack. He must've fucked something up again."

I laughed. "You have fireworks like that around here often?"

"Now 'n' then. They had a blue like that a month ago, always settles down. Gibbo'll get on the grog for a day. Now what about a Merc? Big bugger, should do the job."

We talked trucks and I noted down details about tonnage and fuel and tried to look interested. After a while I eased back, saying I'd be looking around for the best deal. The sun was high now and it was hot. I wiped my hand across my face. "I could do with a drink; what's the best pub around?"

"We use the Travellers." He gave me directions and opened the gate. I asked him to tell Belfrage that I'd probably be in touch; he nodded, but I had a feeling that he didn't believe me. I turned around once on the way back to my car and saw Eddie going in where the rude Mr. Belfrage had gone.

150

The Travellers Arms was a nice old pub about a mile and a half away. The verandah on the second level was supported by thin wooden piles, ideal for the loungers from the public bar to lean against. It had an iron roof from which the red paint was peeling, and a scarred and battered facade that recalled two world wars and a Depression. There was an ancient horse trough opposite the entrance to the saloon lounge.

Gibbons's ute was standing outside along with a scattering of other cars. I parked a little way off, unwound the passenger window and put the Smith & Wesson .38 on the seat under a newspaper. There were ten men in the bar, not counting the beer puller. Two men sat at the bar talking, there was a group of five in one corner and Tommy Gibbons sat near a window with two other men. They were drinking schooners of dark beer. I ordered a glass of light beer, sat down at the bar and pretended interest in my notebook. Gibbons had a long Irish face, and although his hair had retreated on the sides there was still plenty of it. He was wearing a sports shirt and slacks; his arms had been developed by work and his body looked firm. One of his mates was a skinny, ginger-haired character wearing a tattered tracksuit top and jeans, the other looked like a retired Rugby League forward; he was massive in the shoulders and upper chest, but a roll of beer fat around the middle made his torso cylindrical. They finished their schooners and Ginger came across to the bar for his shout. The heavy man leaned forward to hear what Gibbons was saying, and then made a muscle-bound flexing movement on his shoulders. "Well, why didn't ya?" he said.

Gibbons shook his head and looked across toward Ginger, he saw me but nothing registered in his face. They started on their round and I was wondering whether to order another when the red phone on the wall near the school of five rang. One of the men answered it, and shouted for Gibbons. He came across and listened, looked over at me once and I started to move toward the door. Gibbons shouted "Get him!" The redhead stepped in front of me and I swung and got him on the side of the head and he went down. Gibbons was putting down the phone but the front row forward was after me and moving pretty fast. I sprinted to the car and he wasn't far behind; I slowed down a bit to let him gain, put my hand in for the gun and swung around. He was about to grab me when I split his upper lip with the muzzle of the .38.

"Stay there, fatty, or you're dead." He stopped and half-raised his hands. I nipped around to the driver's seat and had the car moving in record time. I had a flash of Ginger and Gibbons on the move and I thought Gibbons had something in his hand but by then I was concentrating on turning, missing other cars and getting out of sight.

I was sweating freely and the beer was sour in my mouth and belly as I headed toward the Dempseys. He was going to have to talk to me whether he liked it or not. As I pulled up at some lights I noticed a truckie looking down into the car at the gun on the passenger seat. I put it away in the clip under the dashboard feeling rattled and inefficient. I hadn't used the gun for a long time, even to threaten, and I didn't feel easy with it. I parked down on the street in front of the house and ran up the drive. I must have looked pretty wild because Rosemary started building defences against me the minute she opened the door.

"No, Mr. Hardy, he's very ill. He can't . . ."

I pushed her aside not too gently and closed the door. "He's got to see me, this is all getting very sticky. It'll be shooting next."

I went through to the main bedroom; Dempsey was sitting up wearing some kind of oriental robe and reading a paperback. The room was feminine, and Dempsey, unshaven and with rumpled hair, was the only untidy thing in it.

"Hardy." He looked up quickly and then winced as a shaft of pain hit him. "Look, I'm very grateful for last night, I . . ."

"Skip it," I said. "It was Tommy Gibbons who bashed you, right?"

He looked surprised, and stalled by carefully putting down his book. "Why do you say that?"

"I've just seen him, he's a very angry man, very upset and he's got a gun. I don't think it'll be a third time lucky for you, mate."

"Third time," he said slowly.

"Don't shit me, Dempsey. Gibbons had a go at you a month or so ago, didn't he? You need help, and if I know the cops in a place like this they'll treat a communist stirrer like you as an accident waiting to happen."

Rosemary was standing in the doorway listening and I had a feeling that she might be an ally. They looked at each other across the room and there was a lot in that look—trust and repsect and other things. She gave a slight nod.

"All right," Dempsey said. "Gibbons had a go, as you say, a month ago, and it was him again last night. He told me to drop the campaign, the usual thing."

"Did Gibbons do the bashing?"

"Well, he pushed me around a bit at first, but no, it was the other one, the heavy one, who hit me most. Gibbons seemed to be holding him back almost. But the big one hit me and kicked me and I think he would have done some more except that there was something that scared them off—a light or a car or something."

Rosemary said softly: "You say this man Gibbons has a gun?"

153

"Yeah, and I think he's under some pressure to use it. Belfrage stands to gain if the road goes ahead eh?"

"He certainly does. He controls the trucking, has an interest in the land and . . ." He'd dropped into a lecturing tone and I held up a hand to stop him.

"I get the idea. All this is known, is it?"

"Oh no," Rosemary said. "Bill's told people of course, but it's his research that shows what Belfrage is doing—he's got it all well covered with subsidiary companies and leases and things."

Dempsey looked modest and I tried to picture it—a known communist slandering a respected business man, boring people silly with details of companies and stand-ins. It sounded as if Belfrage was nicely under cover, while Dempsey was in the middle of a paddock without a bush in sight. Silence fell while I did my thinking and Dempsey broke it with an embarrassed cough.

"Look, Hardy, I can't quite see what this has to do with finding Robert. Isn't that why you're here?"

For no good reason I suddenly remembered that I hadn't had breakfast and now it was early afternoon and I was hungry. Also I was curious about Zelda and why she'd taken off so abruptly. You're not supposed to be like this— distracted, thinking of your stomach—in the middle of an investigation, but it happens. I was confused and finding it hard to get a grip on the things I was supposed to be good at.

I muttered something about it being no good to find one brother and lose another, and then asked Rosemary if she could give me something to eat. She looked surprised but drew on her bottomless well of politeness and agreed to make me a sandwich. I asked Dempsey a few questions about his brother whom he barely remembered, but my heart wasn't in it. His eyes drooped and his colour wasn't good and I started to leave the room.

"I am a bit scared you know," he said quietly. "What do you think I should do?"

"I don't suppose you've got any trained fighters on your side—good men with the boot, a gun or two?"

He shook his head. "No, I wouldn't . . ."

"Didn't think so. Well, the thing is to stop Belfrage."

"How?"

"Tell him a story," I said.

I ate a beef sandwich in the kitchen under Rosemary's curious eye. She offered to open a bottle of wine for me, but I refused, I couldn't afford to get into the habit of opening bottles of wine for lunch. I had to get to Belfrage somehow and play the one weak card I had. I told Rosemary about Zelda's behaviour, and she shrugged.

"She's very sensitive, you must have upset her."

"Me? With my manners? Never."

She smiled. "I'm sure you can make it up. She's terrific isn't she?"

I said she was, but I wondered what she meant. Suburbia, you never can tell. I finished the sandwich and drank some coffee. Rosemary touched me on the shoulder as I rinsed the cup and plate.

"We're very grateful for what you're doing, Mr. Hardy. I don't know anything about guns, neither does Bill. And he has children to think of."

"Don't worry about it." I'd heard that line before; somehow your life is worth less if you haven't got children. "If you want to return the favour, tell Zelda what a prince I am."

"I will."

I walked down to my car thinking about the Dempseys and wondering what the mother had been like. I had my hands on the wheel when I felt the blade nip me behind the ear.

"Just sit still, mate," a reedy voice said, "and nothing bad will happen."

I sat. Tommy Gibbons got in beside me and dug a vicious punch into my ribs. "That's for Stewie," he said. A green Datsun drove slowly down the street and Gibbons waved to the driver—the muscle man with the split lip.

"Tell me where the gun is or I'll get my mate to cut off a bit of your ear."

I told him and he unclipped the .38 and put it in his waistband. "Okay, drive."

"Where to?"

"Where you were this morning, you fuckin' spy."

The blade moved away and I started the car and drove. Ginger sat in the back smoking and doing a little bit of work on the upholstery with his knife. The upholstery is shot anyway but I still didn't like it. Halfway across town I noticed that the Datson had fallen in behind us; he stayed back a bit and on my right which cancelled any ideas of leaping out of the car—if I knew Stewie, he'd put the front wheels over me and smile. When we got to Belfrage's place Gibbons directed me down a track which ran alongside the east fence. Near the end, well away from the main building and the trucks, was a gate. Inside the gate was a small shed. I stopped, Gibbons unshipped the gun and we went through the gate and into the shed.

It looked like it had been made out of car crates, the timber walls were rough, and there was a crude skylight instead of windows. The afternoon light fell on Belfrage, who was standing inside, leaning against the back wall.

"Well, well, you did something right for once."

Gibbons stepped forward, he held my gun in his hand and he waved it crazily. "Listen Harry, stop riding me. I won't take anymore of it. He's here, now get off my back."

Stewie came in then, which made five of us in the shack.

Ginger pulled up a packing case and sat down to work on his fingernails with the knife. Stewie sat on an old sea chest and gave me dirty looks. His lip was puffy and he worked with his tongue at a bottom tooth as if it was loose. That left three of us standing; Belfrage was mean, Gibbons was angry, and I was scared.

Belfrage lit a cigarette and coughed as he drew on it. Veins stood out in his face and he let his belly go even slacker when he coughed. He was in bad shape. "Okay, Tommy," he said. "Take it easy. Where'd you get him?"

"Where d'you think," Stewie growled. "At that prick Dempsey's place."

Belfrage blew smoke in my face. "All right, you. You snoop around here, you spy on my boys in the pub, and you hang around with Dempsey; what the fuck are you doing?"

I shot a quick, uneasy look at Gibbons and tried to look shifty. "Well, it's hard to say, couldn't just you and me have a talk about it?"

Belfrage laughed. "Bullshit. Stewie, why don't you show him that I don't like bullshit."

Stewie got up slowly and took up his position about three feet in front of me. I felt sick and regretted the sandwich; being hit by blokes like Stewie is no picnic but it was something I had to go through. I swayed away from the first punch and ducked the second but his third swing got me high on the cheek. I felt the skin open and I went down harder and more clumsily than I needed to. Stewie stood over me rubbing his knuckles and grinning crookedly with his battered mouth.

"What d'you say now, smart arse?" Belfrage said.

I got up, swayed a bit, and rounded on Gibbons. "You bastard," I snarled. "You've got the gun, use it for Christ's sake!"

Gibbons's jaw dropped and he looked down stupidly at the .38 in his hand. "What're you on about?"

It was too much for Stewie who didn't react at all, Ginger stopped excavating and looked at Gibbons. Belfrage was getting that over-heated-look again. "What's this?" he snapped. "What's this?"

I put my hand up to my bleeding cheek and tried to look abject; I was on thin ice and it wasn't hard. "All right Mr. Belfrage, I'm a spy, I admit it. Dempsey hired me. But I'm not the only one. Dempsey's got inside your show properly. He knows everything, Gibbons is working for him too."

Gibbons gave a forced, throaty laugh. "What crap, Harry that's bull."

"Hasn't he gone easy on Dempsey twice?" I said quickly. "Didn't you tell him to put Dempsey right out of it this time?"

Belfrage looked at Ginger. "Well? You were there, what d'you say?"

Ginger didn't know which horse to pick—Belfrage in fury or Gibbons with the gun. "I dunno, dunno," he stammered. "Tommy went sorta easy but . . ."

"He's Dempsey's brother," I said. I'd measured the distance to Stewie's crotch and reckoned I could get to Ginger before he could do anything with the knife. "He's his older brother, and he's a commie as well. They're going to screw you, Belfrage."

"No," Gibbons said weakly, "no, it's not true." But he looked at me, and Blind Freddie could see that he was lying. Belfrage was almost purple now and he bent down and picked up a length of pipe from the floor.

"Harry!" Gibbons threatened him with the gun. "Harry, listen!"

"I can prove it," I yelped. I scrabbled in my pocket and

pulled out the clipping. "Look!" I held it out to Belfrage. "That's him on the picket line."

"So what," Gibbons sneered. "I've done a lot of things, Harry . . ."

I checked my distances again before I said it. "That clipping came from Dempsey's mother, Belfrage. She kept it till the day she died."

"Died!" Gibbons voice was an anguished groan. "Died, no . . ."

Belfrage swung the pipe, I put my right foot into Stewie's groin and nearly tore Ginger's head off with a roundhouse left: the .38 cracked twice and a sharp, acrid smell filled the shack. Belfrage went back, buckled, and went down. Gibbons let the hand holding the gun drop to his side. I bent and looked at Belfrage; one bullet had taken him in the throat and the other had gone through his jaw and up.

I took Gibbons's arm at the elbow and shook it gently; he dropped the gun. "I couldn't kill my brother," he said.

"I know," I said. "Why did you stay here?"

He shrugged. "I don't know, Harry paid well. I've done time. I made a fuckup of everything. I thought I could discourage Bill, talk to him later maybe . . . I don't know."

Ginger was unconscious and Stewie was holding his balls and not taking much interest. Gibbons had a glazed, resigned look and I remembered the proud austerity of the father, the warm hopefulness of his sister.

"Get moving, Robert," I said. "I'll give you an hour. I'll have to tell them you shot Belfrage but I'll put it in the best light I can, maybe there won't be too much heat. Go north, go a long way."

He nodded and went out of the shack. I sat there for half an hour chatting to Stewie and Ginger. When the flies started to settle on Belfrage we went off to look for a telephone.

I told it to the cops pretty straight, leaving out the connection between Gibbons and Dempsey. After our little yarn about assault and abduction Stewie and Ginger were content to let me tell it—Stewie hadn't understood what happened too well anyway. William and Rosemary Dempsey and I got together over some Black Label, and a couple of policemen interrupted us and it took a while to sort things out. The upshot was that Belfrage was officially unmourned for various reasons as much as I was unwelcomed. I got a much better welcome from Zelda; she forgave me for being work-obsessed that morning and we went out to eat and back to her house for a short session with the bottle and a long session between the sheets. Turned out she was work-obsessed too and we left it that I'd go down again to do some swimming when the weather was warmer.

I drove back to Sydney, and Rosemary and Bill came up to have a pow-wow with Susan. They paid me my fee but I never got to make my report to old Hiram: he went into hospital while I was away and the news was that he was in a coma and sinking fast.

Susan came to deliver the cheque in person; she was elegant but subdued, which made her look even more elegant.

"What will you do with the land?" I asked.

"Keep it, Robert might come back."

"Yeah," I said. "He might."

Mother's boy

It was one of those fifty-fifty days in Sydney; half the sky was grey, half was blue, and it might rain or the temperature might hit eighty. Just then, in my office, which has spare lines as to furniture and a draught under the door, it wasn't hot, but my client was sweating. Mr. Matthews was the sweaty type—his suit was a bit tight for his early middle-age spread; he carried too much flesh to be comfortable except perhaps in the bath or in bed. Still, there were no holes in his shoes and he was my first client in eight days.

"He's like a leech, Mr. Hardy," he said. "Like a vampire."

The two descriptions didn't line up for me, did he mean something slug-like and fat or a sleeker, classier blood-sucker? But I got the idea and he was the client, he could use whatever similes he liked. It was his old mum he was worried about.

"I've been told that you're good," he said nervously. "I mean . . ."

"You mean I won't blackmail you?" I said. "That's right, I'm no good at blackmail, I can never find the right words in the newspapers to make up the threatening letter."

His hands were pale and puffy, and he clasped and unclasped them as if he was practising handshakes. He looked even more nervous than before—nervousness is standard in a client, a sense of humour is a bonus.

I sighed. "I'm pretty honest, Mr. Matthews, and I might be able to help you. Tell me more about this leech who has his hooks into your mother."

He looked at his watch and I guessed he was in his lunch hour; leisured clients are a vanishing breed. "My father died six months ago," he said. "He was old, it was expected. He left my mother quite well provided for. She has a house free of debt, his superannuation, and some income from shares and such."

"Do you live with her?" I asked.

"Oh, no, I have a flat quite close. I'm single, but I left home many years ago." He let the words hang there for a bit, awkwardly. "I didn't get along with my father," he added.

"I see. What was this vampire's name again?"

He looked puzzled for a second, the colourful language he'd used wasn't his usual style. "Oh, that was a bit excessive perhaps—Jacobs, Henry Jacobs. He handled the arrangements for my father's funeral, that's how he and my mother became acquainted. He's been dancing attendance on her ever since."

"What sort of attendance?"

"Flowers; I suppose he gets them cheap. He takes her to dinner, it's appalling."

"How old is your mother, Mr. Matthews?"

"Oh, not old, fifty-five I suppose. She was younger than father." Again, he hadn't finished, he seemed to have a need to explain. "I'm an only child."

He was a man of thirty-plus, still referring to himself as a child. It sounded odd and had a scent of parlours and lavender.

"Tell me about this Jacobs."

He described Jacobs as middle-aged and portly. He thought he might be a foreigner from the way he dressed, mentioning particularly his highly polished shoes. His funeral parlour was in Manly where Matthews and his mother also lived. I wrote down the addresses and leaned back in my chair; it creaked dangerously and I came forward quickly; the desk was a bit rickety and the carpet square was arranged off centre to hide the holes. I needed the work but I had to give him a few hard truths first.

"I charge one hundred and twenty-five dollars a day and expenses, Mr. Matthews. I also need a retainer of two hundred and fifty dollars."

He didn't blink. "I'll be happy to pay it," he said. "I have to do *something*." He got out a useful-looking cheque book and I waited until he was writing before asking the next question.

"What does your mother say about Jacobs?"

He looked up. "I wouldn't dream of asking her about her personal life," he said firmly.

Keep writing I thought, and he did. That would be right of course, he wouldn't ask her, she wouldn't ask him, and nobody would ask dad. Clean rooms, neat garden, polished car, and a shandy at Christmas if you were lucky. It wasn't exciting—it was drawn blinds stuff, a high hedge and a smile for the neighbours, but it has compensations, it can make for very healthy building society accounts; I gave him a business-like thrust. "Do you know anything about Jacobs's business associates?"

"Not really. He has a solicitor crony who has an office nearby. He's introduced my mother to him. I'm very worried about it."

"Why?"

"I think he might be trying to get her to change her will."

"Aha," I said.

Manly is like a foreign country to people like me who live on the other side of the water. The roads are wide and the hills are gradual; some of the streets and cul-de-sacs have a European feel. Henry Jacobs's funeral parlour was genuinely Australian, that is to say, a genuine copy of the Californian model. The building was long and low with smoked glass windows and courtyards covered with little white stones. The funeral column in *The News* had told me that a show was scheduled for that afternoon. I parked across the street and watched the people dressed in dark, hot clothes mope about while a couple of gleaming limousines disgorged the living and transported the dead. Jacobs wasn't hard to spot; he had the act off perfect, the slow movement, the solicitude, the Nazi-like direction of the underlings. He was carrying thirty pounds he didn't need, looked swarthy, and seemed to shine somewhat from a distance. His teeth were very white and he showed them a lot. After the cortege had left I walked across the street and strolled past the sanctum; a grey-uniformed zombie standing outside the entrance gave me a hard stare. Next to Jacobs's place was a luxury car showroom, then a Vietnamese restaurant, and then a nasty cream brick building which carried a brass plate in front—W. J. Hornfield, LLB(Syd), Solicitor. A fine profession, I thought; my mother had wanted me to go in for the law and my father had thought I'd make a plumber—I'd been a terrible disappointment to them both.

I turned to go back to my car and saw Jacobs, who'd sent his 2IC to burning, coming out of his establishment. The zombie stepped out of a silver grey Jag which he'd driven up, so the master only had to walk twenty feet to get behind the wheel. He drove off sedately and I re-crossed the road; a woman who'd been gardening out in front of her house was watching Jacobs's car as it cruised off. I bustled up to her fence.

"That was Mr. Jacobs was it, madam?"

"That was him." She was small and old, but not frail.

"Damn," I said. "Missed him again."

"Are you burying someone? Give Henry a miss."

"No, I'm a journalist, I'm writing an article on the funeral business and I wanted to talk to Mr. Jacobs. But that's an interesting comment, madam. Would you care to add to it?"

She smiled, and all the lines on her face responded; they seemed to have been etched by good humour. "I might; is it worth anything?"

"Well . . . expenses . . . I could pay you for your time, say ten dollars for a half hour chat?"

"Come inside."

The house was brick and tile, solid and unpretentious. It was darkish, cool, and well-kept without being fussy. She sat me down in the living-room and went off to make coffee. When she came back I had the ten out and gave it to her.

"Thanks." She put the money on the mantelpiece between some china dogs. "Black?"

"Please." I got out a notebook. "How long has Mr. Jacobs been in business here Mrs. . . . ?"

"Wetherell, Norma Wetherell. Not too long, four or five years, I've been here for forty. It was all different then."

"I'm sure. Why did you say he should be avoided?"

"He's a crook." She put three spoons of sugar in her coffee and stirred vigorously. "A friend of mine buried her husband with him; lovely man he was, it was a shame. I tell you if he'd been alive and heard what that man charged, he'd have punched his nose."

I smiled. "Bit steep is he?"

"Steep? He's a thief. Extra for this, extra for that."

I made some notes. "Umm, he's got a nice car. But I suppose they all make money in that game. No law against it."

She leaned forward. "He's buried two wives since he's been here," she whispered. "Rich ones too I'll be bound."

165

I almost choked on the instant coffee. "How d'you know that?"

She grinned, pleased at the reaction. "Seen 'em, both of 'em. He's got a flat at the back of the place. There they were, shopping, doing the laundry, and then . . . phftt!" She drew a finger across her throat.

"When did this happen?"

"One just after he got here; the other, let's see, about two years back. Had your ten dollars worth?"

"Nearly; how do you know they were his wives, actually wives?"

"Notices in the paper. Course, he didn't lay them down himself. It's a wonder, though, still I suppose he got a cut rate."

I got up. "Well thank you Mrs. Wetherell, that's all very helpful, I won't quote you of course."

"Quote away," she said cheerfully, "All true."

"We'll see. Just one more thing, do you know anything about Mr. Hornfield, the solicitor?"

She was sharp, suspicious at this development.

"Why?"

"Oh, I heard he and Jacobs were partners."

"Could be, the little rat."

"Have you heard bad reports on him too?"

"No, not a word. But you should see him, he's the image of Billy Hughes, image of him. Little rat."

I thanked her again, and went out to my car thinking that I could probably get more from her if I needed it.

The computer is a terrible thing when it's misused for bank statements and rates notices, but it beats everything for saving the eyes and legs of private detectives. A phone call to Harry Tickener of *The News* won me admittance to the paper's computer room and an introduction to the pimply kid who ran the show. He looked about seventeen, but was probably ten years older. I told him I wanted to ask his friend all about Henry Jacobs.

"Classifieds or news?" His hands caressed the buttons on the panel in front of him like those of an archer smoothing the feathers of a shaft.

"Both."

He did all the things they do—punched buttons, looked at screens, ripped paper and swore until he handed me a bundle of tabloid-sized print-out sheets. I looked at it doubtfully.

"More than one Jacobs?"

He nodded. "Several, and that only goes back seven years." He took a Mars bar out of a drawer, peeled it and chewed. "Lucky it wasn't Smith," he said through chocolate and caramel.

Back home, coffee and pen to hand, I poured over the sheets and the coded summaries and they yielded up some of their secrets at last. One of Henry Jacobs's hearses had been involved in an accident five years before; Henry had stood unsuccessfully for the local council around the same time; his wife Gladys had been laid to rest aged fifty-four five years ago and Ellen Mary Jacobs, aged fifty-six, had followed her but two years later. R.I.P. Henry was very busy at his trade; there were hundreds of notices of funerals he'd handled—men, women, and children. After depressing myself with this data for a while I found a tiny nugget of significance—a high proportion of the folk who came posthumously into Henry's care had shuffled off at St. Mark's Hospital, Harbord.

I pecked away at the typewriter for a bit, applying for copies of the death certificates of Gladys and Ellen and enclosing the correct fee and s.a.e. as directed to Dr. C. P. Hardy, c/o Associate Professor P. J. White, Department of

History, University of Sydney. Peter was accustomed to the subterfuge, it amused him to assist what he called the forces of reaction. Then I phoned Matthews; it was after six o'clock, definitely time for a drink, and I wondered what Matthews was doing in his Manly flat. I had the answer when he lifted the phone—a burst of gunfire and a musical crescendo. He excused himself, turned the sound down, and I told him the gist of what I'd learned. I was hoping that he'd tell his mother and that would be the end of Henry. He was too stunned to reply so I fed this idea to him.

"No, it wouldn't work," he said slowly. "She wouldn't believe me. She thinks . . ."

"Thinks what?"

"That my regard for her is . . . unhealthy. I hated my father, as I told you."

Oh, Sigmund, I thought. "Well, I'd better press on. How's your mother's health?"

"First class, she's never been ill to my knowledge. Mr. Hardy, do you think she's in danger, real physical danger?"

"I doubt it. Still keeping well, is she?"

"Oh, yes, as ever." His voice changed and a despairing, fastidious note crept in. "She's seeing him tonight, they're going to dinner. Mr. Hardy, I don't suppose you could sort of keep an eye on them? I'm really very worried."

I agreed to do some surveillance and pick the happy couple up at her place at 8 p.m. I told Matthews to have a few drinks and not to worry.

"I don't drink," he said.

On that happy note I rang Harry Tickener, who stays at his desk until they turn the lights and air conditioning off.

"How'd you go with the computer?" he asked.

"Great. Would there be a human being around there who could do five minutes work? The person would have to be able to read."

He sighed. "That could be tough. Hold on, Martin's

here." I heard him shout away from the phone: "You can read can't you, Martin?" Martin must have replied heatedly because Harry laughed. Then he said: "Okay Cliff, Martin's ready, what is it?"

I told him and hung up. He called back fifteen minutes later—it's an efficient, tidy world we die in—Gladys Jacobs and Ellen Mary Jacobs had both been cremated.

I showered, shaved and dressed; dinner, I was thinking, didn't sound like a bad idea. And a man like Mr. Matthews with no discernible vices should be able to afford the tab. I drove back into that alien territory and parked a little way up the street from Mrs. Matthews's solid residence. It had some nice old native trees in the front of its rather wild garden; the front fence needed paint.

At eight precisely, Jacobs arrived in the Jag. He dropped a burning cigarette in the gutter and didn't bother to step on it with his highly polished shoe. He'd changed from the creeping Jesus outfit into a dark suit; his cuffs and collar gleamed under the street light. He was inside for about five minutes and then he came out to the car with a woman on his arm. She was a surprise; taller than her son and taller than Jacobs, her hair was white but she carried herself well, and her face in profile was handsome. She wore a green dress of some soft material and had a light, lacey thing thrown around her shoulders. Jacobs handed her into the car with an almost professional air and we set off for the city.

The awful truth dawned on me as we crept through the city streets—our destination was the restaurant in the clouds where they charge you for the view, the carpet, the mirrors, and the head waiter's aftershave. I couldn't face that. They parked, I parked and after making sure that they were strapped into their eating seats, I went across the road to a serve-yourself place and served myself. The steak and wine were good and Matthews saved some money.

It was well after ten when they came out; Mrs. Matthews was laughing at Henry's wit, his colour was high but he looked like a virile, mature man who enjoyed life perhaps a little too much. Mrs. Matthews was no weeping widow—her handbag swung jauntily, she exuded style. It hit me that I knew nothing about her other than what her son had told me. I had that floundering feeling, like a man slipping down a steep roof with nothing to grab onto. They walked along the street to the Jag, stopping to look in windows, close together, sometimes touching, like two people who'd known each other a long time. I skulked behind, feeling lonely and voyeuristic. We drove back to Manly; Jacobs piloted the big car well, his wining and dining hadn't affected his driving. They went into Mrs. Matthews's house, lights came on; I sat in my car and wished I still smoked. Lights went off, I drove home.

Next morning I phoned Matthews at his business number. A non-committal female voice told me that I'd contacted the Milton Insurance Company. It sent a shiver through me; I'd worked for a series of insurance companies as an investigator, the companies had got seedier and so had I. Matthews answered his phone with one brusque word.

"Claims."

"Hardy, Mr. Matthews. How's business?"

He ignored the pleasantry. "I won't be able to talk on this line, Mr. Hardy. Did you . . . ah . . .?"

"Yeah, I tagged along. It was interesting. I don't think she's in imminent danger. Tell me, what's her profession?"

"Oh, didn't I mention that? She's a nurse; well, a matron actually."

"Where?"

"St. Mark's, Harbord."

"How long has she been there?"

"Ten, twelve years, I'm not sure. What are you getting at?"

"Too soon to say. You're sure your mother only met Jacobs recently, after your father death?"

He hesitated. "Yes."

"You sound uncertain."

"Well, I don't live with her as I told you. I imagined that was the case. I mean, funeral director . . . who knows such people otherwise?"

It was a typical remark; who knows garbage men, sewer workers, lavatory attendants? Somebody does, somebody loves them, hates them. Matthews said something I didn't catch, my mind was running along murky channels with bends sinister and causeways suspicious.

"Who's your chief investigator, Mr. Matthews?" I asked suddenly.

He was surprised. "We don't have one, this isn't a big firm, we use the Wallace agency. Really, Mr. Hardy, I don't see where this is leading."

"Bear with me. I won't hold you now. I'll be in touch."

I rang off and called Roger Wallace immediately. Roger runs an honest shop and knows how to do a favour for a friend; I almost went to work for him once. After a short wait he came on the line and we exchanged notes on how well we were doing. He sounded tired so *he* probably was doing well at the usual cost. I asked him a few questions about the Milton outfit, and he promised to call me back at my office.

Primo Tomasetti was bent over a sheet of art paper as I came through his tattooing parlour after parking my car out the back. I leaned over his shoulder to see the drawing; there was a heart, a dragon, an anchor, two flags, and the word "Mother" all inter-woven. The effect was bizarre, like a surrealistic sketch of a Freudian nightmare.

"What the hell is that?" I said.

Primo turned to look at me innocently. "The ultimate

171

tattoo," he said. "I'm going for everything, I mean *everything*! How do you like it, Cliff?"

I squinted. "You haven't quite got it."

"Yeah? What's missing?"

"Hell's Angels, a swastika, a knife for the snake to curl around; come on, you're not trying."

He smoothed the paper. "You're right, you've inspired me." He added a swastika. "Tell you what, I'll put it on you anywhere you like—free."

"Put it on yourself," I said.

His eyes opened wide in genuine shock; Primo would die rather than be tattooed.

I pottered in the office for a while until Roger rang with the good, or bad, news—there was a one hundred thousand dollar life insurance policy on Mrs. Matthews, and the beneficiary was Charles Herbert Matthews—my client.

That left me only two places to go. Well, the sun was shining, the breeze was soft, and there are worse places. I drove the long and winding road back to Manly and fetched up outside Norma Wetherell's house. I marched up to the door, hammered on it and held my licence card at the ready. She came to the door with flour on her hands and eyed me through the fly wire screen.

"Back again?"

I held up the licence. "I'm afraid I lied to you, Mrs. Wetherell; I'm an investigator, not a reporter. I hope you'll answer a few more questions about Mr. Jacobs."

She rubbed her hands on her apron, some flour fell on the floor and she looked down crossly. "Why'd you lie?"

"I didn't want to alarm you."

"More alarmed by lying," she grumbled. "Well, make it quick."

No coffee this time. "Have you seen Mr. Jacobs with a tall woman, white hair, about fifty? Well turned out?"

172

"I have, she's there often. Real lady muck."

"For how long have you seen her?"

"Is there any money in it this time?" I produced another ten dollars and she let the catch on the door come open far enough to let the money through.

"Ta. Well, I'd say I first saw her about three years back."

"When the second wife was around?"

She grinned and scratched her head, dusting her wiry dark hair with white flour. "When she *wasn't* around."

Harbord is one of those places that used to nurture tennis stars and swimming champions. I suppose it looks like anywhere else in the rain, but when the sun shines it looks as if God has laid his finger on it. The hospital was in a road stuck high up above the esplanade, the parks and the wide, blue sea. The sea was so blue and the light so strong that just walking along the street felt like being in a movie filmed in Eastmancolour. St. Mark's was a smallish, private establishment, built of stone when they knew how to build and painted white by someone who knew how to do it. It looked like a pleasant place to work or be mildly indisposed in; for dying it would be just like anywhere else.

I parked up the street a little and did a slow reconnoitre. The place was enclosed by a brick fence, head high. The front, back, and one side abutted streets; on the other side the fence was shared with a house that stood on a deep, narrow lot and a block of flats. The land on which the hospital stood sloped so that it had three storys in the back and two in front; around two sides ran a balcony which gave the paying patients a good view of the ocean. There was a trellis covered with a vine of some sort on a section of the back wall; otherwise the walls were notable for an abundance of big windows.

I went through the gates and ambled up the drive toward the impressive marble steps in front of the building. For a plan I had the idea to engage an underling in conversation, and maybe hand over a little of what underlings don't have enough of. There were patients and attendants taking the afternoon air on the balcony above me as I walked up the steps; the doors swung open automatically and then I was being watched from the reception desk by a woman in a smart blue uniform. I looked around at the spit and polish as I fronted the desk.

"Yes, sir?" She was a thirtyish brunette with good teeth. She looked as if she could head up a cabinet meeting or a commando platoon pretty effectively.

"I . . . ah, wanted to know if you have a Mrs. Hardy here?"

"I couldn't say, sir."

"No, well my mother is going to have to have an operation, nothing too serious you understand, but she'll need some care while she's recovering, and Mrs. Hardy writes such good things about the place she's in. She's an old friend of mum's and . . ."

The phone on her desk rang; she said "Just a minute" to me and "Reception" into the mouthpiece. I looked around the lobby which had a spotless parquet floor and a staircase made of the right sort of wood. A set of glass doors swung open and a white-coated man came through talking to a nurse. He was carrying a clipboard and she was listening hard. A woman in a dressing gown was talking on a telephone beside the stairs; a nurse ran in through the front door and bolted up the stairs where she almost collided with Mrs. Matthews, who was descending with a stately tread. She checked the nurse and sent her on her way, came down the stairs, looked over or under me, and went out through the glass doors.

I drifted off after her while the receptionist was still occupied; I was hoping to find a cleaning person to charm or an orderly to yarn with but I never got the chance; two big men in white coats appeared at the end of the passage to bar my way. I turned and saw the receptionist making gestures from the other end of the hall. I didn't wait, I marched back and nodded to her as I passed.

"I don't think mum would like it here," I said.

At the foot of the outside steps I nearly tripped over a parked wheelchair and then the hospital building seemed to lean down and hit me behind the ear. I opened my mouth to yell and got hit again, in the stomach; and I was slammed down into the wheelchair and was moving. I struggled for wind to yell and move with but a hard arm pinned me back. I heard the wheels of the chair grinding on the gravel and we made a turn; a man said something in a language I didn't understand and then my shirt sleeve was ripped and I felt a prick and a voice started counting: I went with it—one, two, three, four . . .

I came out of it in a room; it was a very atmospheric room; I mean it had stark white walls that ran down to the floor from a stark white ceiling. It had character that room, even purpose. I was lying on a bed watching a light above me swing just a little, fascinating. I got bored with it after a while and looked around; the room had no furniture to speak of, a metal cabinet by the bed and a metal chair by the window. I stared at the window wondering why it interested me so; I wasn't usually interested in windows, *fenêtres*, so what? Then it came through to me slowly; I hadn't got here by myself and the door to the room had an uncomfortably tight look to it. I got off the bed and fell flat on the floor so I clawed my way back up onto the bed again. It was like climbing Mont Blanc, west face.

I lay on the bed again, but somehow everything was less interesting. I pushed experimentally at the cabinet, bolted down. The chair would be the same. I'd been right about the

175

window though, it did have something to say—the light coming through it was broken up into eight inch squares by the bars. My throat was dry and my eyes felt gritty, love of mankind was not in me.

The door opened and Mrs. Matthews and two big men came quietly in. They stood and looked at me and I lay and looked at them. Then I sat up and waited for the feeling of treading water to stop. One of the men spoke in that foreign language again so I concluded that they were the wheelchair kids. The woman was carrying something which she threw on the bed—my wallet; I hadn't missed it because it isn't very heavy.

"Hardy," she said. "Private investigator, it says. What does that mean in this day and age?"

"What it says, Mrs. Matthews."

She looked at one of the men who said something I didn't catch; the other man wandered across to the window. I put the odds on my leaping from the bed and knocking them both unconscious at about ten thousand to one.

"How do you know me and why are you following me?" Her voice was nicely modulated with a roughness to it, like a radio announcer who was a drill sergeant at weekends.

"Who said I was following you?"

"I saw you last night and here you are today. That's why you're in the trouble you're in."

It sounded like a pop song but I didn't feel like humming along; the trouble was the truth sounded ridiculous—this Amazon needing protection from plump little Charles Herbert? I couldn't think of a good lie, so I told her the truth.

"Ridiculous," she said. "Charles would never do such a thing. You're lying."

I shrugged. She said: "Dennis" and the guy by the window moved across and hit me with a backhander behind the ear where it doesn't show. I fell back on the bed and felt

176

him use that hard arm on me again. He pinned me down and forced my head back to one side; it hurt.

"Tell me," Dennis said. His breath stank and a drop of sweat from his shiny, red forehead fell into my mouth. I gagged and the pain got worse; I swore at him and he increased the pressure.

"Stop it!" She moved forward and pulled at his arm. Dennis fell back, breathing heavily. The foreigner watched the show with a pleasant smile. Mrs. Matthews said, "Inject him again, we can't do anything now." The foreigner took a syringe and glass bottle from his pocket and mated them. I faked a collapse and let my breathing go ragged. She came close, smelling nice, and lifted my right eyelid roughly.

"He's all right." She shoved her hand inside my shirt. "He's thin though, not too much." I was pricked again and went to sleep.

They didn't give me enough, I'm bigger than I look. Coming out of it this time I knew what to expect and didn't make any rash moves. When eveything was working properly I went across to the barred window, which was now letting in the last few rays of the day's light. The bars were in the form of a one piece grill bolted into the window frame—the worst way to do it. This gives you something heavy to lever against something fragile if you can get any leverage. This depends on the bolts, sometimes they're anchored deep into the wood, sometimes they've worked loose, rusted or are held firm only by an accretion of paint. Here at St. Mark's we had the latter kind. I took a few breaths and applied some pressure to the grill, it moved. I applied some more and it moved a lot. It was hard work for one in my condition but I stuck at it; eventually I'd jiggled and lifted the grill loose on one side. It was heavy but that helped; I peeled it back off the frame like unwrapping a slice of cheese.

I lifted the window sash and let the cool night air playing on my sweaty brow stimulate some thinking. I could stay and fight with the element of surprise on my side, or run. That didn't take much thinking; Mrs. Matthews' friends were big and at least one of them looked canny, and I still had some kind of drug drifting around in my system that might take the power from my strong right arm. Run then, but where to? I had nothing that would interest the cops and there didn't seem much point in knocking on Mrs. Matthews's door and asking for an explanation. Jacobs? Charles Herbert? The names did set me thinking and prompted action. I re-possessed my wallet, buttoned my ripped shirt sleeve, rubbed my sore ear and climbed out on to the balcony to sniff the air.

It was after eight o'clock and quiet the way hospitals should be at that hour given that they wake the patients up with the sparrows. I sidled along the balcony to the back wall and gave the vine I'd noticed before a tentative tug—solid like the Country Party vote. I trusted the vine and the trellis all the way down to the ground.

I slunk along in the shadows, made it across to the fence and followed that along to a back gate. A dog barked across the street as I swung myself over the locked gate, but I toughed that out. Hardy rampant; I tested the physical equipment by jogging back to my car.

I stopped for some medicinal brandy and it was near enough to nine o'clock when I reached Jacobs's place of business and abode. I cruised around a bit sizing it up; there was a section at the back that looked like the flat Mrs. Wetherell had mentioned. I parked up the street, put my .38 in my pocket and walked back. There were lights on in the flat; behind that was a garage big enough to house the Jag and a couple of hearses. I rubber-soled it along the side of the garage and looked in. Some street light fell on the Jag gleaming like a butler-polished tea pot.

178

"What're you doing?" It was the goon I'd seen here before; he was in short-sleeves and bare feet now and he held a hammer. He didn't look in any mood for discussion and I didn't feel conciliatory myself. I felt strong enough and angry enough at the mistreatment I'd had at the hospital to take it out on him. I charged and hit him in the chest with a dropped shoulder; he went back against the concrete wall of the garage and bounced off it swinging the hammer. I kicked a leg out from under him and he went down hard. He'd lost wind when he hit the wall and he fell awkwardly, his head thumped the ground, the hammer clattered away and he lay still. I waited in the shadows but nothing stirred in the flat. I bent down by the man and checked him over in the half light. His breathing was okay, and his eyes looked normal under the lids. I slid him up into a sitting position by the wall—tongue free, nothing constricting neck or mouth, no blood to speak of.

At closer range I could hear music coming from the flat, something classical and relaxing. I imagined Jacobs with brandy and Beethoven—good. I took out the Smith & Wesson and rapped on the door with it. After a while another light came on inside, and a voice came from behind the door.

"Herb?"

I grunted something affirmative-sounding imitating Herb's voice as best I could. The bolt slid back and the door swung open. I crowded him and put the muzzle of the gun into the fold of flesh between his first and second chin.

"There's nothing here," he gulped. "No money, nothing."

"I'm glad to hear it," I said. "You're going visiting."

He was wearing a dressing-gown over his shirt and trousers, his feet were in slippers and he passed his hand over his hair while he looked down at himself. "Now? Like this?" It struck me forcibly that vanity was his middle name; just possibly he was vain enough to tackle the gun. I prodded his neck.

"Now. Come on."

"I can't go out like this."

"You look wonderful; don't make me put blood all over you."

He came out and I pulled the door shut behind him.

"Where's Herb?" he said.

"Sleeping."

I urged him across the street and up to the car; as he lowered himself on to the torn vinyl in the passenger seat he looked like a bedouin without his camel.

Jacobs put a few questions to me as I drove to Charles Herbert's address but I ignored them. He jumped when I checked the .38 over before getting out of the car. It was a street that treated its cars to garages and car ports, but there was a big Fairlane station wagon outside Matthew's place. There were two letter boxes on the front gate and the number one stood out iridescently on the house's front porch. Matthews had given his address as flat two. I opened the gate quietly and we went up the drive toward the back. When we were almost there we stopped as a sound cracked sharply inside the house. It came again, and then there was a long, thin howl like a cat trying to sound human. A voice was raised, then I heard a laugh and the sharp crack sounded again. I pushed Jacobs ahead of me and I could feel him shaking; I felt a bit shaky myself.

The commotion kept up, and I moved fast around the back of the house to a door at the top of a short flight of steps. I motioned to Jacobs to stand still, he watched the muzzle of the gun like a roulette player watching the ball and nodded quickly. The crack again, the howl again, only going up this time, hanging mid-way and breaking. I went up the steps, wrenched the door open and stepped inside with the gun ready and my teeth bared too.

I was in a long, narrow kitchen that had a sink, dresser, table and chairs. Charles Herbert Matthews, with his pants down and his fat, white bum showing, was stretched across the table. The foreigner held his arms and Dennis was standing behind him with a thick leather belt, studded like a dog collar, in his hand. Mrs. Matthews, the angel of St. Mark's, was sitting at the table smoking a cigarette. I pointed the gun at Dennis.

"Drop the belt."

He looked at Mrs. Matthews, who shrugged, and he moved toward me with the belt swinging. I let him come. He whipped the belt at me clumsily, and I moved inside it; I set the catch on the .38 with my thumb and smashed the gun against his cheekbone; he grunted, sagged, and I ripped him hard and low with my left. He went down and dropped the belt. I picked it up and let the heavy buckle dangle an inch above his nose.

"Sit," I said.

The other guy was still holding Matthews, who'd screwed around to see what was happening; there were three or four broad, red stripes across his buttocks running up to the pads of fat at his waist. I jerked the gun up and the foreigner let go. Matthews crumpled down and adjusted his clothes. When his face came up again it was tear-stained, but by no means unhappy. He was breathing heavily, his mouth was open and moist and he was staring at his mother.

I looked at her too. "Assault, kidnapping, conspiracy, you're in trouble, Mrs. Matthews."

She blew smoke at me. "Ridiculous," she said.

Matthews struggled for some dignity. "What are you talking about, Hardy?" he snapped.

His mother gave him a long look. "So it's true," she

said. "I didn't think you'd have the gumption, Charles."
She stubbed out the cigarette and lit another. "Well, Mr.
Hardy, it seems my son employed you to protect me. Do
you think I'm in mortal danger?"

I thought of Jacobs outside in his dressing gown and
slippers. "No," I said. "But others are at that bloody
hospital."

She smiled, she had charm and force of character to
spare. "I'd say that was outside your brief, wouldn't you,
Charles?"

"Yes, mother."

"Jesus Christ! She's been working a deal with Jacobs for
years. She fixes it so he gets most of the business that comes
out of the hospital. She thought you were on to it, why
d'you think you were getting thrashed?"

Matthews said nothing. I looked at the two thugs who had
their eyes firmly on the Matron—quite a woman.

"I wouldn't be surprised," I went on, "if she helps a few
of the old, sick ones along."

"Ridiculous," she said again but it sounded as if she was
thinking hard. She reached across and pulled Matthews
gently down into the chair beside her. She patted his arm.
"He couldn't possibly have any proof."

Matthews smiled back at her, thrilled at her touch. I felt
desperate, like a man playing a game and not knowing the
rules.

"She's known Jacobs for years, she probably got a
special deal on planting your dad."

It was just the wrong thing to say; Matthews shrugged
and his eyes slid off to look at the belt in my hand. I felt
suddenly sick.

"There's proof," I said. "Jacobs's records will prove it—
signatures, names, it'll stink like a sewer."

Then there was a noise outside, and Dennis moved, and I

182

had to talk to him sharply. Matthews was still breathing heavily, still looking at the belt. I wasn't working for him anymore, I was working for myself.

"I've got Jacobs outside," I said. "He'll talk, I'll make him." I lifted my voice and called Jacobs in. Nothing happened. Mrs. Matthews laughed.

Out on the street there was no sign of Jacobs or the Fairlane. I drove wearily toward Jacobs's establishment and was passed by a fire engine on the way. When I got there a couple of firemen were running about and a few neighbours were huddled, disappointed. The fire wouldn't even make the morning news. Mrs. Wetherell, in her dressing gown, was part of the huddle. I went up to her.

"Just a little one," she said. "Back of the flat. Office and that."

I worried about it for a few days and then let it go; they'd had a disturbing amount of aggravation and I felt pretty sure that Jacobs and Mrs. Matthews would dissolve their partnership. What the hell business was it of mine, anyway? Then the death certificates came, same cause of death with minor variations, same doctor signing. I put them away in the file and wondered why my mother had never so much as given me a clip over the ear.

Man's best friend

I was walking along Vincent Street in Balmain, down near the soapworks, minding someone else's business, when a brick hit me, then another brick hit me, then another and I lost count; it felt as if a brick wall had moved out of line and wrapped itself around Cliff Hardy.

When I woke up Terry Kenneally was sitting beside my bed. My first thoughts were that my sheets had got very white and my windows very clean and that I'd finally got Terry to stay the night; and then I realised that I wasn't at home, I was in hospital. I've been in hospital before; the first thing to do is to check that you've still got all your bits and pieces and that they haven't mixed you up with the guy who had gangrene. I moved and wriggled and blinked; everything seemed to work.

"Don't move," Terry said. "They say you're not to move."

"They say that to break your spirit," I said. I grabbed at her brown left arm and the movement sent an arrow of pain through my head. I groaned.

"They're right, I won't move. How did you get here, love?"

Terry showed her nice white teeth. "Someone found Dad's cheque in your pocket and phoned him. I came, he sends his regards."

184

"I'm glad you came and not him, waking up to his face would be a shock. I wonder how your mum stood it."

"Shut up." She was holding my hand now, and it didn't hurt a bit.

"Did they find anything else? I mean my wallet . . ."

"All that," she said. "And your bloody gun; there's a policeman outside who wants to talk to you. I made them let me in first but I can't stay, I have to get back to work." She leaned forward to kiss me and then pulled back.

"Possible fracture, they said." She backed away and blew the kiss. "Be back tonight, Cliff."

She went out, the door stayed closed for ten seconds and then fourteen stone of plain-clothes copper walked in. His name was Detective-Sergeant Moles and, although he didn't have much of a bedside manner, I told him all I could. I told him that I was a licenced private investigator, fidelity bonded and all, and that I was working for Pat Kenneally who is a greyhound trainer. I didn't tell him that I was trying to find out who was doping Pat's dogs. I had a bit of trouble remembering what I'd been doing in Vincent Street, but it came: I'd been going to see the Frenchman. Moles nodded at that, he knew the Frenchman. Pierre Cressy knew all there was to know about racing greyhounds in New South Wales, he'd know who stood to win if Pat's dogs lost.

"Did you see the Frenchy?" Moles asked.

I had to think about it. "No, I was on my way when the wall fell on me. What's your interest?" Moles scratched his ear and fidgeted, the way cops do when you ask them something. They figure ten of their questions to one of yours is about the right ratio. "Bloke who found you saw your weapon, and called in. The boys who answered the call poked around a bit and asked a few questions. Seems people saw a man hanging around that spot before you came along."

"What about the poking?"

"The wall didn't fall, Hardy, it was pushed. Someone tried to hurt you. Any ideas?"

I said "No," and lay there with my possibly broken skull, thinking about it. Moles had talent, he read my mind.

"The Frenchy's okay," he said. "That all you've got to say?"

I said it was and he shrugged and left. I didn't tell him that I was in love with Pat's daughter or that I was afraid of greyhounds; I didn't think he'd be interested.

Doctors and nurses came and went and the time passed slowly. They told me I didn't have a fractured skull, just a lot of bruises and abrasions. I was grateful to them. Terry came back in the evening and we did some more hand-holding.

"Dad's worried about what happened," she said. "He's thinking of calling in the police."

"He can forget about half his income if he does," I said. "You know what the greyhound people are like Terry, any whisper of trouble at Pat's place and they'll pull their dogs out. Most of 'em anyway."

"I know, but if someone's trying to kill you . . ."

I squeezed the upper part of her arm where she has a long, hard muscle under the smooth skin. "I'll be careful," I said. "I'm used to it. Tell Pat to give me a few more days."

"All right." She kissed me the way you kiss invalids, as if they're made of feathers. Terry is tall and brown, as befits a professional tennis player. She has a terrific serve and aced me three times the day we met. She was overseas a lot reaching the finals of tournaments; we packed a lot into the time she was in Sydney, but I came a distant third in her life after her father and tennis.

* * *

186

They let me leave the hospital the next morning and I went home and read books and drank a bit and slept. Pat phoned, and I convinced him that I was fit to go on with the enquiry; Terry phoned, and I convinced her that I was fit to see her the following night. In the morning I took off some of the bandages and admired the deep blue bruises on my arms and chest. I'd been keen enough on the job in the first place on account of Terry, and now it had got very, very personal.

It was hot when I got to Vincent Street and a sweet, sickly coconut smell was coming up from the water, as if the bay were full of copra. I parked and walked up to the Frenchman's place; the crumpled wall had been tidied back on to the empty lot behind it, and soon the grass and weeds would be creeping up to the bricks and covering them like a winding sheet.

The Frenchman's house is a tumble-down weatherboard on rotting stumps; developers and trendies eye it greedily, but Cressy has some kind of protected lease and will die there. I walked up the overgrown path, brushing branches aside and wincing as the movement hurt my head. A tattered brown paper blind moved in the window of the front room; I reached through the hole in the wire screen and knocked on the door. It opened and Cressy stood there in slippers, pyjama pants and a buttonless cardigan. Pendulous breasted, toothless and with long, whispy white hair, he looked like a witch. But the thing in his hand wasn't a broomstick, it was a shotgun. He poked it through the hole so that it almost touched my chest.

"Go 'way," he said.

I backed off a step. "Take it easy. I just want to talk to you. My name . . ."

"I know you. Go 'way or I shoot you."

I looked at the gun; the barrel was acned with rust, it was

green around the trigger guard and the stock was dusty; but that didn't mean it couldn't kill me.

"Why?"

"Don't talk." He lifted the gun a fraction. "Just go."

I was in no condition for side-stepping, ducking or for grabbing shotguns through wire screens. I went.

I was swearing, and my head was hurting as I drove back toward Glebe; if I'd had a dog I would have kicked it. I was driving fast down Cummins Street toward the turn up to Victoria Road, and when I touched the brake there was nothing there. My stomach dropped out as I pumped uselessly and started to flail through the gears and grab the handbrake, which has never had much grip. I fought the steering and felt the wheels lift as I wrestled the Falcon left at the bottom of the hill. The road was clear, the tyres screamed, and I got round. I ran the car into the gutter, closed my eyes and shook; the tin fence at the bottom of the hill had been rushing toward me and what you mostly meet on the right around the corner are trucks—heavy ones. I felt as if I was walking on stilts when I got out to examine the car: there was no brake fluid in the cylinder. It's not a good way to kill someone; what if the victim thumps the brake a few times in the first hundred yards? But it *is* a good way to scare a man, like pushing a wall over on him. The more I thought about it the angrier I got.

I flagged down a cab and went back to Vincent Street. There was a lane running down behind the Frenchman's place, and I went down that and climbed over his decaying fence. The yard was a tangle of pumpkin vines, weeds, and many, many strata of animal, vegetable, and mineral rubbish. I crept past a rusting shed and almost whistled when I saw the back of the house: there were about twenty broken window panes on the glassed-in verandah, some smashed completely, others starred and cracked around neat holes.

I got my gun out and sneaked up to the side of the verandah; the Frenchman was sitting in a patch of sun at a small table with a flagon of red wine and a racing guide on it. A breeze through the bullet holes was stirring the paper and he moved his glass to hold it down. I couldn't see the shotgun. I wrenched the door open and went in; the Frenchman barely moved before I had the .38 in his ear.

"Sit down, Frenchy," I said. "I think I'll have a glass with you. Where's the popgun?"

He jerked his head at the door leading into the house and I went through into the kitchen, if you call a stove and sink a kitchen. The shotgun was leaning against a wall and I broke it open and took out the shell. I rinsed a dirty glass in rusty water. Back on the verandah the Frenchman was marking the guide with a pencil stub. He ignored me. I poured out some of the red and took a drink; it was old, not good old, stale old. It tasted as if it had been filtered through old tea leaves. I poured my glass into his. "Who did the shooting?" I said.

He shrugged and made a mark with the pencil.

"Don't come over all Gallic on me, Pierre. I've had a wall drop on me, a shotgun pointed at me, and my brakes taken out, and it all has to do with you."

He looked up; his eyes were gummy and hair from his nostrils had tangled up with a moustache as wild as his backyard. "I don't know what you're talking about. The shotgun? I protect myself, that's all." He put some of the red down his throat as if he liked it.

"Protection? From me?"

He shrugged again. "He shoots my house all to hell and tells me don't talk to you. So I don't. Now you have the gun, so I must talk to you."

I put the gun away and sat on a bench under the window, then I realised what a good target that made me and I moved across the room.

"Who told you not to talk to me?"

"On the telephone, how do I know? Bullets everywhere, then the phone. Don't talk to Hardy. Hardy is tall and skinny with bandages. So." He opened his hands expressively, they shook, and he put them back on the table.

He was scared but he drank some more wine and got less scared. I offered him fifty bucks and cab fare to Central Station and he accepted. He said he could go to Gosford for a few days, and I said that sounded like a good idea. After I'd given him the money he got out a bottle of wine with a respectable label on it and we drank that. He gave me names of people who'd profit if Pat's dogs lost. The names didn't mean anything to me. I asked him if these men would dope dogs, and he smiled and said something in French. It might have been "Do bears live in the forest?" but French was never my strong point at Maroubra High.

I spent the early part of the afternoon getting my car towed to a garage and persuading a reluctant mechanic to give it priority. Then I went home and rested; the red wine buzzed in my head as a background to the throbbing pain, but after a sleep and a shower I felt better. I collected the car and drove to Rozelle to confer with Pat and pick up Terry who was visiting there. Pat's street is narrow and jam-packed with houses, but the blocks are deep, and Pat keeps his dogs out the back. He once showed me the kennels and the mattresses they sunbathe on and the walking machine they use when it's too hot or wet for the roads; it was like a country club except that the members were thin and fit. I didn't like them much and they didn't like me; without their muzzles I liked them even less.

Terry was out the front chatting to the neighbours when I pulled up. They'd known her since she started knocking a ball against the factory wall opposite, and even though they saw her on television now their attitude to her hadn't changed nor hers to them—it was that sort of street. Terry and I went inside to talk to Pat, who was drinking tea in the kitchen.

Pat is a widower of five years standing but his house-keeping is as good as the Frenchman's was bad. Terry made coffee in the well-ordered kitchen; Pat tried to talk about my injuries but I wouldn't let him.

"The Frenchy gave me these names." I said. "What d'you reckon?" I read him the names and he chewed them over one by one. He sipped tea and smoked a rolled cigarette: Pat is small, brown, and nuggety, his wife was six inches taller than he and gave her build and looks to Terry. Pat must have contributed warmth and charm because he has plenty of both. He was loyal to the game he was in too; he ruled out all the men I named as non-starters in the doping stakes. Two he knew personally, one was decrepit he said, and another was too stupid.

"It's none of them, mate," Pat said. "Could be some new bloke the Frenchy doesn't know about."

"Yeah, I'll have to check that angle. Takes time though; this'll be costing you, Pat."

"Worth it." He puffed smoke at me and I coughed. "Sorry, forgot you were a clean-lunger, like Terry. Good on you." He drew luxuriously on the cigarette.

Terry and I went to a pub down near the wharf in Balmain. You can eat outside there, and hear yourself talk above the acoustic bush band. They have a couple of very heavy people to deal with the drunks and the food is good. Terry seems to eat mainly lettuce, and drink hardly at all; I was manfully doing my share of both when she told me that two of Pat's owners had pulled their dogs out.

191

"Hear about the doping did they?" I said.

"Yes."

"I thought that was a close-kept secret."

"So did I, so did Dad. What does it mean, d'you think?"

I ate and drank and thought for a while. "Sounds as if the doper spread the word."

"That wouldn't make sense." She took a tiny sip of wine, as if even half a glass would ruin her backhand.

"It might, if the idea is just to put Pat out of business, not to actually fix races. Does that open up a line of thought?"

"No."

"Well, try this; it could be revenge."

She almost choked. "On Dad? Come on." Then she saw that I was serious. "Revenge," she said slowly. "We go in a bit for that on the circuit, but it's not common in real life, is it?"

That's another thing I like about Terry, although she's serious about her tennis she doesn't think it's "real life"; she won't go on the gin when it's over. "No, it's not common," I said. "In fact it's rare. 'Maintain your rage' and all that, people can't do it mostly. But it does happen; we'd better ask Pat about his enemies."

"I'm sure he hasn't any."

"Everyone has." She didn't like that too much; she doesn't like my suspicious nature or the work I do, really. It's a problem, and we spent the rest of the dinner talking about other things and getting over the bad spot.

Back in Rozelle Pat was still up, working on his books. We went through the tea and coffee ritual again and I asked Pat if he'd made any enemies in the game.

"Few," he said. I glanced up at Terry.

"Any that'd want to put you out of business?"

He blew smoke and deliberated. "Only one I reckon. Bloke was a vet and I gave evidence against him for doping. He didn't like it, and said he'd get me."

"Why didn't you tell me about him?"

"Couldn't be him, mate. He's in gaol; he went to Queensland, got mixed up in something, and I heard he got ten years."

"When was this?"

"Oh, four, five years ago."

"He could be out, Pat," I said.

Terry and I went back to her flat at Rushcutters Bay, near the White City courts, and she acknowledged that I could be on to something. We left it there and went to bed; it hurt a bit, what with the bruises and all, but it didn't hurt enough to stop us.

The ex-vet's name was Leslie Victor Mahony, and it took me two phone calls and half an hour to find out that he'd been released from gaol in Brisbane three months back having served four and a half years of a ten year sentence for embezzlement and fraud. I spent the next two days confirming that Mahony had come to Sydney and failing to locate him. There was a definite feeling that Doc Mahony was in town, but no-one knew where, or they weren't saying.

At the end of the second day I was dispirited. Terry was playing an exhibition match but I didn't feel like going, and I didn't feel like reporting my lack of progress to her afterwards. The case was turning into a fair bitch and, weakling that I am, I got drunk. I started on beer when I got home, went on to wine with my meal, and on to whisky after that. I woke up with a mouth like a kangaroo pouch. I stood under the shower for fifteen minutes, telling myself how not smoking reduced hangovers. All that did was make me wish I had a cigarette.

I was drinking coffee, and thinking speculatively about eggs when the phone rang.

The voice said: "I hear you're looking for Doc Mahony."

I said: "That's right, who's this?"

The voice said: "Nobody. How well do you know Heathcote?"

"I know it."

"You get there, and pick up a road that runs along the railway, going south. Where the bitumen stops you go right on an unmade road for two miles. You take a left fork, go down a dip, and there's a shack on your right. Mahony's there."

"You a friend of his?"

"I wouldn't piss on him. If you want him, he's there."

He hung up and I tried to remember whether I'd heard the voice before, I thought I had but I've heard a hell of a lot of voices. I didn't like it at all; it looked to me as if a .22 had been used on the Frenchman's windows and a .22 bullet can kill you. An anonymous phone call, a shack in the bush—it sounded like a trap. It sounds crazy and probably had something to do with the brain cells I'd burnt out the night before, but I just couldn't get too frightened about a vet. I checked over the .38 carefully, took some extra ammunition, and went to Heathcote.

I've heard people talk fondly about Heathcote as an unspoiled place of their childhood; it's hard to imagine it like that now. The sprawl on the western side of the highway is the standard sterile, red brick horrorland where the garage dominates the outside of the house and the TV set the inside. Over the highway and the railway line though, the area has retained some dusty charm, if you like faded weatherboard houses with old wooden fences and roofs rusting quietly away. Up to a point I followed the directions I'd been given, but I'm not that green; I had a map of the tracks leading into the National Park behind and beyond and I marked where the shack would be and circled up around behind it. I stopped at a point which I calculated would be about half a mile from the shack; it was a still, quiet day with the birds subdued in the sun. I closed the car door softly and started down the rough track toward a patch of forest behind the track. Things jumped and wriggled in the grass beside the track and I resolved to be very, very careful so that they wouldn't be jumping and wriggling over me.

The shack, as I looked at it through the trees, was exactly that—an ancient, weatherboard affair that had lost its pretensions to paint long ago. Grass grew in the guttering and sprouted out through the lower boards. I squatted behind a tree for ten minutes soaking up the atmosphere— no sign of a car, no wisps of smoke in the air, no coughing. I did a complete circle of the place at about seventy-five yards distance, the way they'd taught me in Malaya. Still nothing. There are two theories on approaching a possibly defended place like this: one says you should keep circling and come in closer each time; the other has it that this causes too much movement and you should come in straight. The first way was out because there was a clear patch about fifty yards deep in front of the shack and I'm a straight line man myself, anyway.

I made it down to the back door without any trouble. The building was a tiny one-pitch, three rooms at most. The noise I could hear inside was snoring. I gave it a few minutes, but it was real snoring, complete with irregular rhythm and grunts. I eased the door open and went in; floorboards creaked and the door grated, but Doc Mahony wasn't worried—he was lying on a bed in his underwear with a big, dreamy smile on his face—maybe he was dreaming of when he was young and slim and sober, which he wasn't anymore. There was an empty bottle of Bun-

195

daberg rum on the floor and one half full on a chair beside the bed.

It was a dump comparable to the Frenchman's and the rural setting didn't help it any; you could hardly see through the dusty windows and the kikuyu poked up through the floor. I couldn't find the .22, which worried me, and I was also worried by the empty tins and the food and water bowls in the back room—I hadn't seen any sign of a dog. I filled the empty rum bottle with water and went back to the bed chamber. The Doc tried to ignore the first few drops but then I got some good ones down his nose and into his mouth and he spluttered and coughed and woke up.

His face was pale, grimy with dirt and whiskers, and lumpy like his body. He had a few thin strands of hair plastered to his head with sweat, and a few teeth, but much of the beauty of the human face and form was lacking. He opened his eyes and his voice was surprisingly pleasant-sounding.

"Who the hell are you?"

"I'm a friend of Pat Kenneally, Doc. You remember Pat?"

He remembered all right, alarm leapt into his pale, bleary eyes and he made a movement with his hand. He changed the movement into a grab for the rum but I wasn't fooled. I pushed the bottle out of reach and felt under the bed, and came up with a shoe box. I took my gun out and pointed it at Doc's meaty nose.

"Lie back. Get some rest."

Inside the box was a notebook with Pat's address and phone number written on the first page. The next few pages were taken up with the names and descriptions of grey-hounds. Some dog owners were listed with telephone numbers and addresses. Also in the box was an array of pills and powders, a couple of hypodermics and some bottles of fluid with rubber membrane tops.

"Nasty," I said. "Poor little doggies."

He didn't say anything, but reached for the bottle again. There were still a couple of inches of water in the bottle and I poured enough rum into it to darken it up a bit. I handed it to him.

"You'll ruin your health taking it straight. Now, let's hear about the bricks and the car and the bullets through the Frenchman's house."

He took a long swig of the diluted rum, swilled it around in his mouth and spat it against the wall. He followed this display of his manners with a racking cough and a long, gurgling swallow from the bottle.

"I don't know what you're talking about," he gasped, and then took another swallow.

I tapped the notebook. "What's this—research for a book?"

"I wanted to get Kenneally," he said in the voice that was all he had left of his profession and self-respect, "but I don't know anything about that other stuff—bricks and bullets."

"It's God's own truth, Hardy." The voice came from behind me; it was the voice on the phone and now I didn't even need to turn around to know who it was. I felt something hard jab the nape of my neck. "Put the gun on the bed, Hardy. Do it slow."

I did it very slowly, and then I turned. Johnny Dragovic had scarcely changed at all in the past six years since I'd seen him in court when my evidence had helped to get him eight years for armed robbery. Johnny was a tough kid from Melbourne who'd decided to take Sydney on; he knocked over a couple of bottle shops, and moved up to State betting agencies, with some success. The betting authority hired me and some other private men, and I got lucky, heard some whispers, and we were waiting for Johnny at the right time and place. Blows were struck, and Johnny turned out to be not quite as tough as he thought. But he was tough enough, and the automatic pistol in his hand made him even tougher. I said "Dragovic," stupidly.

"That's right," he said. "Glad you remember."

My guts were turning over and I concentrated on getting my balance right and watching him carefully, in case he gave me a chance. I didn't think he would.

"What's it all about then?" I said.

"It's about eight years, five at Grafton." The way he said it spoke volumes, he wasn't there to thank me for rehabilitating him.

"Put it behind you," I said. "You're not old."

The gun didn't move. "You bastard. I've kept going by thinking what I could do to you."

"Thinking like that'll get you back there."

"Shut up! I was nineteen when I got to Grafton, what do you reckon that was like?"

"Scarey," I said. I thought that if I kept him talking something might happen, he might even talk himself out of whatever he had in mind.

"That's right, scarey. That's why I got you with the bricks and fixed your bloody car—to scare you."

"You win. You did it, you scared me. I'm scared now."

"You should be. I'm going to kill you."

"That's crazy," I said desperately. "And not fair, I didn't kill you."

He laughed. "Sometimes, in that bloody hole, I wished you had."

"What about him?" I gestured down at Doc who was listening and clutching the bottle like a crucifix.

"He goes out too," Dragovic said. "You kill him and he kills you. All in the line of duty."

198

"It stinks, Johnny, it won't work."

"It fuckin' will! I've planned this for a while, been watching you until the right deal came up. It'll look like you caught up with the bloke who shot up the Frenchy's house and you shot him and he shot you. You'll take a while to die, though." He smiled and I could see how much he was enjoying it all, and how unlikely it was that he'd change his mind.

Mahony raised himself slowly on the bed and swung his legs over the side. "This is madness," he said. "I don't want any part of it. I'm going." He got off the bed and took a couple of shuffling steps toward the door before Dragovic reacted.

"Get back here!" he yelled. "Get back."

But Mahony opened the door and had half his body outside when Dragovic shot him. He crumpled, and I moved to the left and swung a punch which took Dragovic on the nose. Blood spurted and he blundered back, but kept hold of his gun. I made a grab for mine, missed, and lunged out the door, nearly tripping over Mahony. I staggered, recovered my balance, and started to run for the trees about fifty yards away. I was halfway there when something stung my calf like ten sandfly bites; the leg lost all power and I went down, hard. Johnny Dragovic stepped clear of the doorway, carrying a rifle and started to walk toward me. I lay there in the dust watching him and watching the rifle and when he was about twenty feet away I closed my eyes. Then I heard a shot and didn't feel anything, so I opened my eyes: the rifle was on the ground close to me and Dragovic was yelling and rolling around and a greyhound was tearing at his neck. There was blood on Dragovic's face from my punch, and a lot more blood on his chest from the dog's attack. He screamed, and the dog's head came up and went down twice. I sat up and grabbed the rifle; the dog turned away from the bloody mess on the ground and sprang straight at me. I shot it in the chest and it collapsed and I shot it again in the head.

I hobbled across and bent down, but one look told me that tough Johnny Dragovic was dead. The dog had a length of chain attached to a collar trailing away in the dirt. It looked as if Dragovic had secured the dog, but not well enough. More hobbling got me over to the shack where there was more death. Mahony's eyes stared sightlessly up at the blue sky; his mouth was open and some flies were already gathering around the dark blood that had spilled out of it.

After that it was a matter of rum and true grit. I took an enormous swig of the rum and started on the trek back to my car. When I made it I was weeping with the pain and there was a saw mill operating at full blast inside my head. I got the car started and into gear somehow and kangaroo-hopped it back along the track until I reached a house. Then I leant on the horn until a woman came out, and I spoke to her and told her what to do.

Terry came to see me in hospital and Pat came and Sergeant Moles—it was like old times. The bullet had touched the bone but hadn't messed the leg up too much. No-one wept over Doc Mahony and Johnny Dragovic, although Pat said that the Doc wasn't such a bad bloke, just greedy. Terry went off to play a tournament in Hong Kong, and one solitary night I went to the dog track and won fifty dollars on a hound named Topspin.

Escort to an easy death

The filing card pinned to my office door read "Cliff Hardy Investigations," and I noticed that the finger I used to straighten it with had a dirty nail. Not very dirty, but then the card itself wasn't very dirty and the drawing pin that held it wasn't very bent. But not clean and not straight. These were bad times. People were losing their jobs; people and things were going missing; people were getting more and more dishonest, in big and small ways, and no-one cared. It was all bad news for me: I made a living out of tidying up problems; finding a lost wife or husband, guarding a body for a while, seeing a sum of money safely from point A to point B. Now, tidiness and safety were not expected. I was losing business, and no-one cared.

I pushed the door open, it held on the frayed, lifted carpet while I picked up the mail, and then I flicked it back with my foot. The bills were for the usual things, small, corrective services performed on my body and various bits of machinery, and the baits were the same. I was offered female companionship, life insurance, and a home on the north coast out of the smog of Sydney. I needed all those things; every forty-year-old male whose instincts are within a range of normal does. But to get them I'd have had to be what I was not—prosperous. To hell with them; their market research was lousy. The women were probably ugly and the insurance would have fine print and the house would be sliding into the sea. I shovelled the brochures into the waste paper bin and made out a cheque for the smallest of the bills.

I sat and listened to the sounds of Sydney three floors down. They were busy sounds—trucks and cars and buses, all full of people all chasing a dollar. I'd sat for a whole day like that recently and for a few hours in quite a lot of days. I was a little panicky. As I stared at the office door a shape appeared in the pane of glass. It was a nice shape, not tall or short—trim-looking. The shape stayed there for what seemed like five minutes before it knocked. I let out a tense breath and said "Come in" in my best bass.

It turned out to be a woman with red hair, a red dress, and red shoes. She carried a black shoulder bag and wore a wide, black belt around the dress; when she got up close I could see that the hair was a wig. I watched her walk toward the chair in front of the desk and lower herself into it. She moved all in a piece, not exactly stiffly, but not altogether gracefully either. It was if she'd learned it all from scratch late in life.

"Mr. Hardy," she said, "my name is Trudi Walker."

"I'm pleased to meet you," I said.

"Yes. I want to hire you to find someone." Her voice was what used to be called fruity, she gave the vowels and diphthongs everything she had.

"Male or female?"

She raised an eyebrow that had been plucked to a fine, dark line. She was heavily and expertly made-up; hard to guess her age, forty at least, maybe more. "Does it matter?"

"Not really, but I have more success with women for some reason. I've found thirty-nine out of fifty women but only nineteen out of forty men."

"Perhaps you've just had more practice with women—your statistics suggest that."

"Yeah, maybe."

"It's a man in this instance."

I shrugged. "Well, maybe I can improve on my figures. How long's he been gone?"

"Two days."

"That's not really missing, Miss Walker, that could just be . . . away."

"No! I've seen Gerry every day for the past five years. We are business partners and friends. Something has happened to him."

"You could be right. What's the business?"

"We run an escort service."

And that, of course, was why she hadn't gone to the police and why she avoided the big agencies, which are plugged straight in to the newspapers and also why my fees didn't worry her. She paid over the five hundred dollars retainer and agreed to a hundred and twenty-five a day plus expenses without a frown. In fact she had very few facial expressions, permitting herself the eyebrow, a tight thin-lipped smile and that was about it. Gerry Hadley, she informed me, was an American she'd met when he was on leave from Vietnam. They'd corresponded for a few years while he was in the States and then he'd come over to join forces with her. She gave me two photos—Pfc Hadley, twentyish, in battle dress; Mr. Gerald Hadley, business-suited, well-fleshed, thirtyish. He had a round, corn-fed face with a bright smile.

Gerry and Trudi had separate apartments in the same building in Elizabeth Bay. They ran the agency from a business address in Potts Point, and from their apartments. Trudi still occasionally worked a shift; Gerry didn't, although the agency catered to both sexes.

"When did you last see Mr. Hadley?"

"Three night ago. We had dinner together. He was supposed to come to my flat for breakfast and a discussion the next morning. He didn't come, and I haven't seen him since."

"You've looked through his flat?"

"Yes." She reached into her bag, took out a door key with a red ribbon attached and handed it over. While I looked at the key I was thinking that there was a fair bit of between-the-lines reading to do here, but I decided to play it careful—I needed the work.

"Could you give me a list of your employees, Miss Walker?"

"Not off hand; I could arrange it if you'd call at the office."

Job or not, I was already getting tired of her; the voice was annoying me the way plastic cutlery and Big Macs annoy me. I twirled the key by the ribbon.

"Any of the girls missing?" I said.

The look she shot at me aged her ten years and I put her near fifty. "I don't know," she snapped. "Why?"

"Any of the boys missing?"

She got half out of her chair and her face twisted up; two fissures appeared in the make-up beside her nose. "You bastard," she snarled. "You shit. You can . . ."

I put the key down and came around the desk to pat her shoulder. "Easy," I said, "easy; I'm sorry, but I had to find out how you feel about all this. You were acting till then, doing it pretty well, too."

She sat back and dug in her bag for tissues. After dabbing and wiping some of the control came back, but I didn't have cosmetic-controlled agelessness in front of me now, I had a vulnerable woman with years on the clock and fear in her eyes.

"I'm fifteen years older than Gerry, Mr. Hardy," she said. "I go though tortures to keep up appearances, I eat almost nothing. I love him and everything I've done is . . . I can't bear . . ." The control went again and the tears streamed over her face like a flash flood. I felt sorry for her and realised at that moment that she'd dropped the voice—her vowels were a little nasal now and her delivery had the lazy, easy rhythms of Sydney.

"I'll look for him," I said. "I'll call at your office and I'll look in his flat and I'll ask around. Two days isn't long. Does he have a car?"

She nodded. "A Mercedes, gone."

"Any friends in Sydney?"

She shook her head. "Just me."

"You don't know of any trouble—I mean competitors, the cops . . . any threats?"

There was panic in her face, clearly visible now that the make-up was eroded. "No," she whispered, "nothing."

I gave her a receipt, and she got out a mirror and did a little repair work. I wrote down the addresses and phone numbers she gave me, and we got the whole thing on a business footing. She left and I went to the window and watched her step out on to the street; the first step was faltering but she quickly got into stride and looked like a proud, well turned-out human being as she turned the corner. I decided she had guts and that she was lying about there being no trouble in the air.

Over the next day and a half I did the things I said I'd do: I checked over Hadley's apartment and found nothing that you wouldn't expect to find about a Yank who ran an escort service and had a mistress fifteen years older than himself. He had two girls on the side and I looked them over— nothing. Same result with the four men employed by the

205

Winsome Escort Agency. Two of them were gay and one was black; nothing in the patterns of their lives over the past few days had changed. The seven women were more varied: one was close to Trudi Walker's age with a similar manner, and one looked like a schoolgirl. Two of them had university degrees and one was a hang-glider. I used the phone till my arm ached and knocked on apartment doors with no result. My last call was on one of the girls—Tracey Talbot, who combined being escortd with freelance journalism. I drank coffee with her in her flat at Rushcutters Bay; it was a warm, soft afternoon and the water looked blue, bright, and alive. Her window was full of harbour view. She had posters of world-famous harbours on the walls.

"I love harbours," she told me. "I'm going to have my ashes scattered out there."

"We're all going to have our ashes scattered out there the way things are going," I said. I was feeling gloomy; asking the questions dully, now not expecting sparks. "You've got no idea where Hadley might take off to?"

She shrugged. "Not a clue, Mummy's boy as far as I could see. Tell you one thing though. I reckon Trudi's not long for this world."

"Why d'you say that?"

"I did a story on cancer victims once, she's got all the signs."

I sighed and finished the coffee—ashes and cancer, she'd be a wow of a companion for a night on the town. I used Tracey's phone to call Trudi, but she wasn't at the office and her home phone didn't answer. The receptionist at Winsome said she'd been trying to contact her for some hours without success. I looked at the girl who was dropping cigarette ashes in the dregs of her coffee and stirring them with a finger. I called Trudi's number again—the phone sounded as if it could go on ringing unanswered until the end of the world.

The apartment building was new and shiny; balconies hung off it out over the water like cars on a ferris wheel. Hadley's apartment was on the second floor and Trudi's was directly above it; I went up the stairs fast and stabbed the buzzer. The phone started ringing at the same time and the two sounds blended into a dirge. I pushed the door and felt it give; there seemed to be a lock not quite engaging. I hit it with my shoulder in the middle and applying the pressure upwards the way you should, and it sprang open.

The living room was big and bright; the walls and floor were white as if the room had been designed as a hymn to lightness. There were paintings, a bar, books, a record player, and a TV set. The chairs and settee were white pine and the coverings were cream-coloured, except where Trudi's blood had got on the fabric. She was slumped in a way she'd never have permitted when she was in charge of her body. Her dress had been white, with gold trim, but now half of it was stained a dark red like the costume of a medieval courtier. The dress was also ripped from the neck to the armpit on one side, and on the other side the sleeve was half torn away. I eased the door shut behind me and went up close. She had a big wound in her neck. I looked past her to where a drinks tray sat on a small table; a bottle of brandy was shattered. The bullet had gone through something vital in her neck and there'd been a lot of blood. Her right hand was thrown back across the arm of the settee and it was bloody too; the nails on three fingers were split and broken. Her head had fallen back, drawing the skin tight; her make-up was flawless.

I put my hands in my pockets for safety and wandered around looking. The door was equipped with a heavy dead lock, two safety chains and a light, standard lock—the one I'd broken. The kitchen was uncluttered, the bedroom undisturbed. A cabinet in the bathroom was full of prescription drugs—medicines, capsules, pills. I didn't recognise most of them but they indicated a serious illness or powerful hypochondria and an obliging physician. In a second, smaller bedroom there was a single bed, a chair and a desk with a lot of locked drawers. I went back to the living room, located her bag and keys and unlocked the desk. The drawers were full of stationery, business letters, tax records, old cheque books. I flicked through the cheque stubs which told me that she spent a hell of a lot of money on clothes. There were records of a couple of fixed deposit bank accounts with a few thousand dollars in each. The papers provided only one surprise—Trudi owned her own apartment and the one Hadley lived in, for which he paid her rent of one hundred dollars a week.

This was all taking time, because I was using a handkerchief to pick things up and a knife blade to turn over the papers. The bottom drawer held a fountain pen and a big bottle of ink. A few small drops of ink had spilt in the drawer—it was the closest she'd come to being messy. I lifted the bottle out, uncapped it and probed inside with the thin blade. A little fishing brought up two small keys on a thin ring. I dried them on a tissue; one had serial number, C140, on it, the other did not. I took the copy off the ring and dropped the original back into the ink. Then I prowled around the apartment looking for signs, bent twigs, freshly broken blades of grass. I found it down behind the TV set; a section of the high skirting board was hinged and swung out, a strand of hair from a mop or duster had caught at the spot. The safe, about six inches square, was set in the wall behind the board. I dialled C140 on the combination lock and the key turned smoothly. Inside was a reel of movie film and a plastic envelope. I closed the safe and took the stash across to the window. The film was a standard Super 8 job; the envelope contained about a dozen paper squares and rectangles, some brightly coloured and some dull—postage stamps.

I put the stuff in my pocket, walked out of the flat and down to my car where I stowed it away under the back seat. Then I went to a public booth and called the police, asking for Grant Evans. He came on and I said what I had to say, and he told me to go up again and wait for him.

Grant was puffing a bit when he got to the top of the stairs. He had a youngish, slim policewoman with him and he'd been showing off for her.

"Cliff," Grant said. "Why'd you call from the street?"

"Didn't want to touch the phone."

He grunted and we trooped inside. I told Grant the story while he poked around. He made a few disbelieving noises here and there, just to remind me of the unspoken terms of our relationship—I don't tell him outright lies and he doesn't frame me for things. It's a better set-up than most. I didn't have to feign surprise when Grant slid open the built-in wardrobes, we both whistled. The space was crammed full of dresses, coats, blouses, slacks and other things I don't know the names of. There were six fur coats and fifty pairs of shoes, maybe more.

"Gotta be jewels with this lot," Grant said. "You see an insurance policy, Cliff?"

It was a neat trap, but I saw it in time. "No, I told you I didn't touch anything."

"Yeah, and Borg can't hit backhands." We went back into the living room. "Well, she put up a fight. Look for a guy missing some skin. How do you see it? Reckon this Hadley bumped her?"

"Could be."

"Has to be. Look at those locks—she let him in."

"She was a professional escort remember, she might've let lots of people in. I don't like Hadley, too obvious."

"Well, the obvious happens, Cain bumped Abel, Ruby bumped Oswald."

"Yeah, but what did Oswald do?"

Grant sneered and asked the policewoman to inspect the rest of Trudi's personals. We were looking at the view when she came out with a jewel box. Grant opened it.

"Good stuff?"

Her expression was wistful. "Very good, worth thousands and thousands."

"Scratch robbery," Grant said.

After that the white coats arrived and then it was down to Headquarters for a statement and the usual carry-on.

"You'd be kissing this one goodbye, would you?" Grant said after the formalities.

"Not quite. She paid for about three days' work and she's only had one and a bit. I think I'll stay with it for a while if you don't object."

He shrugged.

"I gather I won't have a lot of competition in the field then?"

He shrugged again and pointed to the stack of folders on his desk. I nodded and went out. I wasn't being quite fair to Grant; he'd like to solve every murder in the city and be the same weight he was at twenty-one, it's just that both are impossible.

Primo Tomasetti has a movie projector at his tattooing parlour. He shoots a lot of film himself and buys films from overseas—he says they give him inspirations for designs. I told him I wanted to see a film and he rubbed his hands.

"Okay, okay. You bring a bottle and I'll lay on a coupla girls, nice girls. You finally learning to live a little, Cliff? Ten o'clock, okay?"

"Not okay. Now and no bottle, no girls; this is business."

He shook his head. "I shoulda known. You have great love inside you, Cliff. But all that comes out is hate and work. How come?"

"I'm saving myself. Where's the gizmo?"

He showed me and helped me hook up the reel, then he went back to drawing designs on cartridge paper. I blacked out the little room and ran the film.

He filled the screen, and I'd seen him on TV so many times that it seemed natural to be watching him on film, even though what he was doing couldn't exactly be called natural. He was naked and very excited and the act he was performing with the young blonde was expressly forbidden by the Bible and the law of the land. It went on for a few minutes, boring after the first few frames because of the single camera angle and the lack of plot. I stopped the show and re-wound the film, thinking that all men have something to hide. Sir Peter Barton, ex-Lord Mayor of the city, racehorse owner and homme d'affairs, always poised for a big take-over, would probably have a lot to hide, it would be expected of him; but kinky carnal knowledge of juveniles was a bit exotic.

I thanked Primo, ignored his revised offer, and hoofed it downtown to a philately establishment I'd passed a hundred times and never entered. A thin, wispy man was leaning over a glass counter under which hundreds of stamps were displayed. The counter was wired and the glass was thick; the stamps would have been as hard to steal as the crown jewels. He looked up at me baring tobacco-stained teeth.

"Yes?"

I hauled out the envelope and started to pull a stamp out with my fingers.

"No! No!" He picked up a pair of tweezers and held out a hand for the envelope. He eased several of the stamps out and aligned them on a glass plate. Then he reached up and swung down a magnifying glass mounted on a moveable arm. He peered at the stamps, darting his eyes up to me as he passed from one to the next. He straightened up.

"Well, sir," he said. "Very nice indeed."

"They're worth something then?"

He was so surprised he almost dropped the tweezers. "I should say so."

"How much?"

"Oh, as to that, well it would take some time . . ."

"Round about," I said. "Err on the safe side."

"These five would fetch twenty thousand dollars, easily. May I ask, are they yours to sell?"

"No, they're not mine at all. I'm conducting an investigation, these are part of the evidence."

"Evidence," he breathed. "You won't be quoting me in court, I trust. I could give you exact valuations, be happy to, but as I say it would take time. Are you with the police?"

"I'm working with them. Can you tell me anything else about these stamps—would they be stolen property or anything like that?"

"Shouldn't think so. Let's have another look."

He arranged the whole stock, which amounted to thirteen stamps, and looked at them all. "Curious," he said. He dug under the counter and brought up a heavy loose-leaf volume and flicked through it. After a few minutes of this he looked up at me.

"This is an intriguing collection. These stamps are each

worth about four thousand dollars give or take a bit. So you have about fifty or sixty thousand dollars worth here—a bit more allowing for inflation."

I grunted, which seemed to nettle him. "What is more," he said firmly, "I should say they were purchased at regular intervals over the past two years, say, at two monthly intervals."

My look of interest gratified him. "You can be that precise?"

"Oh yes, very valuable items like these are listed and their sale recorded. These came from a single collection which has been put up for auction at two monthly intervals over the last three years. It was a very famous collection."

"Would the auctioneer know who bought them?"

"Probably not; it's a secretive business, proxies are used. Even if he did know he would not divulge the information except on the highest authority."

I thanked him and he tweezed the stamps back into the envelope, which I put back in my pocket.

"They should be in a safe," he said.

It was after five o'clock and the streets were starting to fill up with suburbanites bound for home and fun-lovers staying in the city. I walked up through the park, tying things together in my head: Trudi, it seemed, was putting the squeeze on Barton and buying stamps with the proceeds. There wasn't a better way to accumulate valuable assets that took up no space and didn't depreciate. I had two questions. Why was she doing it? She had a prosperous business to judge from her other assets and it looked like she was a very sick woman. Why bother? The other question was the original one—where was Gerry Hadley? Somehow, all things considered, I didn't give much for his chances.

Barton was rumoured to have heavy criminal connections and eliminating the partners in the Winsome Escort Agency would be like opening a can of beer for him.

Home is where the booze is, and also the darts board and the books and the food. I used all these things in moderation and was reading the paper with clear eyes in a clear head when the phone rang at 9:30 A.M. It was Grant.

"How's your investigation going?" he said.

"Quietly, how's yours?"

"Just a snippet I thought you might like. The lady's will turned up, four copies to be exact."

"Yeah? Who?"

"Hadley, every cent. Now what can you tell me?"

"Nothing, but thanks, Grant; maybe I can use that to flush him out."

"Cliff, you've got today. After today you don't owe her a thing."

He hung up and I dialled Sir Peter Barton's office. A secretary with a north shore voice and manner tried to brush me off, so I became rather rude and left a message which I thought Barton might respond to. He called me back half an hour later.

"Mr. Hardy? I understand you have business with me?" His voice was slow, soft, and pleasant, he'd have to do something about that if he got into Parliament.

"You might say that, yes. I want to see you now. Tell me where you are and I'll come over."

"I'm in my office. Come by all means. Ah . . . will you be bringing anything with you?"

I didn't answer. I drove to my office in the Cross and locked film and stamps away in the safe. Then I caught a cab to Clarence Street where Barton had an office in a glass and aluminum tower which he probably owned. I was passed from one sycophant to another until finally I was in the presence of the great man. He stood about six foot four, which gave him four inches on me, but he was beginning to lose the battle with his waist. He was standing behind a half-acre desk and he waved me into a chair in front of it.

"Mr. Hardy, it's a little early for a drink, can I offer you coffee?"

"No. I've got the film."

"Yes?"

"You paid Trudi Walker a lot of money."

"True, and now I suppose I have to pay you?"

"Maybe, I haven't decided. I might just show it on TV for fun. But I don't care much who puts what in who, I was working for Trudi Walker and I think you had her killed. I'm much more concerned about that."

The imperturbable mask slipped a bit, and there was an edge in his voice. "I certainly did *not* have her killed. Why would I? You know what she had over me, killing her would only introduce complications, such as yourself."

"I assume something went wrong. Look, I'm not green, extortionists get killed, it's a risk they take. But she hired me to find someone and she paid me and I haven't done it. I'd like to tie that up, then I can think about other steps."

He was looking puzzled, probably at having to deal with someone who had something on his mind except money. "I don't see how I can help. Find someone you say? Who?"

"Gerry Hadley, the business partner. Now, I'm just guessing, but it looks to me as if you decided to wipe out the whole operation. Maybe you removed Hadley to frighten the Walker woman, I don't know."

The mask was back, nicely in place. He got up from the desk and walked across to a drinks cabinet. "It's early as I say, but I'm going to have a drink. Join me?"

I shook my head; he poured himself a solid whisky, added water, and came back behind the desk. He sipped the drink. "You'll forgive me if I see a ray of hope in all this unpleasantness," he said. "If I convince you that I did not kill Trudi Walker or Hadley, is there a chance that you'd hand over the film?"

"There's a chance," I said.

"Hadley is alive, I can have him brought here inside an hour." He lifted a phone and spoke three crisp sentences. He worked a bit more on his drink and looked at me.

"What do the police think about the Walker killing?"

"They think Hadley did it."

He smiled. "They're right for once. Hadley killed her but he didn't intend to. This is a very messy business, Mr. Hardy, and I can't afford messes just now."

"Too bad," I said. "You should take up jogging and cold showers."

"Perhaps. I'm going to be frank with you. I'm a blackmailer myself in a way. I hold a lot of paper on Hadley, gambling debts."

"I'm glad I live a blameless life," I said.

He ignored me. "I persuaded Hadley to approach Trudi with a view to getting hold of the film. He did, they quarrelled, he shot her. An accident."

"What did you do?"

"I didn't believe him; I thought he'd grabbed the film himself and was going to run the show. I had him roughed-up, shall we say? His car was taken and his money. I told him he had two days to produce the film. He was very frightened, now I know why."

"Hadley was missing for two days before the killing. You have anything to do with that?"

"Yes indeed. I told you that Hadley had to be per-suaded."

"You're a prime bastard. You've kept your eye on Hadley since?"

"Round the clock, I thought he'd crack and get the film. He's been scuttling about, I suppose he's heard that the police are after him. His situation has been unenviable, he'll be relieved by this development."

I looked at him, wondering how much of this to believe. One thing I knew, if Hadley had killed Trudi his face would be marked.

We sat there uneasily; Barton answered the phone a few times, wrote things in files on his desk and signed things a secretary brought in. He finished the whisky and didn't make another. I was thinking about taking him up on the drink offer when the door opened and two men walked in. One was big, with a blank, hard face. The other man, much smaller, was pudgy looking and pale; his soft brown hair was cut short and his expensive clothes looked slept in. His expression was timid; he wasn't the laughing GI of yesteryear but he was Gerry Hadley just the same. There was heavy sticking plaster down one side of his face and along his jaw.

When he saw me he buckled at the knees and the guy with the cold eyes had to hold him up.

"You can't do this," he babbled. "I haven't got it, I . . ."

"Shut up, Hadley," Barton said. "Put him over there, Carl." The big man dropped Hadley into a chair, Barton waved at him and he went out. Hadley's hands were shaking as he tried to light a cigarette. Barton got up and helped him. When the smoke was in the air he clapped Hadley on the back.

"Your lucky day, Gerry, I think. Now I just want it exactly as you told me."

Hadley looked at him uncertainly. "You mean, like everything."

Barton nodded. I got up and poured myself some whisky, Hadley nodded when I looked across at him and I poured him one too.

"Thanks. Well, I went to see Trudi like Sir Peter wanted and I tried to find out where she kept the film." He drank and tapped the glass. "I had a bit of this before, Trudi could be a pretty scary dame you know."

"Go on," I said.

"Well, I took along a gun just for show. I told her what was up and she went wild, she wouldn't even listen."

"What did she say?"

"She looked as if she didn't believe it. I'd always sweet-talked her, you know? I guess she was in love with me."

I felt sick and drank some whisky. "I asked you what she said."

"Not much. She cried, then she laughed. She laughed at me and I got mad. Then she did this to me." He lifted his hand to his face. "I saw red and the gun went off." He finished the drink and looked down into his glass like a man staring into his own coffin.

"Did you look for the film?" I said.

"No. I panicked, the phone started to ring, and I ran." He looked across at Barton. "I guess you told him what happened after that."

"Yeah," I said. "Tell me one thing—how did you feel about Trudi?"

It came to me then that Hadley wasn't very bright. He looked desperately from me to Barton wondering how to play it, looking for a clue.

"The truth," I said.

"Oh, I don't know, I guess I was sick of her, you know? She was a hell of a lot older than me, and she clung so close;

I mean she just stuck there all the time." He waved his hands helplessly. "She was so old you know?"

"And she charged you rent?"

"She sure did!" Grievance made him jerk his head up and tighten his soft jaw. "She was the tightest bitch in the world. I had only ten per cent of the operation; most of what I had was leased, the car and all. She kept me tied up tight."

I had to smile then because I could see how to handle it and because of the irony of it all. I stood up.

"Come on, you two. We're going to have a little look at something you'll want to see."

But Barton had had enough. His hand moved on the desk, and the guy who'd escorted Hadley in came back again. I guessed that he was Barton's persuader. Barton jerked his head at me. "Carl, restrain him."

Carl came across walking light and bouncy and reached for me. I swivelled away and hooked him near the ear. He fell back, looked surprised and came in again with his hands up and moving in and out as if he was almost clapping. One hand whipped out at me and I felt the wind of it as I went under. Carl bent too and dug me savagely in the ribs with a stiff hand. I wasn't in the mood; I kicked him in the crotch and when he went down on one knee I brought my knee up under his chin. His head snapped back and clicked nastily and he stretched out on the deep pile carpet.

"Too fancy," I said. "Stop playing games, Barton, you'll get your film. Come on."

Barton got up, pulled Hadley to his feet and we all went out like the best of friends. Barton collected keys from the front desk and we drove to my office in a white Mercedes.

"Where's *your* Merc, Gerry?" I asked him, but he didn't reply.

We went up the three flights of stairs and into my office. I pushed Hadley down into a chair while Barton looked distastefully around him.

"What do you *do* in here?" he said.

"Make an honest living, or try to." He laughed, took out a handerchief and dusted off the edge of the desk before sitting down. I unlocked the safe and took out the film and the stamps.

"Now this," I said to Barton, "is you in your starring role, and these are stamps Trudi bought with the money you paid her. There's about seventy thousand bucks worth here and they're not getting any cheaper. In five years they'll be worth double that and so on."

Hadley looked greedily at the envelope. "I don't get it," he said.

I laughed. "You're so right, you don't. Let me tell you two things, Gerry—Trudi had the big C, she was on the way out. And she made a will leaving every bloody thing to you—the business, the jewels, this handy little number, the lot. You should have been patient."

"All very interesting," Barton said. "But, ah . . . the film."

I tossed it to him. "Show it to your mates in the boardroom." He caught the packet and turned it over in his hands like a gold nugget.

"That's about it," I said. "You can both go."

"The stamps," Hadley said.

"Oh, yeah," I shook them out into the glass ashtray, lit a match and put the flame into the little nest of paper. Hadley stood up and rushed me but I stiff-armed him back. The paper burned and a wisp of dark smoke curled up to join the other stains on the ceiling.

"Go away," I said.

* * *

Grant called that evening to tell me that they'd picked up Hadley trying to get on a train to Melbourne. His story was that he and Trudi had quarrelled over business and that the gun had gone off accidently.

"Ten years," Grant said, "out in five and we'll deport the bastard. He can't inherit the loot of course. He's really pissed off about that."

I laughed. "You can see his point of view. Well, he did everyone a favour except himself."

"How's that?"

"Trudi had a slow death coming, he saved her that."

"That's her, what's this 'everyone'?"

"Just an expression."

I sat in the office the next day and didn't get any business. Before leaving I picked up the ashtray, went to the window and let the ashes float out onto the warm air.

California dreamland

I hadn't liked finding the body. It was under the house in a spot which the foundations and the hot water pipes had made as dry as the desert. It was shrunken and mummified by the dryness, and when I pulled her out the woman looked more like a leather, laboratory specimen than someone who had laughed and drunk and made love.

Rosa Torrielli had done all of those things in good measure, and there were still some faded shreds of the clothing she'd done them in clinging to the corpse. A crumbling fragment of lilac silk, a silver thread.

The house was one of a hundred in a street in Lilyfield—weatherboard up on high, brick foundations—and I'd traced Rosa there through a series of interviews with landlords and boarders and drinkers that seemed to stretch on without end. But it had ended, and the de facto husband who'd put her under the house had ended his life in prison. All neat and tidy—a Cliff Hardy Investigations special.

Tony Torrielli had hired me to find his mother, and as he'd especially applied for the job in the U.S. Consulate in Sydney to look for her and had saved money for the work, I was glad I'd found her. Torrielli had been taken back to the States by his father, who was Rosa's third or fourth husband, and he was as American as cherry pie.

"That was fine work, Mr. Hardy. I sure am obliged to

you." We were in a pub near my office in the Cross and he was holding his glass carefully so as not to spill anything on his light grey three piece suit.

"I'm sorry it turned out so grim," I said. It hadn't, for me. I had his cheque in my pocket covering my modest daily rates and the expenses racked up on the road and in the boozers.

"Fine work." He bought another round, drank half of his Scotch and left. I finished his drink along with mine, and wondered what he'd do with the knowledge that his mother was a good-time girl who probably hadn't given him a second's thought since his dad took off home.

My next two jobs flowed from the Torrielli case by recommendation. The first was a simple bodyguarding of a very rich and very nervous visitor to Sydney from Las Vegas. The second started when the biggest man I'd ever seen knocked on my office door on the hottest day in Sydney since they started keeping records. The temperature hit eighty around 9 o'clock in the morning, and kept climbing. His knock shook the door so hard I thought the heat might be expanding the old building and splitting it like a paper bag.

I bellowed "Come in," to show that I was half an inch over six feet, 170 pounds, and used to having sledge hammers hit my door.

He opened the door very gently and ducked his head the way he must have been doing since he was fourteen. If he said he was six ten you wouldn't have argued with him, and if he was lighter than 240 pounds it would only have been by a glass of beer or two. I stood slowly as if the size of him had pushed me up on a beam balance.

"Nice to see you," I said. "Take whatever you want, say whatever you like, spit on the floor."

"Tony Torrielli said you were tougher than that," he said. "Said you had to be heavy with some people when you were lookin' for his mom."

"I write my own reports," I said. "Sometimes I use poetic licence."

"I'm interested in your licence to investigate. Mind if I sit down?"

"Try it." I waved expressively at the only other chair and sat back down myself. His chair held, but he might have been doing complicated isometrics.

"I'm Wesley Holt," he said, "engineer." It came out in a voice that rumbled like a big train in a small tunnel. He used that upward inflection that makes Americans sound uncertain, but I was pretty sure he was Wesley Holt, and if he said he was an engineer that was good enough for me. I nodded intelligently.

"Came down here to a job in Queensland because I wanted to see my daughter. She came back here after her mother and I split up."

He told me he'd graduated in 1956 and taken jobs all over the world including the Pacific. He'd met Coralie Burnett from Wahroonga in New Guinea. He lit a cigar, maybe in honour of Coralie. I refused one and opened a window, being a clean-air person these days, but good-mannered about it.

"Didn't last," he said blowing smoke at the windows. "Year and a half and she was back here in Sydney with the kid."

"Didn't like the tropics?" My ex-wife Cyn hadn't cared for them: I'd taken her to Fiji on a half-business, half-pleasure trip, and it had been a full-time hell: one mosquito bite and she turned red, two and patches of her hide developed the texture of half-cooked porridge.

"Loved New Guinea," he said. "Hated me. I was a wild

224

guy in those days—booze, broads, and work, that was me. Coralie was smart, I don't blame her."

"This is about the daughter then?"

"Yup. Diane. I've only seen her a couple of times and not for the last five years. I've got a whole bunch of pictures though." He pulled out a fat wallet that had compartments and divisions like a brief case. He rifled for a minute then pushed a photograph across the desk.

"Bright kid," he said. "Cleaned up everything in school here last year. She was supposed to go to university in Sydney this year."

The photograph distracted me from what he was saying; the image was of a big, young woman who looked fully endowed with brains, good looks, and life itself. A blonde with a face that was all eyes, cheekbones, and mouth: it was a candid shot, she was sitting in a chair, waving her hands, and talking. It would be hard to imagine anyone within view not looking and listening.

"Which one?" I said. "Which university?"

"There's more than one?"

"Three," I said, but I knew which one he meant; the old one, the one with ivy and tradition, the one I hadn't dropped out of.

"Law school," he said. "Going straight into law school. Sounds funny to me, but I was looking forward to talking to her about it. We wrote each other plenty, I felt like I knew her, sort of . . ."

"What happened?"

He squashed out his half-smoked cigar in the little ashtray on my desk, and sighed. Just for an instant, with the breath leaving him, he seemed oddly vulnerable. "Her mother died last year, cancer. Di was real cut up when she sat those exams. I wanted to come out for the funeral and all, but I couldn't get away. I wrote that I'd get work here so that I'd be around, she seemed real pleased."

"Did your wife marry again?"

He shook his head emphatically. "Never got divorced, one of those things. Di moved in with a girlfriend after Coralie died. She was going to live in college she said—a scholarship, that right?"

I nodded. "You keep saying what was going to happen—what did happen?"

"I got here early December, soon as I could. She'd been gone a week when I arrived."

"Gone where?"

"To the States, would you believe it? She took off with some kid to California and here I am stuck, just locked in up there in Queensland for the first eight weeks solid."

He'd used his American connections to make the initial trace. Diane Holt had U.S. citizenship and a passport from a trip to New Caledonia she'd made with her mother. She left Australia on Pan Am bound for San Francisco on 27 November at half past five in the afternoon. She had a cabin bag and a light suitcase which had been carried for her by one Vincent Harvey.

"He's Australian," Holt said. "Graduate student at Stanford, that's . . ."

"I know, university in California. Felix Keesing, anthropology, Roscoe Tanner and McEnroe, tennis. Does Di play tennis?"

"Sure, plays everything." He pulled a sheaf of papers from the pocket that hadn't held the wallet. "All I know about him and some stuff about her is right here." He gave me the papers and wiped a hairy arm across his face. "Shit, it's hot."

We coped with that in the saloon bar of the big hotel down the street where Holt was staying. He said he was a retired drinker but he must have been a title-holder in his day: I drank light beer and he had beer with whisky chasers.

Holt had used Raymond Evans's agency to do the basic digging on Diane, her mother, and Harvey, and I was impressed with the results. We had a straight teenager with the usual tastes and habits and no shadows, until the six months of her mother's illness came along. Raymond's report said: "Ms. Holt appears to have moved into a kind of top gear when she learned of her mother's cancer. By all reports she worked extremely hard at her studies and alternated periods of intense nursing with heavy socialising. Drink & drugs—moderate & experimental; sex probable (see Harvey, V.); politics—radical; criminality—negative."

Harvey had taken a B.A. in history and psychology and an M.A. in sociology at the University of Sydney. He'd done his course work for his Stanford Ph.D. on "Advertising, the media and opinion formation in Australia" and when he carried Di Holt's suitcase at Mascot he was going back to write up his fieldwork for the dissertation. Raymond reported that Harvey had met Diane Holt when he was interviewing the father of one of her schoolfriends who owned an advertising agency.

I tapped the papers and forced down some more beer. "This is good work," I said. "But I think you might need a California man on it now."

"Tried that," Holt said. "San Francisco private eye found out Harvey had dropped out of Stanford. Big deal. Said he couldn't find Australians, charged me high."

"Jesus. Did he call himself a private eye?"

"Yeah."

"Must be the fog. Still . . ."

He broke in impatiently. "I'm a Stanford man myself, got a friend on the faculty there. He tells me this Harvey has

227

gone political—makes speeches on the campus time to time."

"Radical politics," I said tapping the papers again.

"Yeah, beats me. I just figure it might be best for an Aussie to talk to them and find out what the hell's going on."

"Why didn't Raymond handle it?"

"He recommended you."

And that was how I came to be on Flight 532 out of Sydney for San Francisco via Honolulu. I had a visa which would allow me to go in and out of the U.S. as often as I liked for the next five years. It sounded like a treat. I watched *Chariots of Fire* for the third time and admired the way they gave you two of the cute little bottles when you ordered a gin and tonic. I didn't eat any of the food, which was all the colour of raw liver. I read *The White Hotel* on the second leg of the flight, and couldn't sleep afterwards.

It was raining in San Francisco and the cable cars were out of operation being overhauled, but it was Sunday and a lot of the city was working, and that was novel. I checked into a Fisherman's Wharf motel and caught up on some of the lost sleep. After a shave and shower I went out and bought some of the Gallo chablis I'd been reading about for years in American novels. I also bought a turkey and avocado sandwich big enough to choke Phar Lap and went back to the motel to review the case. The wine was fine, a bit fruity; the label said it was 12 per cent alcohol and I confirmed that with a few solid belts. The sandwich was excellent—survival in these foreign parts was assured. The thinking didn't take long; the only lead I had was to Stanford University in Palo Alto. Twelve per cent is an assertive wine—I had another nap.

* * *

It was well into Monday when I presented my international driving permit and American Express card at Hertz and took possession of a red Pinto. The freeway to Palo Alto wasn't any worse than the Sydney versions and the low, exhaust-blasted structures along the road looked like Haberfield with a dash of Barcelona. Since the energy crisis hit they've dropped the speed limit and everyone drives slowly to save petrol. They were forgiving about my hesitations and sudden surges of doubt about the automatic transmission and which side of the road to travel on.

I put on dark sunglasses and blinked a lot and told myself that Palo Alto with its gum trees and ordered streets was nothing like Canberra. I drove cautiously onto the Stanford campus, learning that here joggers and cyclists rule.

At Students' Records a bored woman with a lot of gold chains round her neck told me that Vin Harvey had not enrolled for the new quarter. When I asked why not, she got sly and started demanding ID. I left after getting a squint at the address on the VDT screen—72 Manzanita Park. I located it on a campus map and walked there dodging the bikes. It was an eye-opener amidst the affluence. Low cost student housing covering an acre or so. The buildings, box-like, pale cream corrugated iron jobs were like beached whales. I felt a wall and judged it to be more tin than iron. The layout reminded me of the army and the atmosphere reminded me of caravan parks at home where I'd gone looking for people who couldn't afford to hide anywhere else.

Number 72 was no different from the others except that it had a poster on the outside advertising the delights of the Santa Cruz boardwalk. Pasted to the rippled surface the picture of the boardwalk and the sea had a disjointed, chaotic look. There was also a poster for a recent on-campus Grateful Dead concert, but there were plenty of those around.

A tall, stringy black youth answered my knock. He wore a light grey track suit and sneakers and he bounced just standing there in the doorway.

"I, ah, was hoping you might know something about Vincent Harvey."

"Who was hoping?"

"Name's Hardy, from Australia." I pulled out the investigator's licence and was just balanced and quick enough to avoid the kick he aimed at my head. I stepped back and he came after me, leaping with the hands out ready to smash me down. The leap took him through the doorway but left him a bit close to the wall; I used the space I had to push him into it, hard. He hadn't learned coming-off-walls and I showed him lesson one, which is to avoid going-into-same-wall-again. Lesson two is much the same and it can go on until someone gets tired. He did.

"All right," he gasped, "you're bruising me."

"Truce," I said. "Parley."

"Okay." He got to his feet and I watched all of him carefully.

"Why did you do that?"

"For practice. You guys are supposed to be on guard at all times aren't you? It's hard to find anyone on guard."

"Shit." I stuffed my hands down tight into the pockets of my jeans. "I am officially offguard—all right?"

"Sure. You're good, man, what was that you wanted to know?"

"About Vin, my compatriot."

He nodded and ushered me straight into a room which was like a good-sized motel room, except that it had a bookcase, which I've never seen in a motel.

"Beer?" He bent to the door of a compact fridge which fitted in between the bookcase and the stereo system.

"Thanks." He handed me a can which had more pictures on it than a Walton's catalogue. Coors didn't seem like much of a name for a beer, but it was good. He watched me as I took the first sip.

"Terrific," I said.

"That's what Vin thought."

"Good man is he?"

"Was."

"And you are . . . ?"

"Percy Holmes." He flexed a bicep and jutted his jaw. "More Holmes than Percy, if you take my meaning."

"I do. You know Vin well?"

He scratched his chin and stayed in the squatting position, giving the thighs a workout. "Just because you whipped me doesn't mean I'll spill my guts to you. What's the problem?"

"I'm not sure." I drank some more of the beer and decided it was *very* good. "Diane Holt's father hired me to find her. You know her?"

He nodded. "Sure, a young fox. She was around when Vin came back and pulled outa here. And gave up beer. He was different, like weird."

I'd seen a photograph of Harvey, courtesy of Raymond Evans. He had dark hair, a short beard and what you might call brooding eyes, but he didn't look weird.

"This is nothing heavy," I said. I waved the nearly empty beer can and tried a smile. "Di's dad seems like a man of the world to me, know what I mean?"

His dark brown brow furrowed. "No," he said.

"I want to find out if the girl's okay and what's happening. I won't touch Vin or even speak to him in a loud voice unless he's making her do what she doesn't want to do."

He seemed to find that very funny. He let out a short laugh and then a longer one. He reached into the fridge, got out two cans of Coors, tossed one to me and popped the other himself.

"You got it round the wrong way man. That Di, she's got him here." He gripped his crotch.

We both drank some beer and I started to put together an easy scenario for myself: Australian-raised girl with fantasies about America grabs the first chance she gets to take the trip, rages for a while, gets sick of it, and is happy to come back to good old Sydney University with dinkum detective. Then he had to go and complicate it.

"She wanted to go to Santa Cruz," Holmes said. "That was the place for her, 'dreamland,' she called it. They had the biggest fight right here."

"Santa Cruz—what's that?"

"UC campus—south of here, funky place."

"Harvey can't transfer his Ph.D. there can he?"

He shook his head. "No way. Look, I roomed a while with Vin, he's okay. You sure that's all straight—just findin' the chick and all?"

"Yes." I finished the beer to prove it.

"Okay. Vin, he's through with the Ph.D., he says. He says it's meaningless, I'm not sure why. He's pretty freaked out, that's why he put Santa Cruz down so hard. A cop-out he says. He's into, like anarchy, you know? And the chick wants to hang out in Santa Cruz, shit."

He seemed to remember that he wasn't exercising anything at the moment while sitting on the floor. He did some squats, it was time to go before he started shadow-boxing in the confined space.

"So where did they go?" I said.

"San Francisco—where else?"

"Driving what, Percy? Living where?"

He grinned. "Drives a Volkswagen van. Ah'm sorry suh, ah don' know the number."

"Okay, okay, sorry. Do you happen to know where he lives in San Francisco, Mr. Holmes?"

"No, Mr. Hardy, I don't; but you're in luck, he's going to be right here tonight." He got up and rummaged among papers on top of the bookcase. He handed me a roughly printed notice which said that Harvey would be giving a lecture entitled "Owning the Air" on the subject of the media and politics. The lecture was sponsored by the Stanford Committee for Responsible Social Science and was scheduled for that evening at eight P.M.

"Will you be there?"

"Not me. I'll be playing basketball."

"Are you tall enough for basketball?"

"No, I play for fun."

I drove back to Palo Alto and found a place called a Creamery in which you could eat and drink and read. I ate a salad, drank a beer, and read the *San Francisco Chronicle*. The food and drink were better than the paper but I did learn that Michael Spinks was defending his cruiserweight title against nobody that afternoon on TV. I asked the kid behind the counter if I could watch it and he nodded and turned on the set mounted high on the wall.

"Who's Michael Spinks?" he said.

"Brother of Leon."

I let him bring me another beer while I watched the fight. The beer was fine but Spinks wasn't so good. His opponent was a dark, chunky guy who looked like a blown-up middleweight and Spinks took about three rounds longer than he should to put him away.

I did the crossword in the paper, had another beer, walked around for a while, and filled up with gas. I drove very cautiously; all the cops I'd seen so far wore black uniforms with big guns tucked up high, wicked-looking nightsticks and discontented expressions. Cops have a way of spotting men who are in a similar line of work, and of being nasty to them. I wasn't licenced to blow my nose in California and I knew what one of those nightsticks in sweaty hands could do to a sensitive man like me.

I gave a boy and his girlfriend a ride to the campus because they looked so forlorn walking. Everyone else was in a car or on a ten-speed cycle. I asked the kid if he was going to the media lecture.

"Naw," he said.

"Freaks," the girl said.

A campus patrol car came alongside and the boy waved insolently at the driver. I swore silently at him but the cop just gunned his motor and cruised past.

"Pigs," the girl said. I wondered if they limited themselves to one-word statements. I dropped them near one of the student dormitories; the boy waved, he was a good waver, the girl said "Thanks."

I was a bit late finding the lecture room and I wasn't ready for Vin Harvey. Evans's photograph was the sort that would let you recognise someone in the street and not much more. Harvey appeared a dark-haired young man with a heavyish face and a short beard; his eyes were said to be blue and his build was said to be light, but all that did was distinguish him from brown-eyed truck drivers. The man addressing the crowd in the room might have been dark with blue eyes and slight build, but why hadn't anyone said anything about charisma? He had it. He was tall unless he was standing on a high box and his beard-framed face didn't look heavy.

He worked at talking—his voice was pleasing with a mid-Pacific accent and he moved his shoulders a little for emphasis. He wore jeans and a white T-shirt and his arms and hands moved like an orchestra conductor's. I took a seat up at the back of the steeply sloped room and listened.

"They are not faceless," Harvey said, "never think that. You can see their faces in the business magazines and newspapers they own. Their faces are on the screens, coming at you from the TV stations they own. Then there are the faces of the men and women they own—the lawyers, politicians, and newsreaders." He suddenly stood quite still and the movement dramatically underlined his words. "But more important than the faces are the words." His voice went a bit deeper as if concern were forcing it down. "Last year, there was a meeting. It was held in Sydney, Australia. All the media corporations had representatives there, the political people, a few of the union people. You'd recognise some of the names if I mentioned them. For public consumption the meeting was to organise aid for the under-privileged of the Pacific. That's a hell of a lot of people and for all I know they might get some water to villages in the Philippines. But the real talks, the ones the journalists didn't get in on, weren't about water—they were about direct access to your minds."

The room was very quiet and still, everyone was listening and I had to jerk my attention away to check the audience. When I'd been bored rigid in my law lectures twenty years before I used to count all the people in the room. That's why I'd sit up the back with the widest view I could command. Then I'd split them up into groups: sex, rebels, conformists. It passed the time, and I sometimes did bad sketches of people who took my eye. The old habit re-surfaced and, as Harvey went on, I found myself sketching.

"At that meeting they agreed to experiment with sublim-inal advertising and propaganda through TV. A couple of scientists there had been researching it for years." He

235

paused. "They can make you believe things and disbelieve things, they can make you angry or passive." For the first time he lifted the volume. "They can tune you like a TV set, and they're doing it right now."

One sketch showed two men sitting together near the front. They had an air of forced casualness as if the denim shirt of one and the T-shirt of the other weren't normal dress. The T-shirt one made a tie-straightening movement twice and the other plucked at the hair which sat on top of his ears. The T-shirt was taking shorthand notes.

My second drawing was of a young woman with blonde hair pulled back into a frizzy pony tail. She was in the front row and stared up at Harvey as if she was trying to count the pores in his nose. I caught the glint of a gold chain around her neck above the creased and stained collar of the shirt that had DO IT printed on it in big red letters on dirty grey. *End of the road*, I thought, but it didn't feel like that, not with her looking at Harvey like that and the other two keeping a record and with him saying what he was saying.

"I have tapes from that meeting and photographs of the participants." He help up his hands, palms out. "Not here, not any one place for very long. It moves, like the rockets in the silos, or did they decide not to move them? Or did they decide not to decide? Or not to tell you whether they decided? One thing's sure, they won't tell you the truth."

He had them all now—the blacks and the whites, the students and the faculty. He went on spelling out the details of the nastiness and I surveyed the audience again. Sitting next to Diane Holt were three guys who looked a little like cleaned-up Hell's Angels. They had that same air of being there for the beer, and ready for trouble. One was prematurely bald, the other two were fair, they looked middling-tough. Next to them was a dark Hispanic character I dubbed the Dark Stranger. He wore dark blue clothes, was slim, and looked very tough indeed.

"You can do something," Harvey was saying, "you can refuse to read their papers, you can turn off the tube and tell them so at ratings time. You can stop putting classifieds in the papers and you can protest against people who *do* advertise. There are lots of ways to do that. But there's a bigger and better protest you can mount, a protest that can be immediately and massively effective. If you've been convinced by what I've said tonight you'll want to be part of it; and I'm sorry for this, but you're going to have to wait. I'll tell you soon about it, real soon, and I'll tell you in San Francisco where it's going to happen. Be there! Goodnight."

The muscle moved fast, they were up and blanketing Harvey before anyone else moved. The T-shirt put away his shorthand pad and sat still. I moved as fast as I could but Harvey and Diane Holt and the minders were getting into a Volkswagen van by the time I got out. I couldn't walk up to him and say I was taking his sheila back to Bondi, I couldn't do anything. My car was a mile away. One of the boys handed a bundle of paper down to someone in the crowd and then the van groaned and choked itself into life. As it churned away I saw the two men in diguise follow it in a dark Buick that made hardly any noise at all.

The bundle turned out to be a roughly printed handbill for an "event" in San Francisco in three days time. The message was a little vague but the faithful were urged to be at Golden Gate Park at noon. I took one of the sheets back to a motel in Palo Alto where I drank most of a six-pack of Coors and watched *Guns of the Magnificent Seven* which had none of the panache of the original.

I started early the next day, driving back to San Francisco, checking into a cheap hotel on Sutter Street and surrendering the Pinto because I knew I'd be spending money and wanted to make it stretch. I bought a .38 Smith

& Wesson at a place I'd been told about, where the only credentials they care about have numbers on them and fold easily. Then I bought an imitation leather holder and a star that looked so real I felt like going out and eating a couple of steaks and drinking a lot of beer.

Instead, I went to the Goldwasser Printing Shop, the name of which had been stamped in small letters on the handbill. I found it on my tourist map and walked there—more economising. The print shop was jammed in at the back of a supermarket and accessible only from the lane behind. It had a furtive air, but that might have been because it still used ink and moving machinery instead of fancy photography. As I went up the narrow wooden stairs I could hear the thin sound of a pinched cough from the printshop—that was good. I wasn't feeling at all physical and the morning fog had brought me close to coughing myself.

He was dark, small and stooped from bending over his work. He straightened up as far as he could and peered at me over his half-glasses.

"Yeah?"

I put the handbill down on the cluttered bench where it became about the millionth piece of paper.

"So?"

"I want to know who you did it for."

"Who wants to know?"

I let him see the gun in its holster when I got out the shield which I flapped open and shut in front of him. It made a flip-flop sound like thong sandals on cement.

"Trouble?"

"Not for you. No dirty words, no pictures. Who was the customer?"

"You talk funny."

"I used to be a tennis player, we pick this talk up from the Aussies."

He reached for a rag he had hanging out his back pocket, wiped his hands and took a few shuffling steps across to an old grey filing cabinet under the dusty window. The boards creaked under his hundred and ten pounds or so, and I wondered how safe it was to have the heavy old press here in the room—I was doing fine at feeling like an official.

"I got it here." He help up a docket and I got further into the role by pulling out my notebook and getting set to write.

"Give me the name and address."

"Enquiry fee ten dollars."

I looked at him for a minute and then got out a ten; he reached and I let him take it while I grabbed the docket. He said "Shit," but the cough started and shut him up. I wrote Pedro Moreno and the address. There was no phone number. I handed the docket back.

"Thanks."

"I think that shield's a fake," he said.

I turned back on my way to the door. "Do you care?"

He shook his head. "Get you a better one."

The address was in the district up behind the University of San Francisco; I gave it to the taxi driver and asked him what kind of neighbourhood it was.

"Bo-ho," he said.

"Huh?"

"Kinda slummy but not a jungle. I'll take you right there. Some places I'd just drop you close."

We went over some hills and I got glimpses of the water before the next dip snatched it away. The street was a mixture of residential—apartments dating I guessed from the 1920s, when they re-built after the earthquake—and shops and blank, anonymous buildings whose functions I couldn't guess at. The number I had was one of the apartment blocks; stucco with grey peeping through the white paint and water-stained from the rusted guttering. I told the cabbie to go on a little.

"Undercover huh?" he said as he made change.

"Mafia."

He struck his forehead lightly. "I shoulda known. Spread to South Africa, eh?"

I didn't tip him.

Brave men march up to the front door; men in their forties who think it might be interesting to live into their fifties go around the back first. Along the street and down the lane, and we weren't bo-ho anymore. The back part of the apartment building had been scarred and broken by a fire. Windows were boarded up, woodwork was scorched and charred; and the wooden handrail that had run beside the metal fire escape was gone, leaving the steps naked and dangerous.

I stood behind a car in the lane and looked at the ruin and let the bad feeling creep over me. There was no VW van, but sticking out of an open window on the top floor was a hand. The hand wasn't stuck out to feel for rain, it wasn't doing anything.

I went up the fire escape feeling like a tight rope walker without his pole. I had the gun but you use a gun for ballast rather than balance. The back door to the top apartment was half-open and I listened at it for what seemed like an hour. There was nothing to listen to there and nothing down below where the building had been gutted. Up here there were signs of life of a sort, if you count an ashtray brim full of butts on a window ledge inside.

I pushed open the door and walked down the short passageway on broken boards laid like a walkway on top of charred bearers and between water-streaked walls. In the kitchen the water came in through a hose and went out through a hole. The floor was a sea of wine jugs, news-papers, and take-away food containers.

240

In the room at the back I got my first sight of American flies in any number. They had four bodies to swarm over. Two men lay on their faces along one wall. Big pieces of their backs were missing and their T-shirts were gory ruins. The hand sticking out the window belonged to the Dark Stranger; his dark clothes were darker and glistened where the blood had soaked in. He'd taken two in the body but had still made it to the window. He and the other pair were neat compared with Vin Harvey: he was lying naked on his back in the middle of the room. He'd been worked on with cigarettes and razor blades. One eye was a black ruin. Thin and bearded he looked like something El Greco might have dreamed up on a bad afternoon. All the fingernails were missing on one hand, and I recognised the object nestling in the congealed blood of his left nostril as a front tooth.

I went over to the window for some air; and after I'd got some and was trying for some more, I heard the dark man speak.

"*Muerto,*" he whispered, or something like that.

I bent down, it seemed impossible that he could still be alive.

"English," I said, "no Spanish."

"Ozzie," he said, like in the Nelsons.

"That's right, where's the girl?"

"Away. *Afortunado.*"

"Harvey told them?"

The movement he made was slight but it looked like a nod. Some blood seeped out of his mouth to join all the blood from everywhere else. The flies buzzed so loudly I had to put me ear down near his mouth.

"*Agua,*" he whispered. I knew that much and went out to the kichen to the hose. I brought it in a throwaway cup that should have been thrown away. His lips were nearly black and the glint in his slitted eyes was from pain. I wet the lips but he couldn't swallow.

"Priest?" I said.

"Shoot me. I beg you."

I realised I still had the .38 in my hand although I could have been holding it by the barrel for all I knew.

"Where's the girl, where did she go?"

"Shoot."

"I can't."

"Shoot," he breathed.

"The girl?" I didn't mean to make it sound like a condition but maybe it did.

"Dreamland." He'd echoed Percy Holmes. His voice was just a touch stronger, as if it had synched with the last beat of his pulse. There was no need to shoot him.

The smell of the guns was still faintly in the air, the dead were still warm and the vomit around Vin Harvey's body was fresh. The killing and torturing had happened a few hours ago at most. There was a light dusting of something on the floor near the wall where the two dead men lay. I didn't touch it and haven't seen enough of it to be sure, but it looked like heroin. Insurance. The thing could look like a drug dispute, a little extreme maybe.

There wasn't much else in the place. Every possible hiding place had been ripped apart. Books, notes, and manuscripts were torn and there were a couple of piles of ashes. There were student clothes, student food, and a little grass. There was a .22 handgun in the kitchen in a drawer that stuck. Vin Harvey had seriously over-matched himself.

Two things worried me: the poster on the wall in the passageway was the same one I'd seen at Stanford, singing the praises of the Santa Cruz boardwalk. The hit men might make something of that. The second thing was the absence of the third muscle man I'd seen at the lecture. That could mean a lot.

I felt like Bony examining the road and car marks in the

dimming light. It wasn't hard to read: a big oil stain showed where the van usually stood and fresh oil drops showed where it stood briefly. These led away over the rubber laid down by a car leaving in a hurry.

No one saw me in the apartment or the lane; if they did they decided not to make it their business. I got a taxi back to my hotel, picked up some money and hired another Pinto. I bought a jug of wine with a narrow, drinkable-from neck and a box of oatmeal cookies and set them up carefully on the passenger seat. I studied the map carefully and set out for Dreamland.

After some false turns around Daly City I picked up the Cabrillo Highway which hugs the coast all the way south to Santa Cruz. Along the way Moss Beach and Half Moon Bay were nice names to roll off the tongue and the road had that hopeful, optimistic feel coast roads have. I drove just above the speed limit and drank wine from time to time. I felt more at home when I passed the greyhound track and had some wine and a cookie on the strength of that. A signpost to Bonny Doon amused me more than it should have, and I laid off the wine.

Santa Cruz was quiet; it was after eleven and everyone was inside watching the news about the poisonings and muggings and the fires in the trailer parks. I drove fast along Pacific Avenue down past the back of the Greyhound depot. The town shops were mostly new and or newly appointed and half of them seemed to sell things made of leather. Beach Street was at the end of Front, past the used car yards and the tyre repair place that had been in business since 1937.

It was a wide, palm tree-lined boulevard swinging around in front of three quarters of a mile of beach. I drove slowly south past closed cafes, a big parking lot, and several motels. The VW van was parked just short of where the road followed a narrow bridge across a creek. I stopped on the other side of the street a block away and watched. There were a couple of other cars in the street under a high half-moon and some desultory street lights; but nothing moved. I took the gun out of the glove box, put it in my jacket pocket and walked up to the van. It smelled of oil and food and age but there were no bodies in it.

At this end the boardwalk was given over to a roller coaster and other rides and it was locked up. I went down onto the sand and walked along parallel to the boardwalk wall, looking for a way up. Two men with torches and two dogs were running a metal detector over the sand. It beeped and hummed and they paid me no attention. A set of wooden steps took me up onto the boardwalk where there wasn't a board in sight; it was a concrete walkway about twenty-five yards wide with the sand on one side and a long row of amusement places on the other—shooting galleries, ice cream parlours, a haunted castle. All closed, all deserted except for the castle which had a drunk sleeping with his back up against the portcullis and a wine bottle clutched to his chest.

I moved quickly, checking the dark recesses. The ferris wheel cast a giant shadow like a spiderweb across the cement and I could hear rats rustling in concealment. The boardwalk ended at a vast amusement parlour which was locked. I jumped down onto the sand and skirted the building which had a high Moorish dome topped by a Gothic turret with a flagpole on top of that. The stars and stripes hung limply in the still air.

Up ahead the pier was like a dark finger against the moonlit sea and sky. I squinted and saw movement on it. I sprinted across the sand dodging the volleyball posts and took the steps up to the wharf three at a time. It was about fifty yards wide with a solid white fence running along both sides. A crane loomed up about halfway out and I saw a public works sign. Then there was a flat, no-cover stretch with patches of light and shade formed by the wharf lights, of which about one in four was burning. I ran, crouched and ducking out of the light. Past a low line of fish cafes and anglers' needs shops the wharf narrowed to its last stretch which was about seventy-five yards long by twenty-five wide. The water slapped against the pylons and I could hear a strange barking sound further on.

A woman with blonde hair was bending over the end rail looking out west over the dark Pacific. The barking was louder as I got nearer and there was splashing with it. There were some openings in the tarred surface of the pier about ten feet square with waist high post and rail fences around them. At the first opening I found out about the noise: seals were jumping on and off the pylons twenty feet below. At the second opening a man was crouched with a gun resting on the rail; he was sightling along it at the blonde woman's back.

I moved quickly up behind him and tried to slam the side of his head with my gun butt. He heard me, very late; he fired but the flash went high, he ducked a little and my blow hit him high and glancing. He went *oomph*, bent over, and shot himself up through the chin. I already had another punch traveling; I pulled it and it turned into a push and he went over the rail. He bounced once on a cross beam and a seal barked and jumped into the water, and then he went in too.

She was standing with her back to the rail, facing America with Australia over her shoulder. I put my gun away and walked forward.

"Diane Holt?"

She nodded. "Are you going to kill me?"

"No," I said. I pointed down to the water. "But he was."

The seals which had gone quiet after the big splash, started barking again. Closer up I saw that she had a lot of blood on her face and that she was rigid with fright.

"Your father sent me. It's all right."

"My father," she said.

"Are you hurt?"

She touched her face and looked at the blood. "No, I get bloody noses when I'm upset."

I took her arm and brought her away from the rail, we passed the opening and she pointed.

"What's that?"

I looked down and saw his gun lying on the tar. I kicked it into the water and a seal barked.

We got back to the van and I told her to take off her blouse and a shoe. She did it like an automaton. I wiped blood from her face with the blouse and her nose started up again and the cotton got well soaked. I put the shoe and the blouse in the VW, muffled up my .38 and fired a shot into the passenger seat.

She came out of her trance at the sound of the shot. "Why did you do that?"

"We need a mystery here," I said. "We want some people to stop worrying about you. I hope it works."

She grabbed a bag out of the van and we left Santa Cruz in a hurry.

She filled me in on the drive to San Francisco. Harvey was getting together a big show for his day in the park. He was going to put some of his films on a big screen and play some of his tapes. He was going to name names.

"Some of the biggest people," she said. "Top people."

"Don't tell me," I said. "Forget them."

"I got scared, and I didn't trust Ramsay. He's the one . . . back there. Vin and me had a fight and I split."

When she came back to the apartment she saw what I'd seen.

"Pedro was still alive," I said.

"I just ran."

"It was too late anyway, but he helped me to find you."

She cried then, deep and long, most of the way to San Francisco airport. She stopped crying and wiped her face.

"Why did you go to Santa Cruz? That boardwalk looked pretty tacky to me."

"It's innocent," she said.

She had some clothes in the bag and she cleaned up while I bought her a ticket to Los Angeles where she had an aunt. She was in some kind of shock but there was a strength in her that kept her functioning. She phoned the aunt.

"Go straight home," I said. "Tomorrow, today, whatever. I'll cable your dad."

She nodded, said "Thanks" in broad Australian, and caught the flight.

I sent a wire to Wesley Holt from the hotel and worried about the untidy ends. I worried about things like the muscle man's car, the clean slug in the VW seat, and the tides off the Santa Cruz beach. But there was nothing I could do about any of them.

About the Author

Peter Corris is a former academic turned journalist, thriller writer, and jogger. Born in Victoria, Australia, he is now an enthusiastic resident of Sydney, Australia, which has provided the inspiration and locale for all of his Cliff Hardy mysteries.